WEST TO THE SUN

It stretched out there to the west—the endless, silent, savage wilderness only a fool or a brave man would challenge. Or a desperate one.

Dan Shankle was no fool. He was brave and his mission made him desperate. For somewhere in those killing plains lay hidden the *contrabandista,* the man who traded guns to the Indians and sent them forth to pillage and massacre across the frontier.

The *contrabandista* had to be stopped, and they sent Dan Shankle to do it. Westward he rode, into parched badlands where the Indians massed—Camanches who first would lift a man's scalp, then stake him out to die by inches.

West to the sun, into bitter country that gave no quarter, rode a man who had no time to give—or ask for—mercy.

WEST TO THE SUN

Noel M. Loomis

GUNSMOKE

First published by Collins

This hardback edition 2003
by Chivers Press
by arrangement with
Golden West Literary Agency

ISBN 0 7540 8228 8

British Library Cataloguing in Publication Data available.

Printed and bound in Great Britain by
Antony Rowe Ltd., Chippenham, Wiltshire

Chapter One

IT WAS JUNE, 1773. The weather was hot and humid, and Dan Shankle studied the vast stretches of swamp as the two canoes traveled slowly against the brown water.

"She looks like aguey bottoms to me," he called back.

"She's full of fever," Simon Jeffreys agreed from the second boat.

They had worked against the Mississippi current for two weeks, and that morning the Choctaws had paddled the big canoes up the wide bends of the Arkansa River, through a heavy, oppressive atmosphere that made the sweat run in streams down their copper skins.

And Dan had not failed to note that the Choctaws, who had been full of nasal talk among themselves as they started out from the British bank of the Mississippi that morning, now were watchful and silent as they progressed toward Osage country. It was a relief from tension to hear one of them aspirate the word for heat:

"Lashpa!"

Dan continued to search the shore on both sides, as far ahead as he could see. "It'll get hotter when summer comes," he said.

Simon growled from behind, "If it gets any worse than this, I say let the Quapaws keep it. A man can't make an honest shilling in this kind of weather."

Dan looked back briefly. "I never saw you pass up a chance to make any kind of shilling." He turned back to keep his careful lookout. When Indians were nervous, no white man but a fool would fail to keep his eye peeled.

Kneeling in the bow, he was tall and singularly thin, but he seemed to fill the fringed buckskin hunting shirt rather well, and the hair that showed long from under his coonskin cap was light brown except where the ends were bleached by the sun.

All morning they had traveled through a heavy inundated

5

forest of tall cypress with thick, buttressed trunks, and of
tupelo gum with its pendulous clusters of olive-like fruits not
yet turning purple. There were frequent breaks in the river-
banks, and the water poured out through them into lakes and
bayous and cypress swamps, so that it was a wilderness of
great trees and dense undergrowth, of vast stretches of quiet,
ominous brown water. It was spread out so much that a man
had to watch sharp to keep the channel of the river.

Dan held out his hand. The Choctaws quit paddling. The
twenty-foot canoe with its two thousand pounds of goods lost
its slow headway, and the second canoe came alongside.

Dan looked at Simon Jeffreys. They were dressed about
alike, but Simon was shorter and darker and a little fat.

"My knees are gettin' sore," said Dan.

"I told you at Natchez you better stuff a deerskin full of
leaves."

"How much farther to Arkansa Post?"

"Can't be far."

"*Poco más allá,*" Dan grumbled. "You've been in Louisiana so long you're beginning to think like a Spaniard."

"You'll learn it soon enough," Simon said sourly. "Your
first lesson is up ahead."

The Choctaws went to work again, and the canoes moved
upstream side by side for easier communication. Presently the
talkative Indian said in a low voice, "*Holihta kallo.*"

"What's that mean?" asked Dan.

"A fort," said Simon. "Up ahead there—Arkansa Post."

He pointed, but Dan had to look carefully, for the stockade and the cabins, built of weather-worn cypress and
thatched with grass and leaves, so blended into the background as to be easily missed.

A stockade of upright posts marked the seat of government
in the Arkansa country—the only law between St. Louis and
Natchitoches. The posts were old and weatherworn, and had
fallen over in places, especially at the gate that marked the
river-front entrance. Within the square were a dozen clustered buildings, and far beyond the square, a few men and
women worked in the fields. A dog barked at the canoes, and
a Mexican in a big straw hat woke up slowly from his siesta
in the shade of a thick stand of birch trees. He saw the canoes
and stared for a moment. Then he scurried to a large cabin
while Dan's canoe slid to a stop with its bow high on the
clay.

Dan jumped out and pulled the bow a few inches higher.

6

The Choctaws sat impassive but watched with glittering eyes. Simon's boat slid up, and Dan pulled it beside the first.

Simon muttered, "Comp'ny's comin'."

"Trouble?" Dan asked, pushing his powder horn back to his side.

"His coat is lined with light blue—a lieutenant of hussars."

"Is that worse than cavalry?" Dan asked with an attempt to treat it lightly.

Simon said uncomfortably, "Don't underrate this gent. He represents the King of Spain." He whispered urgently. "Don't keep your back toward him any longer."

Dan turned slowly. The black-haired Spaniard was a young, handsome man, filled with the animal vigor of youth and the arrogance of a Spanish official.

He was flanked by four Spanish soldiers, all black-haired and bright-eyed and all bearing flintlock muskets. Dan scrutinized them. The officer was impeccably dressed, but the soldiers were not. They were infantrymen, to judge from the red feathers in their hats, but their uniforms were sloppy. One wore moccasins, another had no powder horn, and a third had no blunderbuss in his belt.

The Spaniard stopped six feet from him. *"Quién es usted, señor?"*

"I'm Dan Shankle, an Englishman. These are my men."

"Your home, señor?"

"Wyoming valley, Pennsylvania."

The officer's eyes narrowed slightly. "Your business?"

Dan motioned toward the boats behind him without taking his eyes from the Spaniards. "I came to trade."

"Your passport?"

Dan shook his head sadly. "I did not know a passport would be required on the Arkansa."

"A passport is always required of foreigners in New Spain —particularly of Englishmen," the officer said stiffly.

"Are you the commandant here?" asked Dan.

"I represent Don Fernando de Leyva, commandant of this district, with full power to discharge his duties."

"We aren't looking for trouble," Dan said.

"You have trade goods, no?"

Dan nodded.

"May I see your license to trade?"

"I didn't know—"

The officer said sharply, "For a man who has invested perhaps four thousand pesos in goods, you know very little,

7

señor. May I ask with whom you expect to trade in the Arkansa country?"

"Indians."

"What tribe of Indians?"

Dan shrugged. "Any tribe."

The officer considered. "Since you are so ignorant of His Most Catholic Majesty's regulations, perhaps you have brought some nice rifles to trade to the Osages, *verdad?*"

Dan shook his head. "I know you don't want rifles up here. I didn't bring any."

"You have a rifle in the bow of your boat, señor."

"For my own use." Dan nodded toward Simon. "He has one too. Beyond that we have none."

"You have knives, undoubtedly."

Dan nodded. "One apiece."

The black eyes drilled into him. "But none in your goods?"

Dan met his stare. "None."

"The law is the law," the officer said implacably.

Dan tried to look apologetic. "We aren't aiming to violate the law. We just come to do some harmless trading."

"You will submit to inspection of your cargo?"

"Sure," Dan said. "Help yourself. If I've got something that doesn't belong in there, you can keep it."

A quick gleam appeared in the officer's eyes. He barked an unmilitary command: *"Vayanse!"* without taking his gaze from Dan's face.

The four soldiers slouched away.

Dan allowed himself a deeper breath. So far it was going according to schedule.

"I will inspect your cargo," the officer said, "but I warn you that firearms will not be tolerated."

Dan was a little relieved. The very fact that his goods would be examined, though he was without a passport or a trading license, was indication that Simon had known what he was talking about. "I understand the English are working out of the Illinois country, trading rifles to the Osages."

The officer looked sharply at him. "That is true. Farther up the river the Osages are well supplied, and we have not enough force in this post to stop it."

"Aren't the Osages out of your territory, anyway?"

The officer shrugged. "It is an involved affair. The Osages travel to the Red River of Natchitoches, halfway between here and Santa Fé, and raid the Taovayas or Wichitas. The

8

Wichitas in turn demand more firearms from the authorities in Bexar."

"Why not let them have them?"

The officer sighed. "It is not that simple. The Wichitas trade firearms to the savage Cayugas and Camanches, and these in turn raid the Spanish settlements, to the great displeasure of the Viceroy. If the Camanches had access to plenty of gunpowder and rifles, the Spanish in Texas would be wiped out."

"Then it is good that rifles are not permitted up the Arkansa."

The officer looked at him sharply. "What city have you sailed from?"

"Baltimore."

"Arkansa is a long way from Baltimore. This is a vicious country—very wild, very primitive," the officer explained. "The Osages are *muy malos.*"

"I been fighting Indians all my life."

The officer shrugged. "You are of age."

"Have a cigar?" asked Dan, pulling a bundle of eight from the wallet formed by the overlap of his buckskin hunting shirt.

The officer's eyes widened a little as he saw the rounded ends. "Habana!" he said appreciatively.

The officer cut the brown cord with a small dagger that came from somewhere in his uniform. "You will have one, señor?"

"Gracias, no." Dan pulled a half-chewed carrot of tobacco out of his shirt.

The officer looked and nodded. *"Fuego!"* he called in a high, clear voice, and a soldier came out of a cabin bearing a hot coal between two green twigs. He held it to the cigar while the officer puffed. The officer nodded, and the soldier went back. "Now," said the officer, his head in a cloud of smoke, "shall we inspect your cargo?"

Dan knew they were only sparring—*platicando,* Simon had called it, warning him that it was a part of the Spanish way of life. "At your leisure," he said, turning to the boats.

Simon and his Indians were unfastening the canvas in the second canoe. The officer turned to it. He ran an eye over the contents while they held the canvas up at one side. The Spaniard's sharp black eyes scanned the contents. "Beads, cloth, vermilion, looking glasses—the usual goods," he noted, and turned away.

9

The Spaniard walked over to Dan's boat. Dan hastened to lift the canvas and held it high. The Spaniard's quick eyes took in everything.

"What's in the small buckskin bag there on top?"

Dan stared. "I don't know," he said slowly. "I've never seen it before."

"Very curious," the officer said. He did not take his eyes from the bag.

"You'd better examine it."

The Spanish threw him a swift glance, and Dan saw the bright gleam of avarice in the black eyes. The Spaniard leaned over and lifted the bag. "It's quite heavy."

Dan cut the rawhide string with his knife. The bag opened up like a water lily and lay in the Spaniard's hand. The Spaniard glanced at them and up at Dan. "Pesos—pieces of eight," he said.

"Are they of legal coinage?"

"They appear so," the Spaniard murmured.

"I make out about forty of them."

"Part of your trade goods, no doubt."

Dan looked up, wide-eyed. "I never saw them before," he said.

"A strange thing." But the Spaniard did not seem astonished.

"Strange enough—but since they are not mine, perhaps it would be proper for you to keep them for the rightful owner, while I take my outfit on up the river."

The Spaniard weighed the bag in his hand. Then he stepped back. "Very well. I suggest you get far enough up the river to avoid interference with my men. *Vaya bien, señor.*"

Dan nodded. He jerked his head at Simon, standing at the bow of the second canoe.

Dan braced his legs, lifted the bow of his canoe, and gave it a powerful shove. He followed it into the water and leaped in. The Choctaws paddled, and the big canoe began to move upstream. Dan glanced back. Simon was following. Neither one of them looked back toward the fort.

Chapter Two

THEY ROUNDED a bend, and a stand of cypress trees along the edge of the brown water cut them off from the sight of

Arkansa Post. Dan took a deep breath and motioned the Choctaws to stop paddling until Simon came alongside.

"For a minute," he said, "I thought he wasn't going to take it."

Simon's lips twisted. "They always take it—if it's enough. The Spanish colonial policy would strangle the life out of every settlement in New Spain if the officials didn't allow contraband to go through. In the first place, the duties are so heavy they make legal goods cost two or three times what they should. In the second place, Spain is no industrial country. All the goods not needed in Spain could be shipped over here, and the settlers still would be hungry for stuff. They've got to have English and French and Dutch goods. Unless they're rich, they live like animals; they have almost nothing but food and shelter."

"Then they really *need* contraband."

"They've got to have it—and some officials are financing the *contrabandistas.*"

"Up here on the Arkansa?"

"Sure. This post is a plum, for the commander can make enough outside money to get his debts paid. And they do the same down along the rivers in the New Philippines, or Texas country, whatever they call it."

Dan dipped his paddle into the water as a kingfisher dived into a tangle of cypress roots. There was a convulsive threshing among the roots, with only occasionally the wing tips of the bird showing above the tangle.

"Are we through with Arkansa Post?" asked Dan a moment later.

Simon bit off a chew. "I think so. The only thing worried the lieutenant was that you might be a spy for Unzaga. You look too honest to be a *contrabandista.*"

The kingfisher flew out of the trees and crossed the river about two paddle-lengths above them, a small snake dangling from its beak.

Dan watched it go out of sight. "Good thing I ran across you in New Orleans; otherwise I'd have tried to go through Natchitoches."

"That way you'd have been tied up, for De Mézières is one official who can't be bought. Without a passport you'd have been sent back; *with* a passport you'd be tied hand and foot because you'd have to conform to all the regulations." He put the tobacco in his shirt. "If you've got to trade with the Indians, this is the way to do it. Provided you get past the post, and provided you don't rub the fur of the *contra-bandistas* the wrong way, you can trade as you please, come and go as you like, answer to nobody. By the way," he said, a shade too casually, "you never did tell me what you came down here for." He watched the stream ahead. "You didn't come all the way to Arkansa just to trade glass beads to the Indians."

Dan, also watching the river, did not answer.

"There's two more hills to climb," said Simon finally. "The *contrabandistas* and the Osages."

"What about the *contrabandistas?*"

"They're the worst bunch of outlaws in Louisiana."

"How do they get rid of the slaves and horses they get from the Indians?"

"Run them down to Little Manchac if they're in a hurry —same place you bought your stuff. More goods go through Little Manchac than through New Orleans, and every bead is contraband."

"Where does the stuff go from Little Manchac?"

"To Pensacola, and that's British. But if they're not in a hurry, they wait for a licensed trader to come up from New Orleans."

"How does a licensed trader get around the regulations?"

"He isn't trading with Indians," said Simon.

A grunt came from one of the Choctaws. Another answered him.

"What are they talking about?" asked Dan.

"Scalps," said Simon.

Dan looked around. "What scalps?"

Simon dropped into the nasal language of the Indians. *"Himmona?"*

Heads nodded vigorously in both boats.

"Fresh scalps," Simon said laconically. "Osage, by the look of them."

They were now almost even with a dilapidated cabin, around which the only sign of habitation consisted of three black-haired scalp locks hanging on wooden pegs driven between the logs.

"Probably a *contrabandista* lives there," said Simon. "This is Quapaw country."

"The Choctaws don't like it," Dan observed.

"No. It means there'll be Osages looking for hair to even things up."

12

"I thought," said Dan, "the Spanish had the Indians under control."

"How could they, with thirty-two soldiers at Arkansa Post to control thousands of Indians? For ninety years the only good of this post has been as a place for the Quapaws to come for their presents."

"How about the Osages?"

"They get their presents in St. Louis and their rifles from the English."

The next day, three leagues upstream from the post, they were still surrounded by swamp, dormant lakes, and stagnant bayous. "How much farther?" asked Dan.

Simon scowled. "We should be gettin' there. You in a hurry to get it over with?"

Dan realized he was tense. He bit off a fresh chew and put the rest of the carrot back in his shirt. "Like to know where I stand."

"You'll find out soon. That's it, up ahead."

Through the trees Dan saw a blockhouse, bigger and stronger than the fort. "It looks businesslike," he said.

"That's headquarters for all the *contrabandista* trade."

"The Spanish know about it?"

"Sure, but they don't bother. It makes Arkansa Post worth a lot of money."

Dan pointed with the paddle. The Choctaws turned the canoe into a small bay formed by a bend in the river. A sand bar ran across it, and on this grew a thick stand of young cottonwoods.

"Try around the end," said Simon. "It looks like enough water on the other side of the bar."

There were two feet of water beyond the bar. Dan led the way into the protected strip, and the bow of the canoe crunched on sand. Dan got out, pulled up the bow, and turned to look at the blockhouse. It was considerably bigger than the commander's cabin at Arkansa Post, and had about the same group of smaller log cabins around it. Two black-haired Indian squaws with copper bands on their upper arms were scraping a fresh bearskin on the ground in front of the blockhouse, while two red-capped *voyageurs* sat on the ground, one at each side of the door, leaning against the logs and smoking pipes as they watched the squaws. They looked up at Dan, and one called out a name that Dan did not hear clearly.

He heard the obble-obble-obble of wild turkeys from across

13

the river, and turned that way for a moment. On a hill that rose directly from the water, four turkeys—three hens and a rooster—were feeding under an oak tree, and creeping through a thicket of wild plum trees, protected from sight of the turkeys by a slight rise in the ground, were three naked Indian or half-breed boys with small bows and arrows.

The second canoe gritted on the sand, and Dan pulled it up. He looked back at the doorway of the blockhouse as Simon Jeffreys stepped out of the canoe. A huge man was in the doorway. He squinted at the boats and then slowly, deliberately, and insolently came down to meet them, while the two Frenchmen got up from beside the door and fell in behind him.

One of the Frenchmen was tall and concave-stomached; the other was short and square-framed and filled with energy. All three, like Dan and Simon, were dressed in frontier garb: long buckskin hunting shirt fastened with a wide leather belt, with six-inch fringes hanging from the sleeves. The lower portions were black and greasy from long use. Each had a pistol in his belt and a knife on his right hip, and the giant had a brass tomahawk on his left hip. They wore Indian moccasins and long buckskin leggings. The giant wore a shapeless, big-brimmed buffalo-wool hat; the two Frenchmen following him wore red stocking caps.

A fourth man came out of the woods. He was as tall as Dan, with powerful sloping shoulders, and he walked with springy knees. His face was long and narrow but heavily boned; his mouth was a quarter circle turned down above a massive chin. His ears were big and heavy; his nose was big, with a crease across the bridge. And his eyes, so large they almost filled the sockets, were staring, hostile. This man fell in behind the three others.

The squaws, still squatting over the bearskin, had stopped their work and were watching. Dan stood between the two boats. Abruptly most of the noises of the wilderness seemed to cease, and there was left only the erratic gobble of the turkeys.

The men stopped about six feet from Dan. The first big man was rough in the face and wild-eyed; his black hair was uncombed; his face was toughened by wind and sun, his nose aquiline.

His voice was filled with suspicion. "Where you from?"
Dan said, "Down the river."
"What's in the boats?"

"Goods from Little Manchac."

"How'd you get by Arkansa Post?"

"The lieutenant inspected my cargo and told me to go on."

"You got too many answers. You're a liar!"

Dan kept his tongue.

"Pull out of here!" ordered the big man.

Dan looked at him without change of expression. He pulled out the carrot of tobacco and bit off another chew, taking his time. "Unload!" he said to the Indians.

The big man strode forward purposefully. "Not here," he growled.

The Choctaws sat uneasily, not moving.

"Why not here?" asked Dan.

"I got goods to sell. If you want to buy, you can unload here. If you got your own stuff, go on up the river and take your own chances with the Osages."

"That's maybe a good idea," Dan said slowly. "I never liked a fellow who thought he owned the country."

The big man's eyes were flinty and he didn't take the trouble to answer.

"Simon," said Dan without turning, "push off your boat."

"I can push it off," said Simon, but for the first time he sounded dubious. "You're gonna have trouble with the crew, though."

Dan glanced at the Choctaws. Their faces were impassive, but all were shaking their heads. "What's the matter with them?" asked Dan.

"Scalps," said Simon.

"Whose?"

"Their own."

"Afraid of the Osages?"

Simon nodded. "It's midafternoon and they want to get back out of the Arkansa country. They don't like the mosquitoes up here."

"All right, we'll unload. Tear off that canvas!"

The big man moved two steps closer. "There's only one way you can unload here: if you was sent by the right man. And if you was, you better sing out."

Dan paused. He tried to remember the name of the man from whom he had bought the goods in Little Manchac, the smuggling port for Texas. He looked at Simon for help. Simon hesitated for an instant and then said, "Clermont." Dan knew it was a gamble.

15

Dan looked at the big man and nodded. He saw that the big man was taken aback. The guess had hit dead center.

But the big man gathered his wits. "Who was with Clermont?"

Simon answered promptly, "Poeyfarré."

Dan looked at the big man, and what he saw was no good. The big man was grinning. "You mighta said Harry Blundin—but you woulda been wrong, because I'm Harry Blundin. You mighta said Duvivier, because Duvivier is with Clermont this summer, buyin' horses and mules from the Lipan Apaches to sell to the English colonies when the war starts. But you said Poeyfarré—and this is Poeyfarré behind me."

Dan felt his muscles begin to loosen up. He didn't have time to ask, "What war?" because Blundin grappled with him.

Blundin was three inches taller and twice as thick in the body. He tried to break Dan over backward. Dan was lithe but he was tough. He gave a little and then he got his fingers in the man's eyes and nose and pushed him hard. "Your breath stinks bad," Dan said coldly.

Blundin had a big-bladed knife in his hand. "Not as bad as your guts," he growled.

Dan circled. The two Frenchmen and the fourth man were watching, impassive. The Indian squaws had come from their work on the bearskin and were standing, barefooted, watching without expression. These things Dan Shankle saw from the corner of one eye as he circled to the right. Simon was still on his knees in the boat, and the bronze faces of the Choctaws were as impassive as the broad faces of the Osage squaws. There was no sound above the hum of insect life save for the sudden gobble of a turkey under the oak tree across the river. Then Blundin lunged.

He came with the knife blade up for disemboweling, but Dan twisted, and the blade carved nothing but air except for the point, which caught Dan across the underside of his left forearm and left a gash that began to bleed freely.

Dan spun on his left heel. He aimed both fists at Blundin's kidneys and struck home. Blundin grunted and stumbled and went down on his face.

Dan was already falling on him, but Blundin rolled over much faster than a big man should have, and Dan fell on the arm with the knife.

Blundin's breathing was harsh. His hat had fallen off. His

16

dark hair was long and matted and stank of bear oil. He
threw his left leg over Dan and tried to twist on top, but
Dan held onto the knife arm. Blundin reversed himself and
tried to roll to his left and pull Dan with him. Blundin's
big right arm raised from the ground—six inches, a foot
—but Dan held the wrist, the knife blade pointing down.

Blundin clubbed him with his free hand, but Dan braced
himself and strained at the knife. He saw the point driven
into the sand as his weight forced Blundin's arm back to the
ground. He retained his hold on the man's wrist, twisting
it against the knife blade. Blundin's free heel was hammering
the back of his calf, and he felt the muscle curl up.

He relaxed his hold on the wrist, and Blundin surged up.
Then Dan slammed down on the arm and heard a sharp snap
as the blade broke against the sand.

With the knife out of the way, Dan kept his left hand on
Blundin's wrist and moved his right to the man's throat. He
couldn't hope to choke him with one hand, but he planted
his doubled fist under the man's chin and pushed his head
back until it was at right angles with his body.

Blundin's left leg was back on the ground. His body arched.
His left forearm smashed Dan under the jaw, but Dan sank
his chin down against his chest and took the second blow
across the nose. His nose began to bleed, but he turned his
head and took cover against Blundin's side.

The big hand began to flail him in the back of the head,
jarring his brains. He couldn't stand that very long. He
brought his legs under him, turned Blundin loose, and
stomped Blundin's knife hand with both feet. Blundin's fingers loosened for an instant. The stump of a knife dropped,
and Blundin came roaring up while Dan leaped back out of
reach.

They circled each other warily. Blood dripped from Dan's
forearm and from his nose. Blundin's left side and his black,
hairy chest shone bright with Dan's blood, and his dark eyes
burned with fury, but he was cautious. He had sampled the
man from Pennsylvania and he had found he might have
more trouble than anticipated.

Dan made the first rush. He now had the only knife, but
it was still in its sheath and he made no move to use it. He
lowered his head and rammed his skull against the pit of the
man's stomach. Blundin grunted and staggered. He fell back
and pulled Dan with him. He got his big legs under Dan and
straightened them out like a crossbow released. Dan was

17

gouging for the man's eyes when he felt himself lifted free and catapulted into the air. Then he fell into the water between his two canoes, on his back, spread-eagle, while Blundin came threshing after him.

Dan found the sand with his feet and launched himself farther out. Blundin floundered through the water. Dan put down his feet. The water was waist-deep. Blundin was almost on him. His clublike arms began to flail. He caught Dan on the side of the neck and knocked him off his feet.

Dan felt the water close over his face, and Blundin hunting his throat. He twisted under the water, found Blundin's leg, and tried to pull it from under him. For a moment Blundin's big hand was in the middle of his back, pressing him to the bottom. Then he squirmed away and came to the surface.

The big man wheeled, but Dan gulped a big breath and went down, his head between Blundin's feet. He came up behind Blundin, twisted over, and hammered again at the small of Blundin's back.

Blundin stumbled and Dan pushed him. The man went flat on his face, under the surface, and Dan lunged at his head. He got him by the ears and pushed his head deeper in the water. Blundin threshed. One big foot stove a hole in the stern of a boat. Then they were locked, rolling over and over into deeper water until there was no footing.

Here Blundin's weight was no advantage. They locked once more, both treading water. Blundin's big arms were squeezing his lungs together. Their clothes were wet and weighed them down, and Dan's face was alternately under the water and above it. Then he got both arms under Blundin's arms and brought them up to clasp them under Blundin's chin. He forced the big man's head back underwater.

Blundin threshed like a drowning buffalo, but Dan held him there. Blundin's dirty nails took off skin when they struck, but they weakened fast.

Dan held his head under until the man was unconscious. Then he looked around. They were almost under the cliff where the turkeys had been. He gave Blundin a push toward shore. He pulled up in the mud under the overhanging brush. He got Blundin by the hair and held him out in the stream, nose above water. The big man spluttered and struggled.

"Be quiet," Dan said, "or I'll drown you." He pushed his head under and brought it back. "Can you swim?"

Blundin tried to get his feet under him, but the bank at that point was vertical. Dan pushed his head under again.

18

"All right," Blundin spluttered. "I can't swim."

Dan's face was on fire from the scratches of Blundin's nails. He pulled the man toward the bank by the hair, and with his feet pushed out into the stream. He swam across to the sloping sand shore, and walked out dripping wet. He advanced on Pocyfarré and the other Frenchman. "I've still got my knife," he said, "if any of you gents have anything to say."

Poeyfarré's face didn't change. His eyes were small and watchful. He looked up at the length of Dan Shankle, contemplating. Finally he said, "I have notheeng to say," and his arms hung straight at his sides.

Dan turned to the lanky one. "Satisfied?" he asked.

The man nodded quietly. "I am Chamillard. I am satisfie'."

Dan looked at the scowling one in the rear. He knew instinctively that the fourth man was afraid of nothing, and he waited for the attack. But it didn't come. The man looked over the shoulders of the other two. His hand was on the butt of his pistol, but he looked past Dan, and slowly his hand fell away. Dan knew without looking that Simon was covering him.

Dan glanced at the squaws. They were chattering excitedly and giggling, watching Blundin climb the opposite bank. At Dan's stare they quieted suddenly, watching him with big dark eyes, alert, suspicious. They were both young, and looked good to a man who had been away from women for a long time. Perversely, it made him want to hurt them.

"You've got no loyalty!" he said scathingly.

They stared at him without a change of expression. Chamillard said, "Why should they have? He bought them both for one rifle, and in a couple of months he'll get tired of them and sell them down the river as slaves—if he doesn't get mad and kill them first."

Dan turned slowly. "Simon!"

"Here," said Simon from a seat on a cypress root.

"Tell the Choctaws to unload the canoes and—"

"The Choctaws already unloaded the stove-in one, and I let them take it."

"What for?"

"Choctaws are funny cusses," Simon observed, and pulled out his carrot of tobacco. He began to size it up for a chew. "They like to keep their hair. They figgered to get out of Osage country before dark, and I agreed with 'em. For a couple of escudos I'da gone with 'em."

19

Chapter Three

POEYFARRÉ and Chamillard took their time going back toward the blockhouse. Across the river, Blundin was walking down the bank to where a small canoe was tied.

Fifty rods upstream from him was the oak tree, but no turkeys were to be seen under it. The squaws had gone back to their bearskin and now were squatting on each side of it, scraping away the flesh with chisel-shaped bones, and watching him covertly as they talked softly.

They spent an hour moving the canoe to a new spot, and then carrying the already unloaded goods to the willow trees. While they were at it, Blundin came across the river in the small canoe, got out, and pushed it back into the water.

Dan saw three naked Indian children standing at the top of the bank watching. They'd get their boat, all right, although they'd have to follow it downstream until it swung against the other bank. Blundin went to the blockhouse without looking at Simon or Dan.

"You might have more trouble with him," said Simon.

"We won't be here that long."

They piled the goods and covered them with canvas. Simon built a fire with flint and steel, striking it into some charred cloth that he kept in a hollow joint of cane. Dan opened a meal gum, dipped out a double handful of corn meal with a gourd, filled it up with river water, and stirred it with his knife. He put in another small handful of meal to thicken it, while Simon cut some slabs of fat pork. Dan set the gourd of corn meal down by the fire.

"Make some ash cakes," he said. "I'll get some meat."

Simon laid the white strips of salt pork in the skillet. They sizzled when they touched the hot iron.

Dan went back to the sandy beach where they had first landed. The small canoe, paddled by the three naked Indian or half-breed boys they had seen earlier, was pulling around the upper end of the sand bar. They quit paddling as they got into quiet water, and watched Dan. He held out a string of blue and red beads, pointing at their boat. They shook their heads solemnly, holding up their paddles so the boat floated halfway between the sand bar and the beach. Dan

20

held a string of red and blue and green glass beads; then he pointed at them and said, "Obble-obble-obble."

The biggest boy watched the beads. He dug his paddle into the water and brought the canoe in to shore. He held up a fat turkey cock by its neck. Dan nodded vigorously. The boy wasn't over six years old. He tried to climb out of the canoe with the turkey, but it overbalanced him, and he fell into the water.

Dan helped him up. He took .the turkey by the neck and gave the beads to the boy, then waited for his approval or disapproval. The boy grabbed the beads and ran off toward the blockhouse.

Dan returned to the fire beyond the willows. Simon's back was toward him as he shaped corn-meal cakes and dropped them into the greased skillet.

Dan used a strip of rawhide to tie the bird to a tree, then began to skin it.

An argument was arising back at the bearskin. The squaws' voices were high and shrill and vehement.

Simon grumbled, "This is the noisiest place between Natchez and St. Louis."

Dan walked along the shore until he found clay. He encased the disjointed parts of the bird in the mud, carried them back to the fire, and buried them in the ashes.

Simon was watching him curiously. "You get along all right," he noted. "You're a fooler in a fight, and you know your business—but what are you doing in the Arkansa country?"

"You've known me all your life," said Dan. "We grew up together, didn't we?"

Simon said thoughtfully, "When we ran into each other on the levee that day you got in on the Philadelphia boat, you said you wanted to go up the Arkansa to do some trading."

"That's where we are, isn't it?"

Simon used the skillet to level out a place in the ashes. "What I'd like to know is how you were so sure you wanted to come up here."

Dan heard voices and looked up. Half a dozen red-capped men were emerging from the forest, following a well-worn trail. As they turned into the blockhouse, Dan finished pushing the clay-covered pieces of turkey into the ashes.

"I never asked if you had a passport," said Simon, "because if you had had one you'd of gone to Natchitoches."

Dan looked at him across the fire. "I'm looking for a man —a man who's diverting rifles from the frontier in Pennsylvania to the Indians in the Texas country."

Simon looked skeptical. "How can you make any money at that?"

"I won't," said Dan, "but I may save some lives." He stood up. "Ash cake and turkey," he said. "I wish we had something different for a change."

"Yesterday," said Simon, eying him from where he squatted before the fire, "you had catfish. The day before you had buffalo; the day before that it was panther; the day before that it was alligator tail." He scratched his whiskers. "Maybe I'm not no gourmet, but it seems to me you've had a well-set table."

"Meat!" said Dan. "I'd give a shilling for a dozen eggs."

"You would?" Simon got up. "I'll be back."

When he returned he held out his coonskin cap. "Two shillings' worth," he said.

Dan stared. The cap was filled with what looked like eggs, all right, but they were about half the size of a hen's egg and they were round. He picked one up and almost dropped it, for the shell wasn't hard, like a hen's egg, but leathery and tough. He rolled it around in his fingers. "What laid it?"

"A turtle. They lay them in the sand and cover them."

"They're probably not very fresh."

"For a shilling a dozen you can't affort to be finical."

"How do you cook them?"

"You can fry 'em," said Simon, "but I don't recommend it." He broke the shell with his knife point and let it run out into his hand, then held it toward Dan.

Dan sniffed. "It stinks!" he said.

"They eat better than they smell. I'll get some of that clay and we'll roast 'em."

They coated the turtle eggs and dropped them into the hot ashes. They sat back then, Dan against a big cottonwood tree that was just beginning to release cottony puffs that floated everywhere in the air, and Simon against a willow tree whose thick trunk showed a ripe old age.

Simon took out his tobacco from his shirt. "There's still some things make me wonder," he observed.

Dan watched the fire. "What are they?"

"You got by Arkansa Post too easy, for one thing."

"I did just what you told me to do."

"I know. But it went mighty slick, if you ask me."

"What else?"

"You came in here and camped in the front yard of the *contrabandistas* like you owned the place—and this is the toughest bunch of outlaws in all the Spanish colonies."

Dan chewed his tobacco. "Anything else?"

"Yeah. You didn't bring whisky or rifles—just four thousand pounds of ordinary trade goods, which you could as well of taken through Natchitoches."

"You told me yourself," said Dan, "a man can't accept anything but skins from the Indians if he has to come back through Natchitoches."

Simon nodded. His right jaw was bulging from the chew. "All that is true enough. If a man wants to trade for horses and mules and slaves, he can't do it through De Mézières's country. But there's something almighty strange about this trip." He looked at the blockhouse. "If you really wanted that kind of goods, why didn't you bring rifles and gunpowder? How do you figure to compete with Blundin's men when you've got lookin' glasses and beads?"

Dan didn't look up. The sun now was behind a ridge of woods on the west, and the rising hum of mosquitoes had reached a considerable volume. He got up and sliced off some green willow branches and threw them on the fire. Thick white smoke began to pour into the air.

"We're havin' more company," Simon said. "That second Frenchman is tired of bear meat. Maybe *he* likes turtle eggs."

Dan went to the pile of goods and lifted one corner of the canvas. He put something into his shirt and dropped the canvas. Then he went back and sat down.

Chamillard sauntered toward their fire, wiping his greasy knife blade on his woolen pants. He stopped to face Dan, and dropped his knife in its sheath.

"Have a seat. I'm Dan Shankle."

"Merci." Chamillard sat down against the cottonwood and pulled out a pipe.

"Try this," Dan said, withdrawing a full carrot of tobacco from his shirt.

The Frenchman looked up, studied Dan, and nodded as he took the tobacco. He shaved off trimmings with his knife and filled the bowl of the pipe. He snapped off a couple of green

23

twigs and got a coal from the fire to light up. The smell was very pleasant in the evening.

Chamillard looked at him finally, when the pipe was emitting clouds of smoke. "You're a good man in a fight," he said, "and I like you. But maybe," he added coldly, "you're a spy for the Spanish, just as Blundin says."

Dan said with equal flatness, "I'm no spy for the Spanish."

Chamillard pondered. "You look for something special?"

"What special, for instance?"

"It is a violent life along the Arkansa. Sometimes men get killed, and sometimes their friends come hunting the killer." He blew out smoke. "The Arkansa is not a place for a man to hunt revenge. It is enough to stay alive without adding complications."

Dan worked his chew. He got up and pushed a piece of turkey farther into the fire. "I'm not looking for revenge," he said. "I came to trade with the Indians."

Chamillard's eyes dropped to his pipe. "You can go upstream a hundred leagues, into the Trois Rivières country, and trade with the Osages, but they get goods from the English, and so they drive a hard bargain."

"Where is it better?" Dan asked.

Chamillard watched him over the pipe. "A number of us are leaving in the morning for the Wichita villages on the Rivière Rouge, over in the Texas country. We can use some extra men to protect ourselves from the Osages." Chamillard paused. "We raided a band of Osages the last trip and got some scalps and two squaws. They'll be looking for us when we go back."

"I thought the Osage country was farther north."

"The Osages do not confine themselves to any given place," said Chamillard. "They are almost as bad as the Naytanes."

"He means Camanches," Simon said. "Every country has a different name for every tribe."

"The Osages don't like for us to trade with the Wichitas, for they're always on the warpath against the Wichitas and Camanches, and they know that we're the ones who furnish rifles to the Texas tribes."

"The Osages don't like you, then."

Chamillard shrugged and looked toward the blockhouse. "We kill them and take their squaws. It doesn't help."

"How are the Wichitas?"

"Indians, like all the rest, but not dangerous. They raise

24

pumpkins and squash, fight when they have to. They are usually at peace with the Camanches. An Indian peace, that is, with nobody trusting anybody else as far as you can kill a bull buffalo with a tomahawk."

"Why do they even pretend?"

"The Camanches buy firearms and get rid of their stock and their slaves through the Wichitas. The Wichitas make a profit."

"The Wichitas ought to be happy."

"They complain because the licensed traders from Natchitoches don't bring them enough rifles and gunpowder to fight the Osages."

"So they do business with the *contrabandistas?*"

Chamillard nodded. "They have to."

"And the Camanches?"

"They raid the Spanish from Santa Fé to Chihuahua and Bexar; they raid the Apaches wherever they find them. They kill the men, but they keep the women and children and sell them to the Wichitas, and eventually these pass through Arkansa Post and end up in Louisiana." Chamillard blew a cloud of smoke into a swarm of mosquitoes.

"What about these two Osage squaws in camp now?"

"They're Blundin's. You could probably borrow one if you want."

"Have you got any idea where I can get mules to pack my goods?"

Chamillard knocked out his pipe. "See Blundin."

"After the fight we've just had?"

"Blundin's English. He's in business for a profit. He'll sell you mules if you can pay for them."

Dan, squatting on his haunches, looked up at Chamillard through the smoke. "Who's that ugly sinner that stood behind you?"

Chamillard glanced toward the blockhouse before he answered. "He calls himself D'Etrées, but he's not French. He's the most dangerous man on the Arkansa."

"Worse than Blundin?"

Chamillard said seriously, "D'Etrées could whip Blundin with a cup of rum in one hand and never spill a drop. And then he would finish his drink and toss the rest in Blundin's face."

"Blundin, then, is not the boss on the Arkansa?"

"Yes, Blundin is the boss, because D'Etrées does not want to be. Blundin is ver' bad medicine, but D'Etrées is worse."

25

"Is D'Etrées likely to get in my way?" asked Dan.

Chamillard put his pipe in his shirt. "Who knows? He is here now, gone the next minute. He never explains. Nobody asks."

Dan got up. "I'll go with you to see about the mules," he said.

The turkey was tender and cooked through when Dan got back from talking to Blundin.

"You have any luck?" asked Simon.

Dan ripped the baked clay from a turkey thigh and bit into the juicy meat. "I got mules—at a price."

"How much of a price?"

Dan stripped the last meat from the bone and tossed it away. "I traded him half my stuff for twelve mules—enough to carry the other half and you and me."

Simon was fishing baked eggs out of the fire. "Pretty high price for mules, ain't it?"

"About a hundred and sixty-five dollars apiece."

"The best mule on earth isn't worth over a hundred."

"He is if you need him."

"You don't need 'em that bad. You've still got the canoe. We can go upriver a little ways and peddle the stuff to the Osages. You could get mules from them for about a fourth of what you paid."

Dan cracked open another piece of turkey. "As I understand it, these Wichita villages are the trading center for all of Texas."

"For the Norteños, anyway."

"Who are they?"

"The northern tribes—Wichitas, Penateka Camanches, Kotsoteka Camanches, Pawnees, and some others."

"Then they're the people I want to do business with," said Dan. "The Norteños."

"You're sure a hardheaded cuss," said Simon. "Have a turtle egg."

Chapter Four

THEY WERE UP long before daylight. Chamillard and a man named Dartigo came to help them load the mules. Poeyfarré appeared to be the leader of the train. He had twenty-two mules and two men to help him with them, while the rest seemed to be more in the nature of guards.

They were under way by sunup, striking from the blockhouse through the surrounding swamp, leaving the two squaws and their children behind.

Along toward noon Poeyfarré stopped. "Unpack your mules," he told Dan. "We'll let them graze until the middle of the afternoon. Then we'll move on. There's a safe place to camp about three leagues up the river."

"When do we cross over?"

Poeyfarré stuck out his chin. "You ask questions," he said. "We cross in a couple of days, when the river gets shallow. *You* can cross any time you want."

Abruptly there was silence around them, and Dan felt the impact of suspicion and belligerence. He said quietly, "I started with you. I'll finish with you."

Chamillard was building a fire while Dartigo and a man named Poupelinière were taking care of Poeyfarré's mules. Two other Frenchmen, Menard and Brognard, who had dropped out earlier, now came with a gutted deer carcass, which they cut up and hung over the fire while they ate the liver raw.

"Don't sit on the grass," Simon told Dan. "You're liable to come up full of chiggers. They itch like sin."

That afternoon they followed a narrow ridge, with the river on the left and the swamps on the right. Occasionally they had to ford a shallow pass where the water had cut through at overflow time. But the swamps grew smaller as they progressed northwest. It was still humid and hot, but the nature of the country changed. Pine trees began to appear on bluffs along the river, and a vast prairie extended for thirty leagues but still the air was close and stifling in the timbered bottoms. The pines grew bigger and the oaks became more plentiful. They crossed the river but still followed it. The country turned mountainous.

One morning they came across pony tracks that led up from the river and entered the trail from an open, grassy place. Menard, a slender man with black hair, got down and examined the grass. "Ponies with riders," he said. "Most likely Indians. Droppings still warm. They were here this morning, maybe two hours ago."

"How many?" Poeyfarré asked thoughtfully.

"Six ponies."

"Squaws?"

Menard backtracked to the riverbank, looked around, and came back. "Squaws and bucks."

Poeyfarré's heavy jaw worked in thought. "With squaws along, they aren't hunting trouble."

"They're headed northwest," Dartigo said. "And they must have started from the northwest or we'd have run across their trail before."

Poeyfarré stared at him. "So?"

"So they know we're coming, and they've gone back to tell the main tribe."

Poeyfarré squinted at the sun. "They probably won't get there before evening. By that time we'll be ready to turn away from the river."

"Some of these mules haven't got any skin left on their backs," said Villars, a man who limped on his left leg. "They may balk at a long trip today."

"I've eaten worse than mule meat," Poeyfarré answered.

Villars shrugged elaborately.

The country had become less watery and still more mountainous. Down in the bottoms there were a few cypress, but now there were more cottonwoods and sycamores, and cane had taken the place of the impenetrable tangle of undergrowth.

The train was now headed due west, but Chamillard kept looking to the northwest. Dartigo, watching him, said something in French, and Chamillard explained to Dan. "I lived up there a couple of years ago with White Hair's band. They call him Pahuska." He took a deep breath, his eyes far away. "I left a squaw and some children up there."

Dan watched the Frenchman, and sensed something coming that nobody could control. Even Poeyfarré, he knew instinctively, would be powerless.

"You got to remember one thing," Simon said in his ear. "These fellers are the best in the world at taking care of themselves, but they are also children. They take a notion to do something, they do it whether it's reasonable or not."

Dan looked at him. "You think he'll go back to the Osages?"

Simon shook his head. "Nobody knows—him least of all. Just keep your eyes skinned, for he left his squaw. If he goes back now, it means trouble. They'll know he's with our train, and they'll follow him to us." Simon frowned.

Chamillard and Dartigo talked together in low voices. The mules were slowing down, and it took constant beating with heavy sticks to keep them moving. They were keeping to the pine- and oak-covered ridges. "Dry camp tonight," said Simon as Dan dropped back.

Dan looked at the heavy-bellied man. "Better than losing your hair," he said.

A cloud began to form in the west before the sun went down. "We'll stop and make camp for a thunderstorm," said Poeyfarré. "There'll be some weather tonight."

Chamillard showed them how to arrange two pack saddles close together, lay their rifles across them a foot off the ground, hang their bullet pouches and powder horns on them, cover the whole with branches and lay a blanket over the branches, and finally dig a trench around the saddles and their burden. "If it rains, the water will run off," he said. "Dig a trench to one side, and you can sleep within. If it rains, you won't get too wet."

"Your friends from the Six Bull River won't bother us tonight," said Poeyfarré to Chamillard, "but I look for them when it gets light."

Chamillard said absently, "Maybe they won't bother us."

Poeyfarré snorted. "I don't like the look in your eye, you green-shelled turtle. You are getting set for trouble."

There was a peal of thunder, closer than before, and Chamillard laughed the high, crazy laugh of a man who is drunk beyond control. "You never knew a squaw like Oak Leaf," he said in a detached voice.

Poeyfarré sounded disgusted. "I've known more squaws than you ever saw, *enfant,* and I found out one thing: a squaw is a squaw—Slave, Chippewa, Pottawatomie, Osage, or Wichita. If you don' get that damn look out of your voice, I am tempt' to hit you over the head."

Chamillard didn't even hear him. "You never had a squaw like Oak Leaf," he said as if from a vast fund of superior wisdom. "She makes you forget there are others of any tribe."

"Fool!" snarled Pocyfarré.

Menard came up. "It's his own head to lose," he said.

Poeyfarré looked ready to battle. A yellow lightning flash illumined his projecting jaw, and his gray-blue eyes were hard. "I don't care for *his* head. I care for mine. If he goes, he'll bring the Osages on us. That squaw of his will report it the minute he steps out of her lodge."

"We'll be gone before the Osages get here," said Menard.

"Not far enough," Poeyfarré insisted. "Who's watching the mules?"

29

"Villars and Brognard."

"You and I will relieve them."

Dan spoke up. "Simon and I will stand our turn."

Poeyfarré looked at him skeptically. "You know anything about Indians?"

"I been fighting Iroquois for ten years."

"They aren't like Osages."

"Indians are Indians."

Poeyfarré nodded slowly. "One of you pair up with me, the other with Menard. We know this country and you don't."

"All right."

Blackness covered the entire sky. The air was heavy and oppressive, and lightning flashed in all directions, but especially in the west. The intervals between flashes had become so short that at times the sky presented a continuous succession of yellow forks, and a minute afterward the valley below them was filled with rolling thunder. A cold wind struck them from the west. At first it merely shook the tree tops against the backdrop of lightning; then a few drops of rain came down.

Poeyfarré roared, "Get under cover! Stay away from trees! Menard, come with me!" and ran toward the mules.

The wind howled through the trees, and Dan shuddered inside his trench with the blanket around him. The lightning was almost a continuous sheet now, and getting closer. The constant crash of thunder made it impossible to talk. He huddled there waiting for the storm to hit, and thought of Baltimore and Sarah Radnor.

He remembered the first thing he had noticed about Sarah, aside from her startling flaxen hair and violet eyes: She had a light, flowery fragrance, totally unlike his mother and sisters on the frontier, who invariably smelled of sour sweat and wood smoke. It had made him conscious of his buckskin clothes, but Sarah had insisted he wear them, even when she took him to society parties in Baltimore. She had exhibited him as she might have worn a large jewel or a rare locket.

Sometimes it had annoyed him a little, but not too much, for always there were Sarah's laughing violet eyes to look up at him, and when he gazed down at her and saw the light in them that was for him only—for no woman could look that way at more than one man—then he didn't mind being introduced to her friends as a man of the frontier. Sometimes he had heard other words—"primitive," "straight from the jungle," "moves like a mountain cat"—but he did not let those disturb him, for only Sarah's opinion was important to him. The others' were not. It was as simple as that. He remembered the warmth of her lips and knew he was right.

Lightning hit a little higher on the ridge. The wind swirled and howled and blew a sleety gust of cold rain from the south. Then the blackness opened up. The hillside became as light as day, and the big trees shook with thunder. The wind roared back to the west and blew straight up the meadow, driving the rain in horizontal sheets that penetrated everything—blanket, buckskin, meat, and bone.

In the yellow light, Dan saw four men in the meadow holding the mules together. The animals had turned their rumps to the rain and were holding ground. If they drifted at all, they would drift into the wind. Poeyfarré apparently understood this, for he and his men stood far behind the mules with their backs to the rain.

With four men in the meadow, that left four in camp. Dan looked for Chamillard and Dartigo but didn't see them. Simon shouted at him, but Dan could not distinguish the words. They saw a blinding flash of lightning, and with a thunderous explosion the big oak tree under which they had cooked their supper burst down the middle. One half remained standing, while the other half fell toward them with a great wrenching of branches. Then he heard the crashing and threw himself on the ground, rolling downhill.

Simon had been an instant ahead of him. When the half of the oak tree came to earth, only a few small twigs brushed Dan. He leaped to his feet and looked at the tons of fallen wood. Steam and smoke were coming from the split base. Then rain swept through the trees again and for a moment hid everything from sight. . . .

Poeyfarré and Menard came back after the storm center passed over. They built a fire and took off their clothes to dry them, then hung soaked blankets over the boughs of a fallen oak. Dan and Simon took axes and cleared a way to their rifles.

Poeyfarré was grumbling. "Storm like this, a man gets no sleep." He crammed a big pipe full of tobacco. "Only good thing, it keeps the Osages in camp. They don't like

31

this kind of weather any more than we do." He looked up at Dan. "Your rifles dry?"

"Dry enough."

"I saw three-four deer down there under the willows. See if you can get one. We'll be up all night anyway, so we might as well eat."

The hard wind and rain were rolling east. Dan got his powder flask and took out the smaller flask of priming powder. He poured some into the pan and walked cautiously across the meadow, approaching the willows from the uphill side.

In the lightning flashes he saw the head of a buck, watching toward the east. He lay down in the wet grass and drew a careful aim. At the next flash he squeezed the trigger. The buck took one long leap into the water, but did not get up. Two does hit the water with great splashes and kept going. Simon came running down from camp. They carried the deer between them and set it down by the fire. Poeyfarré's knife was already out. "Through the heart," he grunted. "That rifle of yourn shoots dead center."

"It should," said Dan. "It was made by a good workman."

"None of these damn French rifle-makers, I hope."

"English."

"A good rifle," Poeyfarré grunted. "Wouldn't mind having one like that myself."

Dan looked at Poeyfarré in the firelight. "They're hard to come by," he said quietly.

Poeyfarré didn't notice—he was busy hanging strips of deer meat over the fire on green twigs—but Simon looked up sharply.

Suddenly Poeyfarré turned. "Chamillard! Dartigo!" he roared.

There was no answer.

"Menard!"

"*Oui.*"

"Do you know anything about those two idiots?"

"No," Menard said carefully. "I have not see' them."

"You!" Poeyfarré's heavy jaw swung on Dan. "Were they with you when the tree went over?"

"I didn't see either of them."

Poeyfarré uttered a string of French oaths. He called down to the mule herd. "Poupelinière!"

"*Oui,*" came the answer against the background of rumbling thunder and the whistling wind in the treetops.

32

"Is Chamillard down there? Or Dartigo?"

"*Non.*"

Poeyfarré shook his big head in fury. A gust of wind blew a shower of rain down on them from the leaves, but Poeyfarré paid no attention. "They've gone up to the Six Bull to hunt squaws," he muttered, "and if Chamillard finds Oak Leaf, he is certain to bring White Hair's band down on us."

Chapter Five

LONG BEFORE DAYLIGHT they finished the deer, and Poeyfarré gave the order to start packing. "We have got to move," he said. "Chamillard's in-laws will be after us." He groaned. "Why couldn't that damn fool wait until we got to the Wichita village?"

Villars grinned. "Maybe he thought Osage was better."

"There ain't no 'better,' " Poeyfarré growled. "Worst of it is, they took two good mules."

By dawn the train was on a high ridge running east and west. With the sun coming up behind them, they pushed the mules west. The top of the ridge was rocky and inhabited by rattlesnakes and copperheads, and Poeyfarré took the train down below the top on the south side.

They drove the mules hard until noon. "You will have to let them rest," Menard told Poeyfarré.

Poeyfarré grumbled but called a halt.

Dan and Brognard kept watch from the top of the hill while the others cooked a small doe that Dan had knocked over with a club.

"You are very light on your feet," Poeyfarré said.

"We've had Indians up our way too."

Simon and Menard came up to act as lookouts and let the other two eat.

"Are we going on right away?" asked Brognard, a man with a deep scar running from one eye.

"Soon as we eat," said Menard, loading a pipe with tobacco. "We've got to keep moving."

Brognard glanced to the north. They had not seen the Arkansa River all day. "Is no use to run, anyway. The

33

Osages can travel twice as fast as we can, and they can trail us clear to Santa Fé."

They went far over the cutoff that day, and before the sun went down they reached the Canadian Fork. Poeyfarré took the mules down to water, then established a camp in the middle of a sloping prairie between the river and a hillside covered with blackjack.

"Why not in the trees?" asked Dan. "We'd have cover."

"One man might do it," Poeyfarré said, "but a big outfit like this would get murdered. No white man can beat an Indian in the woods, and with six men and forty mules—" He shook his head. "We'll camp in the open. Indians don't like gunpowder and lead. They won't charge an open place like a white man. An Indian thinks every rifle is pointed at him."

"Sounds reasonable," said Simon.

"It's the only way to meet a big force. You spread out in the woods and they'll get you one at a time. But in the open you knock down a few and the rest go home to report."

It was quiet that night—too quiet, Poeyfarré said. He was up most of the night, prowling the camp, going alone down to the river or up toward the blackjack. He got them out before the sky turned gray in the east. They didn't eat, but packed the mules and headed southwest straight up the middle of the strip of prairie. It was good sense, Dan saw, because it would be difficult for Indians to ambush them on the prairie.

The sun had just come up when a faint cry came: "Poeyfarré!"

Dan located the sound across the river. Two men rode mules on the opposite ridge above the blackjack. He guessed they were Chamillard and Dartigo, and he was glad they were back, for Chamillard had been friendly.

Poeyfarré waved at them but kept the train moving. Chamillard and Dartigo turned their mules toward the river—and without warning and without sound the rest of the hillside came alive.

There were redskins everywhere. Each warrior was over six feet tall, dressed in breechclout and moccasins, with a beaver bandeau around the head. They had tattooed V's on their chests and their faces were painted black. Their scalps were shaved to leave only a strip of hair from front to back. And they were not making a sound.

"Like Mohawks." Dan reached grimly for his rifle.

34

"No shooting now!" warned Poeyfarré. "It won't help them, and we've got to keep our rifles loaded for an attack on the train." He shouted, in a booming voice that would have carried a mile, "Chamillard! Wazhazhe!"

There was silence from the blackjack. The hillside was alive with Osages, all moving toward the center.

Simon muttered, "I'd sure like to lay one in there, but Poeyfarré is talkin' sense. There's too many of 'em for us to do any good from here, and we've got our own scalps to look after."

Poeyfarré and Menard were leading the mules into a circle.

"Unpack!" he shouted. "Tie the mules to each other so the Indians can't stampede them!"

A few shots came from the blackjack thicket, almost as a burst, and Dan looked soberly at Simon. "They couldn't have fired but twice," he said.

Simon was watching with narrowed eyes. He shook his head. "There was too many of 'em."

The mules began to graze. The six men spread themselves to face in all directions, using the pack saddles as rifle rests. "They'll come from uphill, most likely," said Poeyfarré, "but watch in all directions. And don't everybody shoot at once. Take turns, so there's always a rifle loaded."

They herded the mules into a shallow draw and waited.

Nothing moved for a long time, while the sun grew hotter. Then high in the air, almost too far to be visible, black dots began to circle over the blackjack where Chamillard and Dartigo had last been seen.

The hills in the distance were emerald green. Dan, watching downstream in the direction from which they had come, saw a cayeute walk up from the river, its nose high to catch the scents on the wind. Then a flock of prairie chickens—twenty or more—got up from the edge of the blackjacks with a curious cackling and flew almost over their heads and across the river to the other side.

Dan scanned the blackjacks and saw the white tails of a dozen antelopes as the animals floated out of sight over the ridge, and he knew then it was coming. "Poeyfarré!"

The big man grunted, nodding his head. "It'll come from there, all right, but you and Jeffreys keep an eye to the river. These Osages are tricky."

The first shot came from Menard. A bronze body with a fox-fur roach fell at the edge of the trees. Menard pulled

35

his rifle down from the pack saddle and began to reload, lying on the ground. A flight of arrows came at the breastworks formed by the goods.

Poeyfarré fired. Another flight of arrows came at them. Dan heard one thud into a mule with the hard zip that he had come to recognize in the East. The mule started to bray, but it stopped agonizingly as blood ran out of its mouth, and it slowly collapsed to the ground.

For a while there was silence. Then a shot sounded from the blackjacks. The ball went over their heads with a crack, and Dan looked for a small cloud of black smoke. He found it in the top of a post oak. He slanted his rifle and pulled the butt back against his shoulder. He saw a gleam of bronze skin, a beaver bandeau. He centered the sights on the bandeau and let it go. An Indian dropped out of the tree, crashing through branches that tipped the body one way and then the other before it wound up sprawled across a rats' nest at the foot of the tree.

Poeyfarré said, "I'm sure goin' to have one of them rifles, Shankle."

"They shoot center," said Dan, "if you hold them right."

Menard chuckled. "If we don't get out of here, you don't need any kind."

"There's no *if*," said Poeyfarré. "I like my own head."

"The buzzards have settle' down across the rivaire," Brognard noted. "I theenk that's all of Chamillard and Dartigo."

There was desultory shooting after that. Another mule got an arrow through both ears, and brayed piteously while it flopped the arrow from one side to the other.

"Let him alone," growled Poeyfarré. "He's not hurt."

Presently Menard observed, "The sun, she's get pretty high."

Brognard scowled. His scarred eye gave him a ferocious appearance. "And hot," he said.

Simon said, "Give me that bladder and I'll go for water."

"There'll be Indians at the river," said Poeyfarré. "That's where they want to drive us."

"Cut that fool mule loose," said Poupelinière. "He's goin' to stampede the others."

Dan went down on his stomach. He reached the mules and stood up among them, watching for stray heels. Arrows began to come over, and two or three rifles sounded. Dan used his knife to cut the rawhide rope that held the ear-pierced mule to the others. Freed, the mule bucked in a half circle around the fort, and an Osage arrow got it in the

36

chest. A dozen more were bristling in its body when it fell.

The mules soon began to bray for water. Poeyfarré swore. "The damn Indians'll know we're short on water!"

"How long will they keep it up?"

"Till dark, most likely, unless they get tired of waiting and try to rush us. Then if we make it hot for 'em—"

"They're come!" screamed Menard.

Poeyfarré shouted, "Stay down and shoot straight!"

Osages erupted out of the trees with hideous yells and exploded across the grass toward the fort. Poeyfarré lay where he was, sighting along his rifle. Menard fired, and a big brave slid forward on his face. Simon got one between the eyes. Dan waited. Menard dropped his rifle and pulled a pistol from his waistband and cocked it.

Arrows were everywhere, but the men stayed down, and the Osages, now on a broad front, wavered. Back in the blackjacks two roached braves stayed, one at each side, and attempted to provide a covering fire for the attackers. But here and there an Osage dropped, and the Indians didn't like it. The line wavered as it reached the dead mule. Menard stopped a black-faced warrior who fell across the mule's neck. Then the line broke. The Osages raced for the trees.

Poeyfarré got up on one knee. His face was black with powder smoke. "They forgot to yell goin' back," he said with satisfaction, and looked around. "Anybody hurt?"

"You got a bad hand," Dan observed.

Poeyfarré swore. "The damn redskins! Why can't they shoot a man someplace important instead of his thumb?"

The thumb was hanging by a shred of flesh. Poeyfarré looked at it disgustedly. He laid it on the pack saddle and pulled out his knife. He took one chop and let the thumb roll into the dirt. "It'll be sore for a month," he growled. "Anybody else got anything?"

"I got a little here," said Dan, and straightened out his leg. The feathered end of an arrow shaft was protruding from his thigh. He began to cut off the end.

Menard said, "You better have a drink, frien'."

Poeyfarré said, "Get the demijohn!"

It was Brognard that planted his moccasin against the back of Dan's thigh and pulled the arrow on through. He looked at Dan and laughed. "You're white in the face, Eenglishman!"

"Give me that jug!" said Dan, suddenly choking.

An hour later he felt better. They had bandaged the wound

with beaver fur to stop the bleeding, and he lay at full length, constantly flexing the leg to keep it from stiffening. The sun was hotter and the mules were braying more loudly.

"There's been no action up there for quite a while," said Menard. "Do you theenk they have retreated?"

"It might be," said Poeyfarré, "but a man would never know, they're so tricky."

Dan watched for a while. "There's a live Indian behind the mule," he announced.

Menard squinted. "The one that fell across the mule's neck, *oui?*"

"We'll have to get him," said Poeyfarré.

Dan took his skinning knife from its sheath and tested the edge. "I can get him," he said, "if you keep them down up there at the trees."

Poeyfarré looked at him doubtfully. "With that leg?"

Dan laid his rifle down beside Simon. "Anybody else got a leg I can use?"

"*Bien.* But don't let that Osage get the jump on you. We need every rifle we have."

Dan was flat, crawling out between two pack saddles. "Keep them down, up there," he repeated.

He got out into the open. The grass was about six inches high and only half covered him, but he stayed flat against the ground and progressed slowly under the sun, now a big yellow ball in a sky that had turned from blue to copper. There was no breeze now. He heard a sandpiper in the river bed below, and from somewhere in the trees came the sad call of a wood phoebe. That was reassuring, for it indicated that if there were any Osages still in the blackjacks, they were keeping low. And yet it was something to wonder about, for it didn't seem reasonable that they would desert a wounded companion. The Indian behind the mule, of course, should have been dead, but Dan had seen two small movements of the roach, as if the Indian were trying to get an eye on them. He was halfway to the mule when a rifle crashed behind him, and he flattened out. An arrow dropped into the ground so close it threw dust into his eyes. A prolonged "ah-ah-ah" came from the blackjacks and ended in a gurgle that sounded as if the Indian had eggs in his throat. Or maybe it was blood.

He lay for a moment, gathering energy, and felt a sting on his thigh. He brushed it, and winced as he hit his leg. He squirmed around and found himself over a nest of big black ants that had been attracted by the blood still coming

38

from his leg. With the knife in his extended right arm, he moved on.

He heard guttural words of Osage from the blackjacks, and he realized they were directed to the warrior behind the mule. That Indian was now warned, and would be ready. He crawled on.

The mule had begun to swell up under the sun, and big blue and green flies had settled around its nose and mouth.

Dan did not risk looking back. He wanted to be facing forward if and when the Osage came from behind the mule. He moved almost without sound. A shadow passed over the ground and he knew the buzzards were circling, waiting for the end.

He studied the position of the mule. He was now less than ten feet from it. It lay stretched out parallel with the river, its head upstream, its four legs toward the trees. The Indian was between the two pairs of legs, and from the mule's body extended a small thicket of arrows.

The logical way to go after the Indian was around one end, but this would expose him to the blackjacks. He considered the situation, inching closer, and decided to go over the arrows. The Indian would get to his feet, and if his companions in the blackjacks fired at Dan, they might very well catch their friend in the back.

He could almost touch the mule. Another shot sounded from the fort. This time there was no arrow, but from up ahead came the sound of a loose arm or leg flopping. Like the Eastern Indians, Dan supposed, the Osages were hard to kill.

He could not see over the mule now, and he dared not raise his head. He began to gather his feet under him. Then a single shouted word came from the blackjacks, and he leaped to his feet.

The wounded Indian leaped at the same time, and for an instant they faced each other across the body of the mule. The Indian was a gruesome sight. He had taken a shot along the side of his head. It had cut a furrow in his scalp, and this had bled profusely, until his face and chest were caked with dried blood already turning black.

Without a sound the Indian jumped at him, swinging a brass tomahawk. Dan saw the shining arc it made under the sun, and knew the end of that arc was intended for his head at about level of his ear. He ducked, and the tomahawk missed him, but the Indian's body hit him. He

39

had braced himself to receive that impact, but he had not taken into full account his injured leg. He tried to turn on it, but he was slow, and then it crumpled under him and he went down.

The bloody Indian dropped on him, tomahawk raised. Dan rolled to free his right arm. The tomahawk started down. Dan blocked the Indian's arm with his left forearm, and drove his knife up to the haft in the bloody chest.

He kept his hand on the knife handle. He tried to pull out the knife, but he must have driven it into soft bone, for it didn't come loose. The Indian's black eyes looked for a moment like the eyes of a cayeute backing away from a club. He tried to swing the tomahawk but failed. The light in the eyes died. The body slumped against him.

Dan eased it to the ground, and went down with it to avoid presenting a target to the blackjacks. He lay on his stomach in the protection of the mule's carcass and worked his knife out of the Indian. Then he began to reverse himself to start back for the improvised fort.

A "Don't!" from Jeffreys stopped him. There were still Indians in the blackjacks, then.

He lay there for almost an hour, while the sun got hotter, the flies got thicker, and the shadows of the vultures crossed the ground with increasing frequency. Finally he turned on his back. The knife was still in his hand. He counted the vultures. There were eight of them now, barely the height of a post-oak tree above him.

Finally there was a rush from the fort. Simon charged across the open space and threw himself at full length beside him.

"You hurt?" he asked.

"No."

"Poeyfarré thinks they've left the blackjacks now that their *compañero* is out of the fight. I brought your rifle. Feel like going to have a look?"

"Sure." Dan wiped his knife on the Indian's bandeau and put it back in his sheath. He took the rifle. "You go up the left; I'll take the right. We'll meet in the middle."

Simon nodded. He glanced at Dan's leg, and watched him get up. "She's pretty stiff," he suggested.

Dan said, "She'll limber up."

They moved out in a wide circle like a pair of curved horns. Poeyfarré and his men were watching. They reached the blackjacks without trouble, and began to move from one tree to another.

They met in the center. "No redskins," said Simon.

Dan shook his head. The leg was beginning to give him difficulty.

"There's some blood up here," said Simon.

"I've got blood."

The Frenchmen got to their feet as the two men returned. Poeyfarré nodded approval and turned to the mules. "Get these birds down to the water. You two—Shankle and Jeffreys—stay here and keep an eye on things. We'll water the mules and then pack and move on. Can you ride?" he asked Dan.

"Don't worry about me," Dan told him. "Get some water into these mules before they bray themselves hoarse."

Poeyfarré grinned. He seemed relieved. He vaulted over the pack saddles, and they began to untie the mules and turn them loose.

Poeyfarré came back leading four animals by the halters. He looked worried. "I think we better cross the river and go up the other side this evening and tomorrow," he said. "If the Osages try to ambush us, they'll wait on this side, for they know the trail."

"What happens to the goods of Chamillard and Dartigo?" asked Simon.

"We divide the goods and mules between us. They don't need them any more."

Within another hour the sun was nearing the western horizon. They took the trail down to the river. "Watch out for quicksand," Poeyfarré told them.

"What about it?"

"Keep moving. Don't let the mules stand in one place or they'll go down."

The water wasn't over a foot deep, but it was loaded with red silt. Dan dismounted and went upstream a way to drink. They crossed the half-mile bed of the river—most of it dry sand—and turned left on the sloping hillside where they had seen Chamillard and Dartigo.

Menard looked up to the blackjacks. His face was drawn. "We ought to hunt for them," he said.

Dan was behind him. "They might be alive."

The sun was halfway down now, and inside the blackjack thicket it was twilight. They rode carefully, searching the ground. Menard swore under his breath and galloped the mule

41

forward. A dozen vultures flapped heavily into the air in all directions when Menard jumped off the mule, grabbed a fallen branch, and struck at the ugly birds. He came back swearing.

"There's no need to bury them, anyway."

"There's not much left to bury," said Dan.

They started after the train. "What happened to their heads?" asked Dan. "There weren't any skull bones."

"The Wazhazhe," said Menard.

Dan stared at him. "They cut them off?"

"That's the way they count coup—especially when they're mad."

Poeyfarré met them with a question in his eyes.

Menard shook his head. For a moment he did not seem to be able to talk.

Dan moved in the saddle to take his weight off of his bad leg. "It looks like Chamillard and Dartigo found what they went after," he said, "but the price was pretty high."

Chapter Six

THEY CAMPED on the ridge that night, out in the open. The next morning again they were up early, pushing toward the southwest. The following morning Poeyfarré led them back across the Canadian Fork, and they took up the former trail.

Some days later they came to the shore of a great river, much wider than the Canadian Fork and carrying many times as much water, though it too was loaded with fine red mud in suspension. They camped near it in the early afternoon.

"This is the Red River of Natchitoches," Poeyfarré told them. "We'll cross here in the morning, and by night we'll be with the Wichitas."

"Why don't we cross tonight?"

"There may be trouble. She's a big river and as tricky sometimes as the Osages."

"I don't theenk we have trouble this time," said Menard.

Poeyfarré studied it. "Maybe not. There is not so much water as last time."

They swam the mules across the next morning before the

sun was up. "If we don't get them across now, we have to wait until noon, because the water reflects the sun when it is low and looks like a sheet of fire, and the mules won't walk into it," Poeyfarré explained.

He led out, feeling his way across, swimming his mule in the deepest part. The pack mules, kept in place by the six men, followed quietly. One or two objected to swimming, but were pulled into the stream by rawhide ropes around the necks, and had no choice. They gathered on the south shore and strung out along the river. By sunrise they had gone quite a distance, and Poeyfarré was satisfied. The country was mostly undulating prairie, and they marked down several small buffalo herds, but Poeyfarré would not let them hunt.

Menard, who had now attached himself to Dan and Simon said, "He's always nervous when he gets near."

"Scared of the Spanish?" asked Simon.

"Eet ees not alone the Spanish. One does not know how friendly the Wichitas may be."

"They were all right the last time, weren't they?"

Menard shrugged. "That was months ago. These *Indiens* of this country arc different from those in the East. These move around and cover big distance. Today you find Camanche vair much north from here; tomorrow in Bexar or even in Mexico. Since they have horses, it is not easy to know where they are or whom they are fighting. A Camanche chief decides to take a Wichita wife. He takes her. The Wichita goes after her and kills the Camanche. Then the Camanche's relatives all make war on Wichita. Wichita fight back. In a few days—poof! The whole country is fighting."

About noon the train reached a smaller stream that flowed into the Red, and Poeyfarré led them up the south bank. It was twenty feet wide by one foot deep, but its water was clear and sweet, and for the first time in several days the mules were allowed to drink all they wanted.

"They've seen us," said Poeyfarré.

"How do you know?" asked Simon.

"Smoke signals." Poeyfarré pointed to the southwest. "See that column of smoke? They make it by throwing green leaves on a fire. That notifies the chief there's company coming."

"That is good sign," said Menard.

Poeyfarré nodded. "If they were hostile, they would not send up a fire where we could see it. They'd already be down on us with about six hundred warriors."

"You think it's the same chief?"

43

"Probably. Old Eyasiquiche was a strong chief. He had a lot of relatives in the tribes, and nobody would dare to kill him." He kicked his mule in the flanks. "Let's get up there. I don't like to have Indians looking for me any time."

"You're scary," said Simon.

Poeyfarré swept off his red stocking cap and bent his head toward them. "You see that? That hair has been there all my life."

Menard laughed, but Poeyfarré went on seriously: "Is one thing I am very finical about: my scalp."

Two hours later they were riding into a large flat space surrounded by low hills and opening on the river—a sort of amphitheatre on the prairie. To Dan's surprise, they rode through fields of corn, pumpkins, melons, squashes, and beans. A mile away across the fields were some two hundred peculiar straw structures, all round and all tapering to a point at the top.

"Looks like a bunch of beehives or hornets' nests," observed Simon.

"Or straw stacks."

"Nobody working in the fields," Menard observed, frowning.

Among the straw dwellings were numerous upright racks made of boughs, upon which hung thousands of dark objects that Menard said were thin slices of buffalo meat, put out to dry. But Menard didn't like the look of things. "The kids are all inside," he said. "Even the squaws are under cover."

"Maybe," said Brognard, "they don't know who we are yet."

"It is somethin' to hope," Poeyfarré growled. "Whatever happens, don't fire a rifle or draw a knife unless I say so."

Chills began to work up and down Dan's spine. One moment the village was seemingly deserted; then suddenly Indians were erupting toward them afoot and on horseback, with fearful yells.

"Keep going," ordered Poeyfarré. "No faster, no slower."

Menard observed, "I don' theenk they on the warpath. Squaws and kids come too. Anyhow, when they fight they hide. They no attack like this."

It seemed that Menard was right. It was frightening to be surrounded by hundreds of Indians whose skins were so dark they were almost black, but they offered no harm. They were shorter than the Osages, and heavier. Their faces

44

were broad and their noses flat, and their hair was long and black and neither combed nor braided.

The men wore moccasins, leggings, and breechclouts or flaps; the women wore moccasins and short bark skirts, with nothing above the waist. Their faces were heavily tattooed, and intricate rings were tattooed around their breasts. The men were not tattooed at all.

Pocyfarré kept the train moving, his rifle balanced across his saddle. A small party of Indians came from within the village of grass huts. These were all on foot but one, who rode a barebacked mule. This Indian was huge and grossly fat. He wore the usual moccasins and leggings, a breechclout, and a blue silk shirt. He pulled up to Poeyfarré, who grinned and said, *"Hartch."*

"Hartch!" the fat Indian said.

Poeyfarré balanced the rifle on his knees while he clasped his hands before him. "We come in peace," he said.

The fat chief nodded. He held his right hand, back up, before his left breast, and moved it briskly to the front.

Menard sighed gratefully. "He says we're welcome."

"Is that the Indian sign language?" asked Dan.

"Sure," said Simon. "You don't see it in the East. This is about as far as it comes."

"We bring plenty of tobacco and gunpowder," said Poeyfarré.

The big chief smiled widely. "It is a long time since the Natchitoches traders have brought us anything worth having. Beads and looking glasses are fine for women, but a warrior needs other things."

"Is that Eyasiquiche?" Dan asked from the corner of his mouth.

Menard said, "That's him."

They palavered for a while, sometimes in sign language, sometimes in Wichita, sometimes in Spanish, with a few French words thrown in, and finally Poeyfarré nodded, satisfied. He turned to them, and all the tenseness was gone from his face. "It's all right. The Chief says we can camp just beyond the village, and tomorrow we'll do some trading. The village across the river will come over too." He rubbed his hands briskly. "It looks good. There haven't been any other traders here since last year."

Simon's eyes were gleaming. "I've heard about this village for years—the great slave market of New Spain. Rifles go

45

west, slaves go east. We should be able to make a few piasters out of that."

"Mind your business and keep out of trouble," Poeyfarré growled. "The Chief will assign you a straw house to sleep in. You can stack your goods around it, and they will be safe."

"When do we start trading?" asked Simon.

"Tomorrow. Any hurry?"

"I'd just like to get it settled."

"If you start swapping too soon, you won't get much. Let these Indians celebrate tonight. Pour a little whisky in 'em, and tomorrow they'll be twice as easy to deal with."

By this time it was dark, and a big fire was built in the center of the village. Dan and Simon and Menard were led to a conical grass-thatched hut. Poeyfarré and Brognard and the taciturn Poupelinière were given a hut across from them, and all unloaded their goods around the dwellings. "You can turn the mules loose," said Poeyfarré. "They will go to the river for water, and the Wichitas will take care of them tonight."

They went up to the fire, and Eyasiquiche, replendent in his blue silk shirt, sat cross-legged on the ground, his vast bulk having long ago popped off the buttons, so that now it was open at the front at least a foot when he sat down.

The braves gathered around the fire, and all ate buffalo stew out of a big brass kettle, fishing out pieces with their knives, biting into them, sometimes throwing them back into the pot.

Finally they passed around a pipe, each Indian and all the members of the trading party taking a whiff until it had been around several times. Then Poeyfarré produced a demijohn. Eyasiquiche's eyes lighted up. He turned up the jug and took a huge drink.

Dan observed, "At that rate it'll be gone before it gets to us."

Brognard's good eye was gleaming. "Don' worry, my frien'. Poeyfarré is no fool. He has plenty of those."

"It won't need to go around a second time," Simon said, "if they all drink like that."

Dan felt mellow when they went back to the huts, but he had hardly sat down on the straw pallet when an Indian came in the open door, unannounced. *"Kah-haak!"* he said grandly.

Menard looked up. In the semidarkness, the only light

46

coming from the fire in the center of the village, Menard's eyes glittered.

"What's he talking about?" asked Dan.

"I got a notion," said Simon, taking a deep breath.

The Wichita turned to him. His left hand was out, fingers together, thumb extended. He closed his right hand into a fist, with the index finger extended, and brought the two hands together, index finger lying between the thumb and other fingers of the left hand.

Dan sat back. "Not for me, I guess."

"You're gonna be lonesome," said Menard.

The Indian stepped aside, and three Wichita girls came in. None was over sixteen. Their bodies were husky and firm, their breasts full. Menard said, "I'll take two!"

Simon held out a hand and said, "One of these is enough for me."

Menard had a girl on each side of him and was talking in low tones when the Wichita came back and fired a string of Indian words at him.

Menard got up on one elbow. "Eyasiquiche wants to know if you weren't satisfied, Shankle."

Dan looked up. "It isn't that."

"He says you can have your pick of the whole village."

Dan said, "Tell him thanks. The women look very good, but tell him I have a wife at home."

Menard talked to the Wichita. Then he said to Dan, "He says you can have all the wives you want."

"Tell him the white man takes only one wife."

More Wichita words. Then Menard chuckled. "He say you the strangest man he ever see. Every man in this village before, when he's been travel' a long time, the first thing he want is wife. They'll think there's something wrong with you."

Dan said finally, "Maybe there is."

He woke up about daylight. Menard's girls were just leaving, and Simon said, "I didn't know you was married, Dan."

"I'm not," Dan said, "but I—uh—"

"Baltimore is a long way from here."

"I know, but I expect *her* to remember *me*."

"Anybody I know?" asked Simon.

Dan pulled on his hunting shirt. "Sarah Radnor."

"Daughter of old Theophilus Radnor?"

"Yes."

47

One of the Wichita girls appeared without sound, flashed a big smile, and set a small kettle of savory meat in the center of the hut.

"That is what I like about the Weechitas," said Menard. "You treat them right, you get fine service. You would not get any better in Baltimore, eh?"

"I doubt it," said Dan.

Simon fished a piece of meat out of the kettle. "Never thought you'd marry a girl like Sarah."

Dan frowned and stared at Simon.

"For one thing," said Simon, stripping a hump rib between his teeth, "she's a society woman. She couldn't live on the frontier."

"Somebody has to live in the cities," said Dan, reaching with his knife.

"And for another thing, she isn't interested in *any* man."

"What do you mean by that?"

Simon pointed the bone toward the open door. "You saw what just happened. The Wichita girl not only stayed all night; she came back this morning with food. Can you imagine Sarah doing anything like that?"

Dan said stiffly, "I don't think Sarah Radnor is to be compared to a savage."

"I don't think she can be compared to *this* savage," said Simon. "But no offense. You can forget this when you get back, and I reckon you better, but all any man will ever be to Sarah Radnor is something to show off, like a piece of jewelry—something that will draw attention to *her*."

Chapter Seven

DAN WENT outside. The air was fresh and clean. Only a few persons were moving this morning, and they were squaws, tending the fire and cooking big kettles of buffalo meat. The three men went down to the stream, and Dan was scratching. Menard looked at him and grinned. "Lice, eh?"

"What do you expect," asked Simon, "sleeping in an Indian bed?"

"Don't your *Indiens* have lice back in Pennsylvania?"

"I suppose they do," said Dan.

"Don't let it worry you," said Simon. "You can get 'em

48

off by scrubbing with sand. Your food will taste gritty for a few days, because every time you move your head a little the sand will drop out, but some people think it's better than lice."

"What about clothes? Burn them?"

"Come weeth me," said Menard. "I show you a very good way."

They walked across the prairie until they found a big anthill. "Take off your clothes," said Menard, "and pile them up on top of the hill. When you get back, you will have only ants to get rid of."

"And you do that by shaking," said Simon.

Dan began to take off his shirt. "I'm going to look funny as hell running around over the prairie naked."

"Don't worry," Menard advised. "These *Indiens* are not afflicted with modesty. It would surprise them if you refused to take off your clothes."

They walked back naked to the stream. The water was clear and sweet, and Dan had one of the most enjoyable baths he had taken in a long time.

A Wichita girl came to the stream with two buffalo paunches for water. She watched them and smiled.

"Only one thing about it," Dan said on the way back to the anthill. "I've got too much Connecticut blood in me, I guess. I'd feel better if the water was more than a foot deep."

They found their clothes thoroughly deloused. The ants had done a good job. They whipped out the ants and put on the clothes.

"You stay out here a few months and you forget the lice," said Menard.

"Is that why Chamillard and Dartigo got their heads cut off?"

Menard shrugged. "It would have been all right if he had never left her. Even an *Indien* has a sense of honor. His isn't the same as yours, maybe, but he has it."

They entered the village. "What do we do now?" asked Simon. "When do we start making a few piasters?"

"Sometime this afternoon Eyasiquiche will be ready—and don't trade cheap. A rifle is worth from ten to twenty mules out here," said Menard.

"I didn't bring rifles."

"Poeyfarré did. They're hidden now for fear of the Spanish, but they are here and Eyasiquiche knows it, or he wouldn't be so friendly."

They got back to the hut, and Dan built a fire with flint and steel and put on some coffee. "What about the glass beads and vermilion and mirrors and sugar? Is that all wasted?"

Menard was lying on his side with his head propped on one hand. "That is standard trade goods, and they'll take it, but if we didn't have rifles, powder, lead, and flints, they'd let us camp out on the prairie and watch our own mules. I've seen a rifle buy four young squaws from the Camanches." He looked curiously at Dan. "You never did any Indian trading down here, did you?"

"No."

"Why then did you risk your hair coming this way?" he insisted.

Dan looked up. He saw Menard's eyes, speculating. He pushed a couple of sticks under the coffee bucket. "There was no guarantee I could get a trading license in Natchitoches," he said shortly.

The village was beginning to awaken. Poeyfarré came from the Chief's tent, looking better than he had looked at any other time since the trip started. "The redskins will be ready to start trading as soon as they get their bellies full and have a couple of pipes," he said. "And good news, Menard: It's been a dry summer, and Toroblanco's band of Camanches are only a couple of days away."

Simon asked quickly, "What does that figure up to?"

"After a dry summer, the Camanches will be impatient to trade. The Wichitas will have a quick turnover, so they can afford to make some good deals."

"We'll go back with plenty of horses and slaves," observed Simon. "There'll be good profit on this trip."

Dan looked at him without seeing him.

The Wichitas ate about midforenoon, and took their time. Poeyfarré was powwowing with Eyasiquiche, and many pipes were passed around. Poeyfarré got two jugs of whisky to follow the pipes. The Wichita women were standing beyond the circle of men. "You can unwrap your beads pretty soon now," Menard told Dan.

But there was a rising murmur of voices through the village, and movement. Menard stood up. "Damn!" he said. "There's another pack train coming."

"From the Arkansa?" asked Dan.

Menard shook his head. "It must be from Natchitoches."

"Maybe Spanish officials."

50

"Maybe, but they won't dare do anything to us out here. The Indians are too strong." He watched. "I don't see any soldiers. It's likely a trader."

Simon swore. "That'll drive prices down."

The pack train approached the village. There were a dozen mules and three muleteers. The village went to meet them, while Poeyfarré sat by the fire. "A mighty lot of good whisky I wasted," he said glumly.

Dan watched. Some of the packs on the mules were made up of long, narrow wooden boxes. Eyasiquiche, with the help of two braves, was mounting his mule and going to meet the train.

Dan straightened. He stared at a black-bearded man who stopped to powwow with Eyasiquiche. Pretty soon the train started on through the village. Dan took a few steps forward.

The black-bearded man looked at him without particular interest at first. Then his eyes widened and he scowled a little. He glanced at Dan's length and then at his face.

Dan took a step forward. "John Meservy," he said. "Last time I saw you was in Baltimore."

Meservy seemed to make his answer cautiously, probingly. "Last time I saw you, you were in Baltimore yourself."

"Things change," said Dan.

Meservy seemed to be studying him, trying to penetrate his thoughts. "It's queer we should end up at the same Indian village—so far away."

"It's queer," said Dan, "but perhaps not unexpected."

Hardness came into Meservy's dark eyes. He turned his back on Dan. "Keep 'em going in the rear!" he shouted.

Meservy's train moved past, and Dan returned to Simon and the Frenchmen.

"Friend of yours?" Simon asked.

"Hard to tell. He came to Baltimore after you left. Supposed to be a broker."

Without warning Simon's low voice sounded in Dan's ear. "There's D'Etrées. I'd know that ugly face anywhere."

Dan stared at the sloping shoulders of the man walking on the other side of the mules. No Indian children followed him. "So the man is tied up with Meservy," Dan noted.

Simon eyed him shrewdly. "Was it Meservy you came out here to find?"

Dan watched the mules going by, followed by a leather-faced muleteer in buckskins, bristling with small arms and knives and a tomahawk, and with a rifle over his saddle, while naked Wichita children, boys and girls up to nine or ten years of age, followed him, darting and chattering but keeping a mule's length behind. "I wasn't exactly surprised to see him," Dan admitted.

"You looked it."

Dan studied the hills across the village. "It was a thing I had thought of, but not a thing I really expected."

Simon worked off a chew. "He's sure going to ruin our business with the Wichitas. No doubt you noticed," he said dryly, "that some of them mules carried rifles."

"It probably won't hurt our business as much as it will Poeyfarré's. We'll still have looking glasses and stuff."

"Maybe this Meservy has too."

Dan didn't answer.

"One thing is sure," said Simon. "We've got him in our back yard and we'll have dealings with him. Maybe you better tell me something about him."

Dan watched Meservy turn into an open place near a stack of hay set up on a framework of boughs so that it was several feet above the ground, curiously protected by a dirt and straw-covered roof like the one on their own beehive dwelling. "Maybe I'd better," he said heavily.

Simon said, with some sarcasm in his voice, "It's nice to learn this is more than just a business deal between you and me."

"I didn't want to draw you into it. I thought, with me putting up the money and you going along to furnish experience and help, it was a fair enough deal. You could make some money, and—"

"The deal was all right, but what about Meservy? What if he decides to eliminate both of us from competition?"

Dan got up and went to one of the packs. He unfastened the straps and got a package of twelve crooked cigars wrapped with a string. He slit the red string with his knife. "Have some cigars?"

"I'll take some for later. Thanks." Simon took the cigars to his pallet in the straw hut.

When he returned, Dan said, "Remember when you and I got back from sailing around the world on the *Caroline?*"

"Pretty well. We anchored to a post off the levee, and everybody went into New Orleans to celebrate. You got in a hell of a fight with the bo'sun over a Creole girl in a saloon. That was just after the Spanish took over Louisiana —1766, wasn't it?"

"Yes."

"You laid the bo'sun over the bar and might' near broke his neck. Then you disappeared with the Creole girl and two others, and turned up four days later looking like a dishrag. You was a pretty good man in those days," he noted, "but now you act like you was ninety years old."

"I can still see a pretty woman as far as you can shoot a rifle and then some," Dan said. "Only thing is, I don't feel free."

"One of them Wichita squaws could help considerable."

"It might be—but I have to see my way clear first."

"Out here," Simon suggested, "you're as good as a million miles away. These Wichita girls don't expect you to marry 'em."

"I know that, but what if I decided I'd rather have one of them, and wanted to stay here on the Red River?"

Simon raised his eyes. "You could do a lot worse. A good man, married into the Wichitas, could make a fortune for himself and his friends."

"That still doesn't take Sarah Radnor's feelings into account."

Simon just stared at him, but his thoughts were plain in his calculating eyes: Why worry about Sarah Radnor? She'd do all the worrying necessary about herself.

Dan frowned. It made him uncomfortable, because Simon was right. Sarah spent a deal of time looking out for herself. Now that he was fifteen hundred miles away in savage country, he could see it clearly. It annoyed him, but he couldn't see what to do about it. After all, he *had* asked her. He got up and went to the fire under the coffeepot. He got a coal, lit his cigar, and puffed it into a red glow at the tip.

"After we came back on the *Caroline*," he said, "and you had shipped out again on that Spanish ship, the *San Luis,* and sailed for Vera Cruz, I shipped out to Baltimore, and when I got home I found my father had been killed in the French and Indian War while I was gone. My mother had been given some land scrip, and she wanted me to go to the Wyoming valley in eastern Pennsylvania. It was a nice valley and fertile soil, and it was near where my father was killed, so there really wasn't any reason why I shouldn't go. The land had cost Mother nothing, and we made good crops, which we generally took to Philadelphia or Baltimore for trade."

Two Wichita girls, full-bodied and full-breasted, passed

53

them carrying empty buffalo paunches. They looked at the two men and smiled. Simon grinned broadly, and Dan nodded.

"Meantime," Dan went on, "John Meservy came to Baltimore and set up as a broker. He claimed to be a Yankee from Connecticut, but nobody ever believed him. He didn't talk like a Yankee. He talked like a Britisher. But he had plenty of money, and so the talk died down."

"This happened while you were in Wyoming valley?"

"Yes."

He watched Meservy stop the two Wichita girls and talk to them. To Dan's astonishment, Meservy seemed to be using the Wichita language. "Nobody ever was sure how he made his money," said Dan, his eyes on Meservy. "He didn't do much brokerage business, but he blossomed out with a fine carriage and fancy clothes and a team of blooded horses. I remember when he first drove down along the docks. I had brought in a wagonload of furs and was buying supplies to take back home, and Meservy was a grand man in his pigtail wig with a red satin ribbon, a three-cornered hat trimmed with ostrich feathers, and blue silk stockings with gold clocks."

Simon spat at the ground.

"And you didn't know where he came from?"

"He arrived on the stage from Philadelphia, but how he got to Philadelphia was always a question."

"What did he have to do with you, aside from the fact that you disliked him?"

"Did I say I disliked him?"

"It's obvious."

Dan sighed. "My younger sister, Georgina, had married a clerk for Theophilus Radnor, and had two children. She was very attractive, as you may recall."

"She was so beautiful that I quit saving myself when I heard she was married, and decided to go to hell the quickest way."

Dan sighed. "Georgina married for love, and her husband was a good catch. He was presentable, worked hard, and would have owned his own business sooner or later. Besides, he could see no woman but Georgina." Dan sighed heavily. "Then Meservy hired him to make a trip to the West Indies for rum."

"And he was lost overboard?"

Dan glared at him. "You're a suspicious man. Yes, the ship ran into the great West Indian hurricane of 1772, and

54

Georgina's husband was lost overboard. The ship itself barely came through and limped into Baltimore with fo'castle smashed and mainmast gone." Dan scowled. "Then Meservy began paying suit to Georgina. He was a clever scoundrel, and it all seemed a very proper thing."

"How did you find out it wasn't?"

"Georgina rejected him flatly. She told me later that he had made improper advances before the news came that her husband was lost."

"Georgina was a girl with spirit."

"She still is." Dan glanced at Simon. "Mother and I and my younger sister Maria were on the farm, and I was the only man, with Georgina's husband gone." He paused. "Some people didn't think Georgina would fit in, being used to fine clothes and parties, but they were wrong. She wore coarse dresses and worked like a farm hand, as any woman has to do on the frontier. She didn't scare a bit when the Indians came in, either."

"Maybe," said Simon, "I ought to go back."

"Then," said Dan, "we got mixed up in a war between the Pennsylvanians and the Connecticut Yankees, and all the time there were Indians—Cayugas, Senecas, Delawares, Shawnees, and strays. For me it was mostly fighting while the women did the farm work. They tilled the fields and took care of the stock, but it was a right nice piece of land and the women did well."

"And Georgina?"

"Georgina minded her own business. Several men courted her, but she stayed at work and raised her kids. I guess she was pretty much in love with her husband."

"But something's all wrong," said Simon shrewdly. "Now there's no man on your place at all, and you're down here looking for some rifles."

Dan smoked for a moment. "A while back our wagons began to return empty from Baltimore. We sent flour and whisky and hog meat down, and got nothing back but money."

"What's wrong with money?"

"No objection to money, but it's no good of itself. It's worthless if you can't use it to buy goods. The Indians were getting rifles from the French and British, and they were better armed than we were. The only gunpowder we could get came in driblets from Philadelphia, and finally one man in the valley set up a powder mill. But saltpeter was hard to come by, and his powder wasn't very good anyway. So I went down to Baltimore to ask Theophilus Radnor why our money wasn't any good. Theophilus was indisposed that day, and they sent me to his home." Dan took a deep breath. "That was when I first met Sarah face to face."

Chapter Eight

HE HAD ridden his shaggy frontier horse into the part of town where well-to-do people lived, feeling increasingly out of place and ill at ease as he passed the fine big houses, lawns and flower gardens (all far better groomed than his horse), and trees planted in straight rows like trees in an apple orchard. He had ridden up the sand-covered driveway of the Radnor grounds, knowing he was out of place but not knowing what he could do about it. He tied his horse's reins to one of the iron weights near the front door, went up, and used the brass knocker. A black woman in a white uniform and little white cap came to the door.

"Deliv'ries at the b——" she said, but then she took in the length of him and breadth of his shoulders, his coonskin cap and long-fringed hunting shirt; her eyes went to his horse and back to him, and when they returned they were considerably bigger. "Did you wish to see somebody, suh?"

"Mr. Radnor—if he's able to see anyone."

"Yas, suh." She hesitated, and again he felt ill at ease. He wasn't used to such fancy doings; on the frontier you either walked in or started ducking bullets. "Mebbe you better come in, suh," she said at last.

The doorway was small for a man his size, and he ducked as he went in. She led him into a very dim room.

"Sit down, please, suh. Ah'll fetch the mistress."

There was elegance even in the maid's appearance, he realized as his eyes became adjusted to the dimness and he surveyed the room in which he was now alone. Elegant was the only word to describe it. The floor was covered with a huge rug of a faded buckskin color, with a many-pointed star in the center and vines and flowers trailing all over. The chairs were somewhat spindly, with round seat cushions probably stuffed with straw to make them stand up so it looked as if a man would slide off when he tried to sit

56

down. There was a long, long sofa along one wall, similar to the chairs but with half a dozen legs along its front edge, and how a man could sit on it was beyond him.

He spied an ornate candle holder in the corner, and finally located the fireplace. It was summer and obviously they didn't use the fireplace for cooking, since the white marble frame was filled in with an old-rose-and-gold panel of some kind that had a very fancy bowl of flowers in its center. Of course, a big house like this would have a separate cabin for cooking, he then realized.

Altogether it was by far the fanciest place he had ever seen. What good it was he didn't rightly know; it made a man think of a king's castle as he imagined it must be, but it was astonishing to find such a thing right here in Baltimore.

He was still standing in the center of the room, surveying its ornate furnishings, when a clear voice asked, "You wish to see my father?"

It took him a while to locate her, for she was only minute size. She was standing in an ivory-framed doorway that he hadn't noticed, and the duskiness of the ivory was a complement to her clear skin and brought out the gleaming highlights in her flaxen-colored hair.

He looked at her again, and found it hard to believe she could be so tiny and yet so obviously grown up. Her hair was brushed back from her forehead, then made into curls on the back of her head and swept down in a long, heavy mass of curls that followed her white neck and came forward over one shoulder. Her eyes were violet and her dress was a dense satin, well fitted above the waist but most voluminous at the bottom, with a front panel of some figured white material. She was quite a sight as she stood in the doorway waiting for an answer.

"I— Yes, ma'am, I came to speak with him."

She moved a few steps closer, almost floating. "At the moment he is uncomfortable with an attack of dyspepsia. Won't you sit down?"

He looked at the highly decorated chairs and knew that he had no business sitting on them in his dirty leggings and hunting shirt, but she moved forward until she was close enough for him to touch her, and he decided he had better sit down. He was careful to sit straight and not lean against the back, and to keep his feet on the floor so his leggings would not rub against the seat cushion.

She sat opposite him, and there was no hint in her voice or manner that he didn't belong there. It gave him a pleasant feeling from the start.

"Does Father know you?"

"Yes, I'm Dan Shankle."

Her eyes widened and took him in from coonskin cap to moosehide moccasins. "You could hardly be anyone else," she murmured. "Won't you take off your cap? You may find it cooler."

He swept off the coonskin and held it on one knee.

"You're from Wyoming valley, aren't you?"

"Yes, ma'am."

"We in Baltimore have heard of your exploits on the frontier, Dan. Won't you tell me about them?"

"There's nothing much to tell, ma'am. We just went up there to make a farm, and the Indians didn't want us there. That's all."

But her violet eyes were glowing in their depths. "How about the time you fought five of them with a knife, and killed the lot? It's all over New England how you vanquished the entire party!"

"Yes, ma'am, I lifted quite a few scalps that day, but they invited it, ma'am. We weren't looking for trouble. They waited at the spring and captured our next-door neighbor about sunup as she went for water."

"And you?"

"Her youngest boy came after me, because the oldest boy was taking a boatload of skins down to Louisburgh on the Susquehanna. I took my rifle and pistol and went after them."

"And your knife?"

"Yes, ma'am, we always carry a knife and a tomahawk."

"And you set out after these Indians?"

"Yes, ma'am. They were Cayugas, and I trailed them back into the woods."

She shuddered exquisitely, and the movement seemed to send waves of perfume around him. He thought perhaps it was lavender.

"Into the woods alone after five savage Indians!" she exclaimed.

"Well, you see, they were burdened with having to handle Mrs. Cotlow as well."

"And Mrs. Cotlow—was she pretty?"

"A woman any man would be proud to have on the frontier, ma'am, but not like you. That is to say, it's hard work living on the frontier, raising half a dozen children, cutting wood, plowing, fighting Indians. A lady has little time to spend on fixing up."

"And yet you say she was pretty?"

"Yes, ma'am, one of the prettiest women I ever saw—except in Baltimore."

"I'm flattered," she said.

"Well, it's only a plain statement of fact, ma'am." He could have said more; Sarah Radnor reminded him of the star-blazed black filly he had fed on corn all one winter and then had curried until her sleek sides glistened. The filly had been small too, like Sarah Radnor, but rambunctious and—

"And you found them?"

"Well, ma'am, Mrs. Cotlow is not a woman who likes to be man-handled. She was putting up a battle, and I trailed them and caught up to them as they were trying to get her across the river in a canoe."

"And you attacked them?"

"Well, ma'am, I fired my rifle, but I didn't dare shoot at the Indians, for they were struggling with her and I might have hit her, so I put a bullet through the boat below the waterline."

"I thought women usually killed themselves when they were captured by Indians."

"No, ma'am, not often. First place, it isn't always easy; second place, there's always a chance to escape."

"But Indians!" she said with a fine distaste in the thinning of her lips. "They smell, don't they?"

"Yes, ma'am. As for that, I guess we all smell after we've been out there a while."

"Tell me about the fight."

He had got over his self-consciousness now, and he began to feel easier. "Not much to tell. I ran up to them and began laying into them with my tomahawk."

"I thought it was a knife."

"Not at first, ma'am. I finished the last one off with a knife, and used it to raise their hair after it was all over, but the main fighting was done with the tomahawk."

"Is that—it—that you have on your left side now?"

"Yes, ma'am."

"Do you mind if I see it?"

"Why, no, ma'am. It isn't much to see—just a sort of brass hatchet with a sharp edge." He drew it from the rawhide loop and handed it to her, handle first. "It's heavy, as you can see, and makes a good weapon when there's room to swing it."

He expected her to touch the hatchet gingerly, but she took the handle in her small white hand and hefted the hatchet to get its balance, and he at once admired her for it.

"You killed four Indians with this tomahawk?"

"Yes, ma'am, in a manner of speaking."

She looked up, bright-eyed, obviously fascinated by the picture of him swinging the tomahawk. "Where do you hit them with it?"

"We generally aim for the top of the head somewhere—try to get through the skull."

She shuddered. "And you scalped them?" she asked.

"Well—yes, ma'am. They scalp us if they can," he said defensively.

"What do you do with the scalps?"

He put the tomahawk back in its loop. "Hang them up in the sun somewhere—far enough away so they don't stink up the house."

"We hear so much about Indian fighting, but I've never seen a scalp."

"I'd be glad to send you one, ma'am, next time I get a chance."

Her eyes held a strange glow. "You mean—one that you cut from an Indian you killed with your own hands?"

"That's about the only way you ever get one, ma'am."

She arose. "I'll have to see about Father. If you will wait . . ."

"Have you given him anything?"

"The physician prescribed grated nutmeg in whisky."

He nodded. "The nutmeg won't hurt, and the whisky might do him some good."

She was gone before he realized it. Like most small women, she moved fast. He watched the doorway where she had disappeared, and in the still dimness of the parlor felt the waves of lavender fragrance sweep back to him.

He now felt at ease. In spite of his buckskin clothing, his coonskin cap, and his moccasins, Sarah Radnor seemed to have a personal interest in him. He was grateful that he had thought to take a bath in the creek the day before he reached Baltimore.

He studied again the magnificence of the room he was in, and then heard the silken rustle of Sarah's dress. She seemed to materialize in the doorway.

60

"Father doesn't feel like talking today, but he suggests that you stay with us a few days until he feels better."

"Well, ma'am, I can't—"

She moved closer. "Of course you can," she said with a smile. "The Indians can wait."

"I don't think—"

"Do you have a wife?"

"No, ma'am, just my mother and two sisters, but—"

"I'm sure they wouldn't begrudge you a rest."

He was suddenly reluctant to leave her. "Maybe."

"All Baltimore is talking about your exploits. Surely you can stay a fortnight and let them have a look at a real frontiersman."

"Not a fortnight. I couldn't stay away that long."

"Then two or three days," she coaxed. "To please me."

Her personal interest gave him a warm feeling. "All right," he said, justifying himself on the ground that he did have to see her father.

A look of satisfaction appeared briefly on her face; obviously she was as much attracted to him as he was to her. "The maid will show you to your room. We'll have supper in about an hour."

He got up. She moved closer to him and took his big hand in her two small ones. "I'm glad you're going to stay," she whispered, her head thrown back.

The closeness of her, the fragrance of the lavender, the lights in her violet eyes, the warmth and pressure of her hands—those were like a great draught of rye whisky on an empty stomach. He knew what he wanted, but did a rough, dirty, uncouth man like him take such a fragile creation in his arms and hold her to him? He said with difficulty, "I'd better see about my horse."

"The groom will put your horse in the stable."

"These are the only clothes I have," he remembered.

She smiled. "I wouldn't for the world have you wear anything else. It would destroy the whole effect."

He didn't quite know what she meant, but he followed the maid to the bedroom. This was a large room, but not so richly furnished as the parlor. A round braided rug occupied the center of the open floor. A dresser stood at one wall, with a heavy china pitcher and washbasin. The bed took up about half of the room. It was huge, with a post at each corner that extended almost to the ceiling, and from a framework around the top hung a silk canopy. A decorated bootjack stood alongside the bed, and a round brass bed-warmer with a long handle leaned against the wall.

Dan took one look at all this splendor and was dubious about sleeping at all the first night, but he would certainly try. He put his rifle in a corner, hung his powder horn and bullet bag on pegs, tossed his coonskin cap on the floor under the bed. There was water in the pitcher, and he washed his face and hands, and was a little astonished at the amount of dirt that came off. He remembered to take the half-used carrot of tobacco out of his shirt and drop it into his coonskin cap under the bed.

The window was genuine glass, and he could look out at the stable and see two blacks currying fine horses. They'd have a time currying his, he thought. That horse never had seen a curry comb; all it wanted was a good roll in the dirt.

He had dinner with Sarah Radnor that night, and used the knife and fork the best he could; he didn't see they were much improvement over a scalping knife. He realized that he'd have to get rid of the tomahawk until he was ready to go back. The thing would be marking up the furniture.

Sarah sat opposite him at the table, and he had never seen eyes with such depth. "Father is still not very well," she said, "though he is improving, and I think will be able to see you tomorrow. But tonight I am taking you to a reception at Lord Thaxted's."

He gulped. "I can't go to a place like that. I'm not properly dressed."

A gleam of intensity was in her eyes. "You must believe me, Dan, you will take Baltimore by storm. They have never seen such a man as you."

Nevertheless, he felt uncomfortable about it, and even the carriage wasn't made for a man of his height.

Lord and Lady Thaxted soon put him at ease, and Sarah possessively took him everywhere and introduced him to so many persons that he could not begin to keep them separated in his mind. They had punch made of brandy and rum, which he discovered was quite as potent as rye whisky or plain peach brandy. They danced the minuet and the Virginia reel to the music of two fiddles and a bass viol, and the ladies gathered around him while Sarah encouraged him to tell of the five Cayugas he had chased to the riverbank.

It was then that John Meservy appeared. He was a tall man, but still three or four inches shorter than Dan. He wore a heavily powdered wig and an apple-green coat with a white ribbed silk waistcoat and a frill of linen filling the V. His black silk breeches were very tight and ended at the knees; his long stockings were white silk with gold clocks; and his leather shoes had square toes, large silver buckles, and red heels. In all this magnificence he looked at Dan, tucked his ivory cane under one arm, took a tiny golden snuffbox from his waistcoat, dropped a pinch of tobacco on the back of one hand, and snuffed it into his long Roman nose.

Dan, suddenly feeling foolish, had stopped his tale. Meservy took his time, getting all eyes on him, and then looked up. "It is quite obvious," he said, staring at Dan's clothes, "that this gentleman is at home chasing Indians through the forest."

Dan hardened and spoke before he thought. All the bitterness of his knowledge of Meservy came out in one harsh sentence. "I send no woman's husband to sea to make her a widow."

He heard gasps around him, and regretted having spoken. But Meservy might challenge him to a duel, and he would welcome a chance to fight the man.

Meservy's eyes glinted, but he didn't take the bait. "I have no redskin squaw in the forest, either."

For a fleeting moment Dan wondered why Meservy had thought of such a retort, which was hardly to be classed as a cause for dueling on the frontier.

There was silence around him for a moment. He glanced at the ladies behind Meservy, and saw faces that tried to appear horrified but eyes that glowed with something he did not recognize. Dan knew he was no match for Meservy at this kind of talk, so he did not answer. He sought Sarah's eyes in the group around him, and was relieved when she smiled. There seemed to be an unspoken understanding between them, an intimacy far above the kind of animosity exhibited by John Meservy. Sarah came up to him and said, "You are really marvelous, Dan. All Baltimore will be agog by tomorrow."

It gave him a warm glow to know that Sarah was pleased, but something impelled him to look over the heads of the ladies, and he saw John Meservy watching them. Meservy turned away immediately, but not soon enough to hide the fact that he was jealous of Sarah Radnor.

That was unexpected, but Dan knew a way to take care of it. When he and Sarah alighted from the coach before the Radnor house that night, he took her hand as the coach rolled off and held her for a moment. She looked up at him in the moonlight and asked, "Is there something you want to say, Dan?"

What he really wanted was to know how she felt in his arms. He started to raise his hands, but then the difference between them overcame him, and he stepped back.

But she moved toward him, and stood almost touching him. "Yes, Dan?"

His arms went around her, and she moved her warm body against his. Her head was back, and he kissed her on the lips. Her hands clung fiercely to his upper arms.

Finally he took a deep breath. "Miss," he said, "I'm asking you to marry me."

"Dan!"

"You aren't very big for heavy work," he said, "but I think we can make out."

"You're surely not serious."

"I surely am."

"Well, I—"

She lost the poise she had maintained so naturally all night, and it endeared her to him to find that she was not always sure of herself.

"There's no use waiting. There's land up in Wyoming valley to be had for the taking. We can build up a mighty nice farm."

"But Dan! The Indians!"

"We've taken care of them so far," he reminded her.

She withdrew with seeming reluctance. "I don't—You—We don't do things so precipitously in Baltimore," she said. "Mr. Meservy has been courting me for months. Do you think this is fair to him?"

Dan answered coldly, "I am not concerned with what is fair to an unmannered man like Meservy. If you are not already spoken for, and if you will consider marriage with me, I will speak to your father."

He thought there was promise in her voice when she said, "Father is asleep now. You cannot speak to him until tomorrow."

He felt himself glowing with warmth as he took off his hunting shirt and got into bed. Perhaps they didn't do things that fast in Baltimore. They could afford a life of leisure, but on the frontier a man never knew whether he would be alive tomorrow. Life was to be lived and not wasted—and waiting until tomorrow might waste it all. Indeed they did do things differently. They had a wilderness to take away from the

64

Indians, to turn into farms and homes; they had families to raise and grandchildren to watch out for, and it behooved any serious-minded man to let no grass grow under his feet.

It was none of his worry that Meservy had so far delayed asking Sarah the question. Meservy was a scoundrel anyway; Georgina's experience was proof of that.

Meservy might yet challenge him to a duel. Dan grinned in the darkness. That would give him the right to name the weapons, and he had no fear of meeting Meservy on an even basis.

Chapter Nine

HE WAS UP early the next morning, but when he entered the dining room he found Theophilus Radnor and his daughter already seated at the breakfast table. Radnor was middle-aged, but he had worry lines that belonged to an old man. He was portly, and he wore black mutton chops and a fringe of chin whiskers that was beginning to turn gray.

"Good morning, sir," Dan said. "I'm glad to see you're feeling better today. I want to talk with you."

Theophilus waved a pudgy hand. "Not now, Dan. Not now. I never mix business with breakfast. That's the one time of the day I don't give attention to anything but food—and you'll find there's plenty of that: ham, bacon, biscuits, butter and honey, coffee and chocolate, melon—everything that's in season and some things that aren't. Take my suggestion and apply yourself to it. I daresay you don't have meals like this in the valley more than once a year."

"We can't depend on gardens," Dan said soberly, "for the Indians raid them. Sometimes they raid our smokehouses, too, so a lot of our food comes direct from the forest. There's usually plenty of it, but there may be only one thing at a time."

"Such as what?" asked Sarah.

He looked at her, envisioning her smallness in a cabin of their own.

"We shoot a deer or a bear or find a wild honey tree, and we eat all we want until it's gone."

"Sounds improvident to me," said Theophilus.

"It isn't really. It's just practical. Meat doesn't keep forever.

65

We eat it and then go look for more. The forest is full of game. I can go out at night and get a dozen big wild turkeys with a club."

After breakfast he rode to the warehouse in the carriage with Theophilus. They negotiated the narrow, crooked streets —some paved with cobblestones that made far rougher riding than the worst-gaited old plow horse in Pennsylvania—and turned down toward the docks. Theophilus sent the carriage home. "He'll pick us up later."

He led the way into his office in one corner of the warehouse. "Good morning, Zachariah," he said, and a man sitting on a high stool, writing in a big book with a goose-quill pen by the light of a candle, said dutifully, "Good morning, Mr. Radnor. I hope your dyspepsia is better today."

"It's as good as a man can expect." Theophilus hung his hat on a peg and sat heavily in a rawhide-bottomed chair. "Now, Dan'l, what's on your mind? Want to borrow money?"

"Not exactly," said Dan. "I want to *spend* some money."

Theophilus grunted. He was turning over some bills of lading, and didn't seem at all astonished. "What do you want to buy?"

"Some of the goods that have been on the lists we've been getting back unfilled."

Theophilus didn't look up. "I suspected as much." He picked up the sheaves of paper and bounced them on one edge until they were neatly square with one another. "Can't fill orders unless I have the goods," he said.

Dan frowned. "You—"

The outer door opened. A cheery voice said, "Good day, Theophilus," and a slight, wiry, sandy-haired man bounced in.

"Good day, Pat," Theophilus said heavily.

The slight man glanced at Dan.

"Customer of ours," Theophilus said. "A dissatisfied customer." He got up and waddled across to the clerk's desk and laid down the bills of lading, then came back. "Pat, this is Dan'l Shankle. You heard of him, fightin' Indians in Wyoming valley."

"Begorrah, yes." The sandy-haired man shook hands. "It's Patrick Evers I am, at your service."

"Dan'l," said Theophilus, "Mr. Evers here is the biggest merchant in Baltimore, and he has as much cause as you to complain about the scarcity of goods." He sat down again. "In fact," he said wearily, "he does complain."

66

"I was told you had a ship unloading yesterday," said Evers.

Theophilus sighed. "The ladings are over there—such as they are. Twenty barrels of rum, half a dozen hogs-heads of sugar, a few cases of iron articles and twelve hundred pounds of liquorice root. Twelve hundred pounds!" he said disgustedly. "When am I going to get something I can sell?"

"More to the point," said Evers, "when are you going to get something *I* can sell?"

"Aren't you getting goods, either?" asked Dan.

Theophilus looked sadly at Evers. "You both come with me," he said, and led them into the outer warehouse. It was vast, and it was empty. Theophilus shook his head. "We get a driblet of goods now and then, like the bills I just showed you, but we are getting almost nothing we can sell to the consumer. Who wants twelve hundred pounds of liquorice root?"

Their footsteps echoed hollowly in the emptiness of the big building. They reached the end and saw the small piles of goods represented by the bills.

Dan frowned. "It isn't a matter of credit, is it?"

"My credit's as good as the Bank of England. It's a question of getting the merchandise. We order it, but I am not receiving it, and no one else in Baltimore is getting any better than I am. And according to the post, importers in other towns are in the same position. We get small consignments of scattered merchandise, but the big shipments of manufactured goods that come from England—those do not arrive."

"How about rifles?" asked Dan. "That's what we need most of all."

"Rifles are very difficult." Theophilus led them back to his office. "During this past winter four shiploads of goods, all containing quantities of firearms destined for Baltimore, have disappeared on the high seas, supposedly captured by pirates."

Evers said, "You heard from the *Matilda?*"

"A good example," said Theophilus, looking at Dan. "The schooner *Matilda* sailed from Liverpool with bolting goods, wine, hardware, and all the rifles turned out by the Watts Rifle Works for the previous year. I made a contract with Watts six years ago, and have taken his entire output ever since. Within six days' sailing from Baltimore she was seen by the brig *Harrison,* under a brisk wind." He watched the clerk enter the bills in the ledger. "That was twelve days ago," he said, "and she isn't here—nor is she likely to get here. She has disappeared from the surface of the sea."

"It's the King's fault!" Evers exclaimed. "He and his infernal profit-minded merchants!"

"Hardly," said Theophilus. "Eventually we find these cargoes are cleared for Baltimore as they should be. But they don't reach port—and I'm sitting here with nothing to sell. I'll go bankrupt if this keeps up."

Evers laughed. "You'll be in the business long after the rest of us have closed our doors. Theophilus," he said to Dan, "has a finger in every pie in Baltimore."

But Dan, sitting there, was getting angry. He got to his feet. "While you two gentlemen are worrying about a profit," he said, "men and women and children on the western frontier are depending on rifles and powder to save their hair from the Indians. We can use animal skins for clothing. We can kill our meat and raise our own corn and mill our own wheat. We can dress out logs to build a house. But we have got to get manufactured goods from the cities. Have you ever," he demanded, "seen the Indians burn a man alive?"

Theophilus looked up, intent. Patrick Evers' eyes were fixed on Dan. The clerk on the high stool turned, his quill pen poised in his hand.

"I have," said Dan. "Along with Tom Cotlow, I was captured by Captain Pipe's Delawares. They stripped him and painted him black and tied him with a long rope and built fires all around him, so he could never get away from the heat. The wood was hickory, and it burns hot. They fired a hundred charges of gunpowder into his skin at close range. They started at the feet and worked up. When they finished that, the fires were hot, and he started running around the stake. When he slowed down, they jabbed him with burning sticks. When he fell down, they scalped him, and a squaw poured live coals on the top of his head." Dan stopped, his face harsh. "They burned him for two hours, and when he was no longer able to get on his feet, they skinned him alive." Dan shuddered. "His shrieks will live in Pennsylvania for eternity."

"And you—"

"They tied me to the same stake with the same rope, but a rescue party came from the valley." He paused. "Now you know why I fought for his widow, Mrs. Cotlow—and you

68

know why it isn't a thing I remember with any taste—fighting for a woman whose husband was killed that way."

"I know that life on the frontier is difficult," Theophilus began, "but—"

"There are no buts," Dan said fiercely. "You live or you die. And living depends to a large extent on getting rifles from men like you. The Indians get rifles from the British. They have better firearms than we." He stared uncompromisingly at Theophilus. "Is that where our rifles go—to the Indians?"

Theophilus shook his head. "Not to my knowledge, though I don't know for certain where they do go. They don't come to me, and I have not been able to determine why."

"Don't you have gunsmiths?" Evers asked Dan.

"We have a few gunsmiths and almost no equipment. To get equipment we would have to depend again on imports."

"Rifles are at a premium all over America," said Theophilus. "In Kentucky a good rifle will bring thirty dollars. In New Spain, if you smuggle rifles past the border, you can get twice that, in gold or horses or slaves."

"Is that why we aren't getting them?" Dan would keep asking that question until they realized what he was up against.

"I don't know," said Theophilus.

"It's probably because the damned Tories are turning them over to the Indians," Evers said hotly.

Theophilus shook his head. "I don't agree with that. I'm loyal to the crown, and I see no reason for this talk of rebellion."

"I said nothing of rebellion," Evers retorted.

"Rebellion is talked everywhere," Theophilus insisted, "and your words reflect it."

Evers' face was red. "Good day, Theophilus," he said, and stalked out with as much indignation as a little man could demonstrate.

Dan said earnestly, "Mr. Radnor, isn't there anybody else in Baltimore who has rifles?"

Theophilus' lips were thin. "Not to my knowledge," he said. "But to satisfy yourself, I suggest you inquire. You might try Robinson or Morris and Draper. They probably would have arms or information if anybody has. Don't take my word alone. Ask at any place that strikes your fancy." He rubbed his whiskers. "It is a serious problem to us all. Our living depends on the goods we have to sell."

Dan walked down the dock to a painted sign that said, "Alf. Robinson, Importer."

Robinson was a tall man with penetrating blue eyes. He watched Dan as he talked. Then he got up and said briefly, "Come with me."

They walked into the big warehouse, and again their footsteps echoed hollowly in a huge empty space.

"You see," said Robinson, "a small assortment of goods on the open dock. That was unloaded this morning from the brigantine *Jonathan*. I got this much from the shipload. The other importers along the dock will get about the same. As you can see, it is pitifully small. We are not getting a tenth of the goods necessary to supply the town of Baltimore."

"What can we do, then, in Wyoming valley?"

"There is only one answer known to me: Find out where the bulk of the goods is going."

"How can a man do that?"

"I don't know."

"I don't either," Dan said, "but one thing is certain: I'm going to find those rifles."

Chapter Ten

DAN SPENT the rest of the morning looking at empty warehouses. He reached the end of the docks and went across the street for a glass of grog. He was just stepping inside the tavern when he was hailed. "Shankle!"

Dan stopped, turned, and scowled.

John Meservy came up the street toward him, picking his way through the dust with his silver-buckled shoes. "I'll stand you a treat of rum," he said.

Dan looked at Meservy's fancy clothes and made no attempt to hide his distaste. "I thought you'd be challenging me."

"Oh, come," said Meservy. "You needn't take offense." With an unexpected turn, he said, "I am as accustomed to leather clothing as you are, but when I live in Baltimore I dress as Baltimoreans do. Come on in with me."

Dan went in, and Meservy ordered Jamaica rum. It was the best, and it was not for children, but he noted that

70

Meservy tossed it off like water. "What's your business?" asked Dan curiously.

"Broker," said Meservy. "The only difference between Theophilus and me is that he orders from England or France or India, and resells, while I take my chances and pick up what I can. If an importer finds himself overstocked on— firearms, for instance, I take them off his hands."

"Rifles!" said Dan. "Do you have rifles?"

Meservy tossed it off. "I used that only as an example." He laughed disdainfully. "More rum," he ordered. "Nobody has rifles," he said with a sneer. "You're a fool for even thinking you can find rifles."

"Why so?"

"The importers, merchants—all are working for the King, and they don't get rifles because the British War Office fears a rebellion. They are afraid to put rifles into the hands of the colonists for fear they'll be turned against His Majesty's soldiers."

Dan fingered his glass. "Maybe I'd do better in New York."

"It's worse in New York," Meservy said. "The only place to solve your problem is in England."

Dan pushed back the second glass of rum. "I serve notice," he said. "I am going to find out where these rifles are going and who is responsible for it. When I put my finger on the man, I will break him in two."

Meservy watched him coolly. "Before you do anything drastic," he said, "remember that the other man will have something to say about that."

"Marse Shankle," said a voice at Dan's back.

Dan looked around at the groom. "Yes?"

"Missy Sarah done send me to find you, suh."

Dan felt the alertness of the frontier come over him. "Is there trouble?"

"No, suh. I don't think so, suh. Missy Sarah done tell me to fetch you, suh."

Meservy downed his drink. "You might as well mind Sarah. She always gets what she wants."

Dan didn't answer. After all, he was her guest. "I'll come," he said, and went outside.

He was let out of the carriage at the ornate front door. Sarah met him in the hallway—cool, fragrant, skin dusky white. "I was frantic for fear you would not get back in time," she said, her small hand on his forearm.

"I had business," he said, looking down at her.

71

She had to tip her head far back to look at him. "There is another reception tonight by the Misses Blakesley, and they have specially requested that you attend, and by all means wear your frontier uniform." She smiled beguilingly. "You cannot disappoint us poor city people who have a knowledge of the frontier only through the lips of adventurous men like yourself."

"I'm not adventurous," he said stiffly. "And it's not a uniform. It's what we wear because it's all we have."

She patted his arm. For a little girl, he thought, she was amazingly confident. "Did you speak to my father this morning?"

It warmed him to know she was thinking about it. "I've been trying to get rifles," he said.

"Are rifles important?"

"They come ahead of food."

"Well, I'm sure Father can manage some. Is it true that you use the rifles to kill Indians?"

"Indians and meat."

"How many Indians have you killed?"

Her inquisitiveness unexpectedly bothered him. "I never kept track," he said. "When the Indians crowd us, we shoot to keep 'em back. When they try to sneak in on you, you have to kill them. There isn't time to count."

"You keep the—scalps, you said."

He thought her eyes were overbright. "We don't always scalp them. They take away their dead when they can. Scalps aren't important, anyway. We only do it because the Indians do it."

She clung to his forearm with both hands. "Tell that to the ladies tonight," she said. . . .

It was midnight when they got home, but he found Theophilus stretched out before the open fireplace in a small room opposite the parlor. It was a cool evening, and Theophilus was toasting his shins and sipping brandy.

Dan went into the hall with Sarah. He kissed her briefly but impetuously, then watched her move through a door, where she turned and looked full at him for an instant before disappearing.

Dan went back to the library. Theophilus glanced up and then back at his brandy. "There's something I want to talk to you about, sir," said Dan.

"I'll talk first," said Theophilus. "But sit down. You're too damned tall, and I'll get a crick in my neck."

72

Dan sat in a big leather chair that was nothing like the highly decorative chairs in the parlor. He was able to lean back while Theophilus poured brandy in a big-bowled glass. Dan took it and stretched his long legs toward the fire.

"You people in Wyoming valley," said Theophilus, "are not the only ones concerned with shortages of goods, especially rifles. You saw how Patrick Evers stalked out this morning."

"Yes, sir."

"Evers is an excellent chap, but his feeling is typical of the turmoil in the colonies today. Most of us know that we are discriminated against by the Crown, but we feel also that the position of the colonists at such a distance from the mother country is a situation that has to be worked out gradually. However, some hotheads, egged on by trouble-makers like Sam Adams, are in a hurry for these changes. They refer to us as loyalists, and when they get angry they call us Tories. In turn we call them rebels—but the truth is that the only difference between the two groups is a difference of time. They are in a hurry; we are more willing to let time work for our ends."

"That's all right in Baltimore, but it means lives on the frontier."

"That is a different aspect of the situation. It brings up the fact that there are many men among us who foster discontent and suspicion to serve their own ends. Sam Adams is so accused, but it is well to note that there are others more dangerous than Adams, for they work behind closed doors and hide their true intent behind smiling masks." Theophilus sighed. "In most cases these men are serving their own personal ends. They have no interest in the colonies or their people."

Dan sipped his brandy. Was Meservy one of those of whom Theophilus was speaking?

Theophilus looked up. "I might as well tell you what little I know and how much I suspect about the rifles."

Dan sat forward.

"All of the Watts output," Theophilus said, "is consigned to me, but it does not reach me. What does happen is fairly common knowledge."

Dan looked at him sharply. "What is that?"

"The rifles are routed to New Spain and sold at an immense profit—not by me or by any legitimate importer or broker in Baltimore."

73

"Meaning what?" asked Dan.

"There is in town a man who seemingly does nothing, but who dresses well and drives a fine carriage. He has plenty of slaves and a stable of blooded horses. We do not know where he gets his money."

"It could derive from an estate in England."

Theophilus stared at him and went on. "This man often disappears for months at a time, with no explanation."

"Do you think he is diverting the cargoes by either piracy or bribery, and selling the goods in the Spanish colonies?"

Theophilus poured them both a second glass of brandy. "We know the Spanish are starving for goods—more so than you are. The Spanish colonial administration is far more bunglesome than the British, and they are afraid to give the colonists weapons to protect themselves. So, since there is a relative plenty of gold and silver in that country, goods bring extremely high prices."

"To speak frankly," said Dan, "what is to prevent legitimate importers and brokers from diverting goods?"

"The fact that our businesses are built up in Baltimore; our homes and families are here; most of us have large estates here. We must continue to furnish goods to the merchants in this town if we are to stay here—and most of us are too old to go to a new country and face the hazards of the frontier. We are not young and vigorous like you."

Dan held the brandy before the firelight. "Eventually, won't these ships have to be accounted for?"

"Eventually is a long time. If these cargoes are being diverted to the West Indies—which includes all of New Spain—it would be very difficult to trace them within an ordinary lifetime." He rotated the glass in his pudgy fingers. "It is difficult for a person not conversant with the ways of commerce to understand the situation in the Mexican gulf. With the Spaniards restricting trade on every hand, even among Spanish colonies, there is a tremendous volume of contraband trade going on. On top of this, there is piracy. Not only are the seas filled with pirate ships and villainous crews who think nothing of sinking a ship and appropriating her cargo, but there are countless ships carrying letters of marque from some neutral country, and these too are hard to control."

"I don't know about that, sir."

"A ship of some neutral country can stop a ship of British

74

registry, for instance, and, finding contraband goods, confiscate them and proceed to a Spanish port, where the goods are turned in, and the capturing ship is awarded a percentage of the haul."

"It seems to open up abuses."

"Nor is that the whole story," said Theophilus, staring into the fire. "British, French, and Dutch ships prey constantly on the Spanish merchantmen with impunity. There are treaties, but what are treaties?"

"It seems to me that a more or less regular disappearance of ships does indicate an organized effort."

Theophilus poked the fire. "It also indicates an organized method of disposal."

Dan sat forward. "Which would account for the disappearance of this man at intervals?"

Theophilus nodded.

"What's the name of the man?"

Theophilus looked at him obliquely and poured a third glass of brandy. "A man who, I am sorry to say, has asked for the hand of my daughter—John Meservy. I understand you met him last night."

Dan sat back. "Uh—yes."

"You're a man who is alive because of your ability to size up other men. What do you think of Meservy?"

Dan's brows moved together. "It is hardly fitting for me to give an opinion of my rival."

Theophilus glanced up. "You too, eh? That makes an even dozen in the last twelve months."

"But Sarah—"

"Encouraged you, no doubt." He reached for the fire tongs and pushed a small log into the center of the fire. "She might have meant it, of course. Sarah's a willful girl. She gets what she wants—and she might want you."

"Would you give your consent, sir?"

"If Sarah wants it. But I don't like the idea of her going up into Pennsylvania when you haven't got rifles to protect her." He frowned. "I suspected this was coming. That is why I told you about the rifles."

"Thanks." Dan nodded, and got back to the first question. "Then it is true you are not able to furnish rifles."

Theophilus thumped his glass on the table. "Why do you think I showed you my empty warehouse?"

"Sorry, sir." He finished the brandy. "Were those rifles on the *Matilda* dated?"

75

"Watts always dates his rifles. They'd show 1772."

"Then they could be identified."

"I'd think so. Since I contracted for his entire output, if I found a Watts rifle with that date, I'd feel certain it had come from the *Matilda*."

Dan moved restlessly. "If those rifles could be located in New Spain, they would be contraband. I could claim them and ship them back to Pennsylvania."

"It seems so," said Theophilus.

Dan was thoughtful. "Could Meservy benefit from a war with England?"

"Yes, because it would add to the general confusion. He could pirate cargoes on a bigger scale and sell them at exorbitant prices to those who could not afford to haggle. That is just one of many ways he could profit."

Dan stood up to the full height of his six feet four. "The crops are in. I will go to New Orleans tomorrow."

"Do you know anybody down there?"

"Simon Jeffreys, who grew up with me in Virginia."

"What is his business?"

Dan smiled. "He is supposed to be running a blacksmith shop, but he's probably as deep in contrabanding as a man could be and stay out of jail."

"You think you can depend on him?"

"If anybody would know things like that, Simon would. And I would trust him with my life."

"It would be helpful to have a contact."

"If we should find the rifles," Dan said confidently, "we can recover them. Then we can backtrack and find the man who was responsible for their getting to New Spain."

Theophilus considered. "It will be dangerous."

"No more so than the Senecas."

Theophilus considered. "I'd suggest you enter at Manchac."

Dan smiled. "I'll take a load of contraband goods and go trading myself."

"That would require money, Dan."

"I've got a little."

"I'll give you more," Theophilus said abruptly. "If you make a profit, we'll divide half and half. If you find the rifles, you'll be doing the colonies a service."

"I—"

"No argument, young man. You've been doing business with me for a long time, and I'm willing to gamble on you. There's a sloop, the *Rebecca*, sailing with the tide tomorrow for Pensacola. I'm quite sure it is destined eventually for the Texas country, for Florida is British now, you know, and a great quantity of English goods enters at Pensacola, finds its way into West Florida, and enters Louisiana at Little Manchac. Once admitted into Spanish territory, it is fairly simple. It goes up the Misicipi to the Red River of Natchitoches and follows that stream into New Spain, or it goes on up to the Arkansa River and enters by the route of the *contrabandistas*. Of the two, Natchitoches is the easier, but the Arkansa is the more profitable. At any rate, no trader would be permitted to take rifles through Natchitoches, and so it seems to leave the Arkansa Post at the point of entry. Since I am gambling anyway, I may as well gamble on that. I would say to go by the Arkansa River to the Wichita villages."

Dan said, "You show an uncommonly good knowledge of the trade in New Spain."

"Contrabanding in that part of the world has been notorious for a long time. All active merchants know the details."

Dan stirred, satisfied, "If I am to leave in the morning, I won't have time to buy trade goods."

"I doubt you could find enough here anyway. Wait until you reach Little Manchac. The English traders have more contraband there than we have honest goods here."

Dan got up. "Very well, sir. I'll be on the *Rebecca*."

"Trade goods come roughly to two thousand dollars a ton, and you might as well take enough to show a profit. I'll send my black with a letter of credit for twelve hundred pounds to the captain of the sloop, and you'll get it from him. You can draw on it in Pensacola."

Dan took a full breath. "Thank you, sir."

"Don't thank me. I may be sending you to your death. The *contrabandistas* are bad ones."

"I'm sure they are no worse than Captain Pipe's Delawares."

"You would be a fool to count too heavily on that." Theophilus got up.

Dan shook his hand. "I'll be back with—news."

Theophilus looked worried. "I wish you Godspeed," he said. "And by the way, John Meservy left Baltimore by stage this afternoon, headed for Richmond, supposedly."

"Richmond!" Dan said. He saw Theophilus' eyes on him. "That could be in the direction of Texas."

77

"Exactly." Theophilus' back was to the fire. "Good night, Dan."

"Good night, sir."

Dan left with the glow of the brandy in his blood and the heady vigor of impending action in his brain. A lighted candle was on a table in the hall. He took it and started upstairs, but Sarah came from somewhere and stood in his path. "You've been talking to Father?"

Her flaxen hair and her violet eyes and her precious smallness were more vivid than ever in the candlelight, and she seemed more fragile. She was a thing to cherish.

"Yes," he said finally.

"What did he say, Dan?"

"Why, he said—" He stopped to enjoy the dancing light in her eyes. "He said I could—" He hesitated, recalling exactly what Theophilus *had* said. They had got off onto rifles. "He said, if you wished it—"

Her eyes were shining. "Dan!" she whispered.

She came into his arms, and he kissed her for the second time. Then he heard Theophilus stirring in the library, and released her.

She stepped back. "Tomorrow I'll send you a tailor who will provide suitable clothes, and you—"

"Suitable clothes for what?"

Her eyes widened. "Your uniform is distinctive, but of course you can't wear it in town indefinitely. You will—"

"I'm not going to be in town indefinitely," he said, more bluntly than he intended. "I'm leaving in the morning for Louisiana."

Dan finished his story and reached for his carrot of tobacco. "You know the rest."

"Somewhat," said Simon. "You came to my blacksmith shop and accused me of using it as a front for contraband activities. I swore on my sacred honor that it wasn't so, because I didn't have enough money to finance smuggling, and then you offered me a job. So what could I do? The blacksmith business in New Orleans was slow anyway."

The two husky Wichita girls had filled the water bags and apparently decided to take a swim, for they had shed their skirts and were playing in the shallow water, giggling and chattering like magpies.

"So now," Simon said thoughtfully, "you want to find

78

some rifles with 1772 stamped on them—and they may be in those long boxes under that cottonwood tree."

Dan took a deep breath. "Yes," he said.

"How do you figure to look at them?"

"He brought them here to trade. Pretty soon an Indian will have one of those rifles." Dan bit off a chew with his strong white teeth. "When he does, it's only a matter of time until I'll have a look at it."

Chapter Eleven

POEYFARRÉ came from Eyasiquiche's place, sat down, rolled a cigarette, and lit it from the fire. "Everybody stick close tonight," he said, "and keep your eyes open, for the Spanish may be trailing this man."

"What's his name?" asked Dan.

Poeyfarré said pointedly, "I do not know what his name really is."

"You've seen him before?"

Poeyfarré glanced up. "I have seen him on two-three other trips. He is well known in these villages."

"I never heard of him," Simon observed.

"Is possible. He may use different names in different places. Anyhow, it's time to watch out. With D'Etrées here, there will be some throats cut before this is over."

He finished his cigarette and tossed the butt into the fire. He got up and went back to the Chief's hut.

Menard came from somewhere and lay by the fire.

Meservy passed them, going toward the center of the village with each arm around a Wichita girl.

Dan watched him go into a hut with them, and looked back at the goods now piled under an oak tree. "Two men left to guard the stuff," he noted. "He doesn't trust the Wichitas."

"Or you," said Simon.

About dark the squaws began carrying up wood and building a big fire in the center of the village. "We might as well go up and see what's on for supper," said Simon.

The slender Menard said, "Best we eat all we can now. It may be a long day tomorrow."

79

Two big pots of stew had been simmering all day, and Dan strongly suspected that most of the meat was dog.

Poeyfarré came over. "There is going to be a big dance and celebration tonight. You men have a chance to make some friends—and maybe tomorrow this man's goods don't hurt us so much."

Menard said, "I'm do all I can, but I'm scare' there is too many girls for even a man like Menard."

"I'll back you up," said Simon.

"Shankle—"

"I'll be on hand," Dan said.

He ate plentifully of the stew, and he had to admit it was good, no matter what was in it. The young squaws were everywhere, looking expectant, but Dan left the fire and kept an eye on the goods under the oak tree. He wanted just one chance to look in those long boxes. If he should find what he suspected, he could then have a showdown with Meservy. Then he could backtrail him and find the rest of the rifles— for Meservy could have brought only a small part of them with him.

Dan went back to the hut, where he could keep an eye on the guards. The two men sat on opposite sides of the tree with rifles across their legs; one was D'Etrées.

He sat there in the dark for quite a while, hearing the monotonous chant of one warrior after another boast of his exploits at the fire, acting them out with body and hands; hearing the murmur of feminine voices; hearing mules biting and running; hearing prairie wolves in the distance. He chewed tobacco and occasionally he smoked, but always he kept an eye on the men guarding the long boxes. They talked to each other from time to time in low tones. They got up occasionally and walked around, but they stayed within arm's length of the tree and the boxes.

Simon returned along toward midnight. He sat down beside Dan and stretched. "It might not be such a bad life to settle down with the Wichitas, if a man could have the squaw he wanted."

"Couldn't you?"

Simon sighed. "She'd cost me too many mules." He yawned and went inside. Dan heard him settling down in the straw.

A couple of hours later the party had tapered off around the big fire, which was nothing more than a heap of glowing coals. Menard came back to the hut.

Dan cast a glance toward the tree. The moon was up and

one of the guards was walking down toward the river. Dan got up and went quietly that way.

He came up behind D'Etrées and smelled whisky. He looked toward the river. The first guard was not in sight. Dan backed off far enough to find a section of fallen limb green enough to use as a club. Then he returned.

Just as Dan raised the club, D'Etrées looked up, and Dan caught him hard across the forehead. The man grunted and then toppled.

Dan let him sprawl on the ground. He stepped over him, picked up one of the long boxes, and started for his own lodge with the box held in both arms.

He stumbled over the club he had dropped, and went halfway to the ground. At that moment something thudded against the box, and he heard the whine of a quivering knife. He dropped the box and reached for his tomahawk.

"Pardon me," said Meservy's cynical voice. "I thought somebody was trying to steal my rifles." He stepped into the moonlight from the side of a meat-drying rack. "I didn't know it was you, Shankle."

"You know it now."

"Drop that tomahawk. I'm holding a pistol on you."

Dan dropped his hand from the hatchet and felt it slide back into its rawhide loop.

Meservy came over and worked his knife out of the wood. That knife would have buried itself in Dan's chest if he had not stumbled and thrown up his arms. Meservy stood up, still holding the pistol on him. D'Etrées groaned and rolled over.

A step sounded behind Dan. "Trouble?" asked Simon.

Meservy said to Dan, "Both of you go on back and mind your business. I've had you watched from the time I got here."

Dan had to accept it, but if he could catch Meservy off guard . . .

But the man knew what he was thinking. He backed up. "Get out of my camping ground and stay out. The next time I won't miss," he said. Dan knew he meant it.

Dan and Simon went back. Simon slowly put his pistol away, saying nothing. Dan was chagrined, but there was nothing he could do. He got his blanket from the drying rack and bedded down in the middle of the floor.

The sun was high when he awoke. He sat up and stretched, finding that apparently he had acquired no lice during that night. A fleeting thought came to him that this fastidiousness in the matter of small insects was a thing oddly out of place, under the circumstances.

He got his flint and steel and a piece of charred linen. He went outside and built a nest of dry twigs and got on his knees to work at the flint. The charred linen began to glow. He got down close to the ground and blew, dropping on a few small pieces of dry straw. The fire flamed up. He got the coffeepot and started for the river. The way led by the oak tree where the guards had been. They weren't there now. Neither were the rifles.

He halted for a moment, assimilating this knowledge. Then he went to the river, washed out the pot, scoured it with sand, and filled it half full of water. He went slowly back to his fire.

One fact was fairly obvious: Those were the Watts rifles for which he was looking. Otherwise there was no point in guarding them, for the presence of the boxes made it obvious that rifles were a part of Meservy's trade goods. The big question was: Where had the rifles gone?

Poeyfarré came out of a grass hut, rubbed his eyes, looked toward Dan, and then came over for the coffee.

"Those rifles disappeared this morning," Dan said.

Poeyfarré didn't look happy. "He's already sold his stuff. But don't worry. He will have to take his pay in buffalo robes and deerskins—maybe some gold and silver." He added with obvious satisfaction: "These fine metals have not come through a crown smelter and are subject to fifty per cent tax." He stared at the oak tree. "A bunch of Wichitas left this morning to take his stuff to the Camanches, and we'll have to wait until they get back—maybe tonight, maybe tomorrow night. There'll be powwows and pipe smoking, and lots of argument over how many squaws a good rifle is worth."

"Tomorrow," said Dan, pouring coffee into tin cups. "That's a long time to wait, when we're here without trading licenses."

"You can't push 'em. Time doesn't mean anything to an Indian. And old Eyasiquiche is a sharp trader. He wants to be sure how much he's getting from the Camanches before he loads up on too much goods."

"What do we do in the meantime?"

"Loaf, visit. You talk Wichita?"

"No."

"It's a good time to learn," Poeyfarré said. "I'll send

82

one of Running Bird's daughters to teach you. You'll learn in one big hurry."

Dan got up. He realized that Sarah hadn't even promised, except by implication, with her lips—which was a pretty good way to imply, as he thought about it now. He looked at Poeyfarré a long time without seeing him, and finally he got up and said, "I think I'll take a ride around the village."

Poeyfarré's eyes were penetrating. "Take Simon with you. It isn't safe to roam around this country alone."

Dan got up and looked toward the oak tree. "You figure the rifles went to the Camanches?"

Poeyfarré didn't hesitate. "But of course."

"Why did he sell so fast?" asked Simon. "I thought there was a bigger percentage if you took your time."

Poeyfarré frowned and looked again at the oak tree. "That has always been true. I do not understand it," he said slowly.

Dan thought he did. Meservy had wanted to sell those rifles before Dan could see the name and date on them.

"In a way," said Simon, "it's a good thing Meservy went back already. Your friend D'Eliées had a big lump on his forehead this morning, and the look on his face woulda curdled Pennsylvania whisky."

"I'm glad we're rid of him," Dan admitted.

Simon had a faraway look in his eyes. "A man with a face like that you never get rid of."

They found their mules grazing along the river. They saddled them and rode out to the south, over undulating prairie country with good grass.

From a high mound they watched Meservy's pack train already winding east, back toward the Red River and Natchitoches.

"Mighty quick turnover for him," said Simon. "Big profit in that kind of business."

Dan said thoughtfully, "Do you think those rifles really went west?"

"Bound to," said Simon. "That's where the Camanches are, and where the Camanches are, that's where the money is in guns."

They found their way through the timber belt and killed a turkey.

"We better cook it here," said Simon at the edge of the timber. "I don't see any wood on the prairie."

The turkey was a big hen that weighed about twenty

pounds. They ate most of it, and threw the rest on the sand. "The buzzards will clean it up," Dan remarked.

"The buzzards won't get a chance at it. The prairie wolves will have it within minutes after we leave."

They rode on east and came to the top of a swell. Dan looked back. Two small dun-colored animals were tearing apart the remains of the turkey.

They rode north, and it still lacked two hours of supper time when Dan saw movement in the timber ahead of them. "Down!" he grunted.

They alighted on their moccasins and led the mules to lower ground.

"What was it?" asked Simon.

"It looked like the east end of a mule headed west."

Simon frowned. "Why would a mule be going west?"

Dan started to follow the bottom toward the timber. "That's what I want to know."

They found out minutes later, when a line of uniformed Spanish soldiers rode through an open spot in the timber. "Jumping Christopher!" whispered Simon. "No wonder your friend got out of here so fast. He knew the *soldados* were coming."

"How did he know it?"

Simon was mounting his mule. "He probably paid the lieutenant to give him a day's time."

"We're in for it," Dan said. "They'll find our goods."

"Not if we get to the village first. We'll stick to the edge of timber north a ways and then cut through. It's slower but it's shorter."

They went through the timber at a trot. They turned north along the edge, but Simon was shaking his head. "He's not so dumb, that lieutenant. Once he got through the timber, he put spurs to his outfit."

Dan studied the ground as they loped north. The bent and bruised grass left a trail as plain as a wagon road. He moved alongside Simon. "Not much use hurrying. We can't go around them now."

"I want to see the finish," said Simon.

They saw it. Eight Spanish soldiers with short fusils or rifles, heavy blunderbusses, sabers, lances, and shields were standing at attention before the huts that held their piles of goods.

Chapter Twelve

DAN RODE UP and alighted from his mule. Simon was beside him. "Who's in charge here?" asked Dan.

A swarthy young man stepped forward. "Lieutenant Antonio Borica Durán," he announced proudly. His uniform, Dan thought, was in excellent shape for having come all the way from Nacogdoches or Bexar. Undoubtedly Simon was right: The Spanish cavalry had been camped about a day's march away, waiting for Meservy to return, and possibly awaiting payment for being so considerate.

"You are English?" the Lieutenant asked.

"No," said Simon quickly. "We're French."

The Lieutenant sneered. "Your names, please."

"Daniel Shankle."

The Spaniard glared at him. "That's an English name."

"You have strange names in your own country," said Dan. "How about Alejandro O'Reilly, the captain general at Havana?"

The Spaniard's lips tightened. "Very well, if you insist." He spun on Simon. "And your name, señor?"

Simon sighed. "Pierre Duval."

"You too look English."

"Remember O'Reilly," said Simon. "And how about Hugo Oconor, the *comandante inspector?*"

The Spaniard's eyes narrowed. *"Bien.* Let me see your passports, señores."

Dan said, "We have no passports."

Borica's eyes flashed. "Without passports—both of you?"

"Both."

Borica showed great satisfaction now. "And your licenses to trade?"

"We didn't know we had to have a license," said Simon, wide-eyed. "We just brought in some ordinary trade goods, to try to pick up some deerskins."

"Silencio!" Borica hissed. "These are your goods?" he asked. "This many piles of goods?"

"Sure," said Dan. "You want to look through them?"

"Is not necessary, señor. I take possession of it all in the name of His Most Catholic Majesty."

85

But Eyasiquiche pushed his huge bulk through the Spanish soldiers. *"Qué hay?"* he demanded.

Borica explained in Spanish. "These two men have no passports, no licenses, but they bring trade goods into Texas. I have confiscated their goods."

Eyasiquiche answered promptly, in Spanish almost as good as Borica's, and Dan's respect for him went up.

"They are my guests," Eyasiquiche said. "It is not a hospitable thing you do, to take the belongings of my guests."

Dan watched them. Eyasiquiche was a smart Indian, all right. He knew that if word got around at Arkansa Post that the Wichitas had let a few Spanish soldiers come in and confiscate trade goods, there would be trouble with the *contrabandistas*.

Borica saw which way the wind was blowing. He watched the Indian with narrowed eyes. "There are regulations," he muttered.

A second Wichita pushed forward—Running Bird, a tall, well-built Indian with cold, hard eyes. "The Lieutenant has in times before accepted our hospitality," he said, "and the hospitality of my daughters. Does he now repay us by taking a few trifles that would amuse our women? These men have no rifles, no gunpowder. They do no harm."

"They have no passports. They—"

A third Indian came forward, a smaller and older man with a crippled leg. "You will listen to One-Horned Buffalo," he said, and the camp went suddenly quiet. "I am an old man and I take little part in these squabbles of children. But my heart is good toward the Spanish. I have made promises not to war upon the Spanish and not to take their women and children from San Antonio de Bexar, and I have kept those promises." His old eyes were filled with fire. "And now a young soldier—a boy who has had no chance to prove himself as a warrior—with eight miserable soldiers comes into our village and insults our guests. Does not the great Spanish father value his friendship with the Wichitas enough to send a man with many medals to insult us?"

Borica was trapped and he knew it. He looked around at the ring of bronze-skinned Wichitas. They were muttering now, hostile-eyed, and Borica looked back at One-Horned Bull. He looked beyond the ring of warriors at the squaws, at the several well-built daughters of Running Bird, and back at Eyasiquiche.

Menard slipped through the Wichitas and stood between

Dan and Simon, shaking his head slightly. Dan was puzzled. There were enough Wichita warriors to tear the Spaniards to bits, and yet—

Borica was not helpless. "It is true we have made treaties with you, and we have promised things, and you have promised things. But you have not always kept your word."

One-Horned Bull stiffened. "Am I then one who talks with two mouths?"

"A few moons ago," the Lieutenant said, "we sent a company of soldiers to your village, seeking those who had ravaged our people near Bexar. These soldiers you killed and scalped, and you captured two of their brass cannon. What do you have to say to that?"

Now there were snickers from the Wichitas, and some of the women giggled.

"Is true," said One-Horned Bull. "When any fighting men come against us, they come prepared to fight. The Wichitas are great warriors, and even the Osages know this." He looked around at the nodding heads and fixed his beady eyes again on Borica. "We have two of your brass cannon. They were captured in fair fight. Your soldiers came against us, looking for trouble. We defeated them and sent them away. Many of them were killed and scalped, and I can show you their scalps."

Borica studied him, trying to figure his way out, Dan knew. The Spaniard was in a bad spot. He didn't have enough men to start trouble, but he would lose face if he backed down.

"We have a great chief," Borica said finally, "as great as you, One-Horned Bull, and he gives me orders. I have to enforce them."

Now Poeyfarré, who must have been awaiting the proper moment, came forward. "Governor Rípperda has allowed this innocent trade to go on for three years," he said.

Borica turned to this new opponent. You had to hand it to the Spaniard, thought Dan; he wasn't afraid of the odds.

"Who are you?" Borica demanded.

The Frenchman shrugged. "They call me Poeyfarré. I have traded all over the Texas country."

"You have no rifles?"

"No."

"You take mules and slaves in trade, though."

"Of course not. Such a thing is unthinkable!"

Borica shifted his attack. "You have a passport?"

Poeyfarré shrugged. He was, Dan thought, enjoying the whole thing, because he too considered there was only one way for the Lieutenant to get out alive.

"You have a license to trade?"

"No," Poeyfarré admitted.

"Then I am forced to confiscate your goods also."

"But Rípperda—"

Borica said, his back like a ramrod, "I do not represent the Governor of Texas, señor. I represent Don Hugo Oconor, the *comandante inspector* whom one of your men mentioned. Don Hugo takes orders directly from the Viceroy in Mexico, and does not serve His Majesty under the Governor of Texas."

Simon frowned. "This thing's gettin' mixed up, if you ask me."

Eyasiquiche, Running Bird, and One-Horned Bull seemed temporarily nonplused. Menard whispered in Dan's ear: "Oconor! That's deeferent!"

Borica barked orders at his men. Like a squad of comic soldiers they snapped to attention around Dan's goods, and Dan began to get his dander up. "I can take a tomahawk and wipe out the whole bunch," he growled.

"Best not be impulsive," said Menard. "Oconor would only send more soldiers."

Dan, Simon, and Menard left the circle. Poupelinière and Brognard joined them, and Poeyfarré led the way to the center of the village. "We are in big trouble," said the energetic Frenchman.

"I don't see any trouble we can't handle," said Dan. "There are six of us. We can lick nine Spaniards without pulling a knife—and if we couldn't, what about the Wichitas?"

Poeyfarré seated himself, cross-legged, near the big kettle of stew that was always hanging over the fire before Eyasiquiche's lodge. "We could take care of Borica and his eight men and not lose a scalp, but Borica represents Oconor, and *he's* a bad *hombre.*"

"The Wichitas—"

"They know Oconor too. All the Indians know him. They call him *el Capitán Colorado,* not only because he is red-haired, but because he is a very hard fighter and he never gives up. If he heard that Borica and his men were massacred, he would probably follow us all back to the Arkansa and wipe us out."

Dan frowned. "Everybody turns tail when Oconor is mentioned! Well, I'm not afraid of him. Those goods represent all of my future and a good part of somebody else's."

"You can make it back," said Poeyfarré. "One good trip is all you need."

Eyasiquiche waddled up and sat down by the kettle.

Poeyfarré moved a little to make room for him. "What is your answer, great chief?"

Eyasiquiche's black eyes were quick and evasive. "We are great warriors. We have beaten the Spanish and we can beat them again. But we have lost many young men to the Osages. Numbers of our squaws are without men now. Should we then lose still more fighters over a pile of trade goods? This is an argument that can be settled peaceably. The Spanish officer does not back down. He is not afraid. One-Horned Bull says his medicine is very strong. Running Bird agrees. We favor peace."

Dan got up, disgusted. "You lose your stuff too," he told Poeyfarré.

Poeyfarré shrugged. "I will be back in a couple of months with more. Borica will be somewhere else."

Dan said, "You had rifles. What did you do with them?"

"We have had this experience before," Poeyfarré said blandly. "The rifles we dispose of at once, one way or another, for we know how the Spanish are about rifles."

"Where did these go?" Dan insisted.

Poeyfarré eyed him. "I will slit your throat from one ear to another," he said calmly, "if you say one word to the Spaniard."

"I don't want to say a word. I want to know what happened to them."

"They are still out in the hills," Poeyfarré said quietly, "well hidden. It is as I told you. We were waiting for the Wichitas to get ready for trading."

"It looks like you waited too long."

"That's the way it looks," said Poeyfarré. "Your friend from Natchitoches came in without warning."

Borica was striding toward them. "You, Shankle"—he had some trouble with the consonants at the end of the name—"and you, Poeyfarré, I am going to arrest for trading without a license."

Poeyfarré stared at the Lieutenant, and Dan knew the

Frenchman had been pushed too far. He quietly elbowed Simon in the back.

But Eyasiquiche looked up at the Spaniard. "I do not think you need to arrest them," he said in Spanish.

Borica's eyebrows raised. He was a young man and he had been so sure. Now he couldn't understand what had suddenly changed the situation. "I have confiscated the goods," he said. "Now I am arresting the men who are responsible."

Eyasiquiche was unmoved. "You have confiscated the goods, but you are a long way from your soldiers now."

Borica stared at him. He looked back at the eight Spanish soldiers guarding the goods, and at the two hundred Wichita fighting men who had closed in between himself and those eight. The Wichitas were armed with bows, and some had arrows against the strings; a few had rifles; nearly all had knives or lances.

Poeyfarré looked up and smiled. "You have made a tactical mistake, my friend."

Borica swallowed, but he had a stiff back. "What do you propose to do?"

"You're the one who has been doing the proposing."

"What's the big Indian going to do?"

"I think it's plain where Eyasiquiche's interests lie. He doesn't care too much who gets the goods; his people will have them in the long run anyway. But arrest is going too far. It would get back to Arkansa Post, and the other traders would not come down here any more. They would instead trade guns to the Osages."

Eyasiquiche nodded gravely.

Borica said at once, "That's exactly what we want to do —stop the *contrabandistas!*"

"You might," said Poeyfarré lazily, "but you might lose your life doing it. Now I'll offer a suggestion: You have confiscated the goods and you have no use for them except to trade them to the Indians. Nobody will know how much there is or what you get for it. You can report to Oconor that you took the goods and gave them to the Wichitas because they are complaining for goods. So who knows if you sell a few of the horses and mules down along the Brazos? Is Hugo Oconor watching everything you do?"

"I could not do that!"

"You could and you would," said Poeyfarré. "Especially when you realize that these Wichitas are only going to let you go so far."

90

"What are you wishing to say?"

"We can take the loss of our goods once in a while," said Poeyfarré, "and we will—but we won't go back under arrest to rot in one of your stinking Spanish prisons."

"You mean there would be trouble?"

"Big trouble!"

Eyasiquiche nodded agreement.

"He knows," said Poeyfarré, "that the minute we stop coming down here we start selling rifles to the Osages—and Osages are heap bad medicine for the Wichitas."

"I am not afraid to lose my scalp."

"Osages don't scalp. They take the whole head."

Borica studied Poeyfarré, looked at Eyasiquiche, and glanced over the solid mass of Wichita warriors. Finally he said to Poeyfarré, *"Bien.* In the interest of peace I will not arrest you—but the next time it will not be so easy for you."

Poeyfarré grinned. "The next time," he said, "you better bring more soldiers."

Eyasiquiche looked up and grunted to the Wichitas. They moved back and made a path for Borica. He strode through, and the path closed behind him.

Poeyfarré got up and stretched. "So we are still free," he said.

"Sure," said Dan. "And I'm out four thousand dollars' worth of goods."

"We still have the mules."

"You may have some trouble getting them back to Arkansa Post," Dan said.

Poeyfarré got up, catlike. "What does that mean?"

"I'm not going back," said Dan.

"Where you go, then?"

"West," said Dan shortly. "I've got business with the Camanches."

Poeyfarré looked toward Borica, who was going on down to the river. "I'll have a lot of mules to take back," he said, apparently thinking of the still hidden rifles and the animals they would bring in trade.

"You better make a deal with the Wichitas, then. I'm leaving for Camanche country in the morning."

"How many men are going with you?"

"I haven't asked."

"I'm going," said Simon. "I want to find out if a man

91

can make any money trading with the Camanches instead of the Wichitas."

"I theenk I go too," Menard said unexpectedly.

"What's got into you fellows—going into Camanche country?"

"I want to see what it says on those rifles that came from Natchitoches," said Dan.

"I would not fool with that Meservy. He's bad medicine."

"I don't need to see him. I want to talk to Toroblanco. All I need is to see one of those rifles."

Poeyfarré glared at Menard. "So what's got into you?"

Menard said lazily, "He'll need more than two, and I remember when he want to help Chamillard and Dartigo."

Poeyfarré swung back on Dan. "Camanches are very bad Indians—worse than Osages."

"Maybe," said Dan. "Tell you later."

Simon smoked a cigar that night. "Do you reckon there's any way your friend Meservy could do us any damage in Camanche country?"

"Not unless he's there himself."

"I don't figure there's any reason why he should be there." Simon frowned. "But he sure outguessed us here."

Chapter Thirteen

THEY WERE UP long before daylight. Dan had made a deal with Poeyfarré to herd his extra mules back to Arkansa Post for half of the mules. "I'll be back for them," Dan said.

"I'm not sure we'll get through Osage country."

"With ten Wichita warriors, you'll get there."

The Wichitas were to return due southwest from Arkansa Post and hit the Mexican River at the Camino Real. This route had the fine virtue of avoiding Osage country, which was anywhere north of the Red River. It would have been a good route for Poeyfarré to take east except for the small matters of passports and trading licenses.

"Anyway," said Dan, "you stand to make money by the deal. If I don't get back to Arkansa Post, you get all the mules."

But Poeyfarré was disturbed. "I don't know what you want to see those rifles for."

"*I* know," said Dan, "and it's a good reason. But I don't know why these other two are going."

Menard grinned. "You need someone to speak the sign language, no?"

"The sign language won't do you any good in hell," Poeyfarré growled.

They saddled the mules. The Wichita village was asleep; only a few dogs were prowling among the lodges in the dark, hunting scraps of food. The three men had rifles, pistols, knives, and tomahawks; each had a pair of saddle-bags, one side filled with dried meat, the other with parched corn. Poeyfarré still objected. "It ain't good sense," he said. "*Nobody* goes into Camanche country. There's no percentage in it."

"That's where you've got your saddle on backward," Simon said, leaning over. "Didn't you ever wonder where all that silver comes from that has no royal stamp on it?"

"I've heard there are mines in Camanche country." Pocyfarré moved up and put his hand on the mule's neck. "But you can't take it out. De Mézières would confiscate it."

Simon said mockingly, "Poeyfarré, you been in Louisiana long enough to know better than that. That's why you're takin' back a lot more mules than you brought."

The square man shrugged against the starlight. "All right. You know it all. I give you one good wish: I hope they kill you quick and not slow." He slapped the mule on the rump. "Get out of here before Borica finds out. We'll tell him you got scared and went east."

"Thanks."

They had directions from Running Bird to go due west until they reached a large mound on the Big Wichita River, which forked at the mound. They should find Toroblanco's Kotsotekas on the north fork. If not, they should follow the fork to its source, cross a low ridge, and they would be on the Ke-che-a-que-ho-no, where it was likely that Toroblanco, being a northern Camanche, would take his band when he moved. By that time, Running Bird said, Toroblanco would have plenty of rifles and he might move on, for no Camanche trusted anybody very long.

"But you be careful," he warned. "Toroblanco is a snake." He made the now familiar wriggling motion with his right hand, drawing it back toward him.

They pushed the mules hard, and by noon they had reached the mound. The river had abrupt banks of red clay and sandstone, and the current looked deep and sluggish. There were a few cottonwoods and hackberry trees, and luxuriant mesquite grass.

"We better let the mules graze a while," said Dan.

"You rather rest up on this side?" asked Simon.

"From what I've heard, yes."

They swam the stream about midafternoon, and Simon was worried. "I expected they'd have a watch around the mound," he said.

"If they want to attack, it would be easiest when we are in the water," Menard noted.

Dan was scanning the grass in all directions. "I don't see anything."

"You wouldn't see Camanches," said Simon.

"Is right," said Menard. "Camanches you do not see. You feel their knives, but he can be everywhere and you don't see him."

"It's a funny feeling," said Dan, standing up in his saddle. "The country ought to be full of them. Maybe it is and maybe it isn't. If it isn't, where are they?"

They found out an hour later. The Camanche camp had been abandoned. They rode through it, surveying the refuse, while the mules nervously fought their bits.

"Twenty-five or thirty lodges," Dan noted, "and they headed southwest."

Menard looked worried. "Running Bird said they would likely go northwest."

"He also said they might go in any direction," Simon reminded him, "and he said not to put any stock in it, no matter how it looked."

"Let's go up a ways," Dan suggested, "and camp for the night. We'll figure out what's next tomorrow."

They camped, and in the morning they went back to the Camanche campsite and let the mules graze while they debated. Dan was strongly opposed to the others' continuing with him. "I can do what I want to do by myself as well as with you fellows," he said earnestly.

"Don't you like our comp'ny?" asked Simon.

"You're both fine to ride with, but I have a feeling we aren't all going back alive."

"Maybe not," said Simon, "but I'll take my chance. I want to get my eyes on them silver mines. Every so often

I've seen a pack train of silver come in from somewhere out here. I'd like to find out where they dig it."

"I do not like to go back," said Menard, "once I have start' somewhere."

"What are *you* looking for?"

Menard shrugged. "What is there besides silver and gold?"

"Women," said Simon promptly.

"It's as good a reason as any."

"Simon," said Dan, "you've got a couple of brothers back in the East.

"They don't like me," said Simon. "Come on, it's getting light. We better move."

They followed the broad trail of the Camanches. They had freely used the travois—two long boughs, one tied to each side of a horse, the rear ends dragging on the ground. They were lashed together behind the horse's heels to carry the buffalo skins for tents, dried beef, or even children, and they left very plain trails.

"What bothers me," said Dan, watching the horizon, "is it's *too* plain. If these Camanches are so slippery, they can do better than that."

"I'm sure Toroblanco knows what he do," said Menard. "He's prob'ly have scouts out behind to see if they are followed, and I will bet you a thousand sous right now he knows we are here and he can tell the color, age, and sex of every mule we've got."

The trail followed the Big Wichita. With women and children, Dan had figured they wouldn't travel very fast, and he would have to look sharp to keep from running into them. But Toroblanco's Kotsotekas were making tracks. They hit the upper waters of the Brazos, and Dan was disappointed to find it loaded with salt.

"Watch the mules," Simon warned. "They drink too much of that stuff, we'll be afoot."

They went west to the Salt Plains. Here the country was level and dry but cut by deep *arroyadas*. The grass grew poor and scanty, and only occasionally did they find a spring of sweet water. The springs were seldom big enough to make a stream, for the water soaked into the sand as fast as it flowed.

"Toroblanco knows all the holes," Simon remarked one day as they ate a deer they had surprised the evening before browsing on the shrunken, bitter, amber berries of a china tree at the bottom of a canyon. Dan, fearing to call attention to their presence by firing a shot, had waited in the small tree with a club all afternoon.

"Toroblanco must know we're here," he said, chewing on a half-raw shoulder. "Otherwise he wouldn't keep moving so fast."

"Camanches always move fast," said Simon. "They always figger somebody might be trailing 'em."

"We could catch them, I'm sure, if we wanted to be reckless."

"Is true," said Menard, "but one cannot be reckless with Camanches. We want to meet Toroblanco on our terms, not his."

Dan looked back toward the east. There was nothing but flat plains behind them. "We've come four days."

"We must be gettin' close to the Yarner by now," said Simon.

"What's the Yarner?"

"The Staked Plains. You come to a big cliff that goes hundreds of miles north and south, and up on top is all level prairie, no water, no wood. If there's any water holes, nobody knows them but the Camanches and the Cayugas."

Menard looked west at the endless flat horizon. "Somewhere that way is Santa Fé." His slim body was poised, his dark eyes alight under the red cap. "Are lovely women in Santa Fé, and they ver' happy for *extranjeros*. The men ver' unhappy, but the women—" He blew a kiss to the west. "Poeyfarré himself has told me."

"The Spanish men might be worse than the Camanches," said Dan.

Menard was scornful. "The *españoles* have sat too long on their hind ends. They carry knives and they will show them if their women make them jealous, but wan good Frenchman with a chair leg can whip a roomful of *españoles*. Poeyfarré has told me so himself," he said, as if that ended it.

Simon tossed a bone into the ashes of the fire. "Keep your eyes this way," he said in a conversational tone, "but behind you, maybe half a mile, are Indians."

Dan went on eating as if he had not heard. Menard paused for only an instant. "How many?" asked Dan.

"I count eight," Simon said presently.

Dan got up and walked casually over to his saddlebag. He got a carrot of tobacco and bit off a chew. He put the tobacco back in the saddlebag and returned to his former

96

place by the dead fire. "I see them. It looks like feathers sticking up over the grass. Seems mighty careless."

Simon looked troubled. "Maybe Poeyfarré was right. Maybe I shouldn't of come on this sashay. But it's too late to go back," he added hastily.

"How can they sneak up on us on a flat prairie?" Dan asked.

"With Camanches," said Simon, "you don't wonder how. If a Camanche put his mind to it, he could steal your moccasins off your feet without waking you up. Only," he added, "they don't go around stealing moccasins."

"I would say," said Dan, "the best thing for us is to stay in open country. That way we can watch them."

Menard wiped his greasy fingers on his buckskin pants. He looked toward Dan, but his eyes were on the prairie beyond Dan's shoulder. Then he laughed. "Camanches! You are get' nervous, *amigo*. Those are not Camanches, those are goats."

Simon let out a sigh of relief. "Antelope," he said. "I should of known. Those horns, curved on the end, look like Indian feathers from a distance."

"So now you quit worry," said Menard.

But Dan still felt the heavy weight of possible tragedy.

The trail of the Camanche camp moved more to the southwest. The land became drier, grass scantier, game scarce, and the water almost undrinkable. Even the running water in the few small streams was as salty as sea water. Occasionally, following the Camanches' trail, they reached a buffalo wallow with a few inches of dirty yellow-stained water. The mules drank this, and so did the men. "Is no time to be fussy," Menard observed.

They killed an old bull buffalo that had been left behind by the herd. Dan risked a shot. "We've got to eat whether the Camanches know it or not."

They ate the tenderloins and the seeds, and tried to eat the tongue, but it was all gristle and fiber and had no food value in it. Menard showed them how to sprinkle the liver with bile from the gall bladder. It was bitter but it made the liver more edible. "Will give you energy," said Menard, "and make brave man out of a coward."

"I'm not so sure," said Dan worriedly, "but what we need something to make us cowards."

The hot winds struck them from the south and southwest —winds that shriveled the sparse grass, that seemed to turn

97

man and beast inside out and hold them up to the sun. The brackish water and the all-meat diet gave them diarrhea. They found a cottonwood tree at a water hole, and Menard took the inside bark, boiled it, and made a tea, which he told them to drink.

"Tastes like hell," said Simon. "It's more puckery than persimmons and more bitter than chinaberries."

"It cure you, though." And Menard was right.

Water became more of a problem. Two days later their mouths and throats were like leather. Menard got down from his horse, cut off the thick leaf of a prickly pear, and peeled it with his knife. He gave them each a piece of the white meat. "Hold it in your mouth," he said. "It is better than a bullet or a piece of copper to draw water."

The hot winds beat down at them, making it hard to breathe. The water holes became mere buffalo tracks with a few spoonfuls of water. And they knew now that the Camanches were all around them, for Menard went half a mile back to their camp one morning, looking for a lost carrot of tobacco, and found a piece of beaded buckskin.

They reached another encampment of Toroblanco's band that evening, and Dan went out around the site of the camp and studied the ground. "They are only one day ahead," he announced when he came back.

"They're not eating reg'lar, either," Simon pointed out. "Look at the bones—turtles, lizards, horny toads, and snakes. Grub is gittin' scarce."

Menard scowled at the west. "We getting near the Caprock," he said. "I wondair if Toroblanco is going up there, or will he go north?"

"It couldn't be much worse up there," said Dan.

"Is worse," Menard said emphatically. "No water, more hot wind. Nothing to eat but the goats—and they are ver' difficult to kill on the high plains, for there is nothing to hide behind. Even the grass is too short this summer to hide a rattlesnake."

They camped back away from a water hole that night.

"Not close," Menard insisted.

His knowledge of the Salt Plains proved itself. During the night Dan was awakened by trampling hoofs and the growl of a panther. He sat upright in his blanket and saw in the moonlight, down at the water hole, a big cat fastened around the neck of a deer. He shot without thinking. The panther

98

screamed and fell to the ground. The deer sprang away into the darkness.

They dressed out the panther and went down in a hollow to build a fire. They sat up the rest of the night, eating every edible part of the panther, including its intestines.

When daylight came, Dan looked at their gaunt, unshaved faces. "We were close to starving," he said.

"Is bad," said Menard, "when Camanches eat rattle-snakes."

"First time I been full in two weeks," said Simon, sighing.

Menard filled his pipe with his last scrap of tobacco. "That deer might still be around," he said wisely. "It weel not go too far from the water."

Simon picked up his rifle. "I'll saunter down to the mud-hole and have a look."

"Watch where you're going," said Dan.

"That's my best trick," Simon assured him.

Menard scowled as Simon walked away. "Is dividing us up. I do not like."

Almost at the same time Dan heard the splat of small hoofs in the mud. An antlered deer jumped from behind a mesquite bush and bounded away over the prairie, to disappear in the northwest.

Simon was near the hobbled mules. He caught his own, jerked off the rawhide link, stuffed it in his heavy wool shirt, leaped on the mule, and went off after the deer.

"He's figure maybe that deer went down in the next canyon," said Menard.

"Maybe it did," Dan said, getting up.

Menard went with him. They caught the mules quickly and saddled them. Dan kept watching the horizon where Simon had disappeared. They left Simon's saddle, saddlebags, and rifle in a clump of bear grass. "He might come back looking for them," Dan said thoughtfully.

Chapter Fourteen

THEY CAME to the next *arroyada*, a dry gash in the alkali earth whose whiteness glistened under the brilliant sun.

"Will be a hot day," said Menard.

The sun was now edging over the eastern horizon like a blazing arc of hot brass.

"There's a mudhole." Dan pointed. "That would be where the deer went."

"And here"—Menard got down—"is where Simon approach' the edge to get a shot."

"But he didn't shoot."

"No. We would hear a shot many miles this morning."

"Then he must be down there somewhere."

"The mule stood back here"—Menard indicated droppings—"and then—"

Dan was down, holding the mule's reins. "All of a sudden," he said, "the mule took off at a gallop. It was scared."

"Scar' of what, I wonder? No panther would be so close, up here on the prairie, or Simon would have seen it."

Dan said in a tight voice, "What if there were a couple of Camanches down in that *arroyada*, watching us? They'd hear him come up, and hide back against the bank. Then they'd find a way out, and come up behind him. That's what scared the mule."

Menard nodded, his eyes narrow.

"The mule snorts and runs. Simon looks around. The Indians are flat on the ground. Simon starts after the mule, and an arrow—"

"An arrow can be merciful," said Menard.

Dan flinched. "There's no sign of blood. It wasn't an arrow. Anyway, he would have hollered."

Menard said, "We can trail him."

"They would leave one man in the canyon to watch the ponies," Dan said thoughtfully, "while one or two of them went after him. While he was chasing the mule, they might have run after him and caught him before he could fire a shot."

"I theenk that is it."

"Then," Dan said grimly, "we've got to find him before they start to work on him."

Menard was watching the ground. "Here the ponies were brought up from the canyon."

Dan nodded. "Three ponies and a mule. Makes a plain trail."

"Is not plain unless they want us to see it," Menard cautioned.

"Well, it's open country. They can't very well stay out of sight up here."

100

"A Camanche can hide behind a blade of grass—but they have to do something with the ponies and the mule."

They followed the trail at a trot. It turned to the left almost immediately, and they found themselves in a shallow draw. A man walking alongside a horse might be invisible from the prairie. They followed the tracks to the bottom of the draw, and came out in a small canyon with white alkali dirt sides. A shallow stream ran through the bottom of it.

Menard tried the water and made a face. "Not too bad. The mules can drink it."

Dan got down. "Where did the tracks go?"

Menard pointed to a hoofprint in soft sand. "Into the stream."

Dan surveyed the water. "Which way?" he asked.

"I would say up. Therefore they probably went down."

They rode, one on each side of the stream, watching for the exit of horses' tracks. They followed the stream for two miles, with the water diminishing in volume until finally it sank into the sand and flowed no farther.

Dan got down and bathed his wrists and his face in the now tepid water.

"There are no tracks," said Menard. "So we must go the other way."

Dan began to feel urgency. "We'd better hurry."

They rode out of the *arroyada* and came up on the plains again. The wind was now smothering hot, and beginning to pick up dust. "If we cut straight across this way," Dan said anxiously, "we should be able to gain on them."

They bore to the left, but the sun was high and the wind was stronger, and tiny particles of gravel began to beat against their hands and faces.

"Is going to be hard to see," said Menard.

"The mules will try to face into the wind," Dan observed. "We'll have to pull them to the right."

By now the dust had risen high above the earth and obscured the sun, and they could not be sure of directions. But Dan felt reassured when the mules stopped at the edge of an *arroyada*.

They found a way to the bottom. There was a tiny stream here too, and they followed it until they reached a place where it seeped out from the base of a high cliff. They examined the ground, and finally Dan shook his head. "If they came this way, they left the canyon before they got up here."

"We follow it down," said Menard. "They have to come out somewhere."

They went downstream for a mile; then the water soaked into the sand and disappeared as before.

"Wait a minute," said Dan. "It isn't as long now as it was."

Menard looked at him thoughtfully. He got down and tasted the water. When he arose he said soberly, "Is not the same water, *mon ami.*"

Dan was incredulous. "You sure?"

"The other water was salty; this is sweet. The mules will love it. But we have found another stream."

"Where's the one we were following?"

"Is the big question."

"Let's sit down and think for a minute. We followed that canyon down, and then we cut across on the north side until we came to another canyon. The water was flowing to our left, so it—"

"It was flowing to our right," said Menard.

Dan barked, "You're lost!"

Menard got out his pipe. He had no more tobacco for it, but he clamped it between his teeth and said, "We're *both* lost."

"It isn't possible. I've seen men lost in the forest, but never on the plains like this."

"There are always new things to see," said Menard, his expression calm.

"In the meantime, the Camanches have got Simon."

Menard did not comment.

Dan looked at the sky, but the dust seemed to fill the air until it was like twilight. "Which way do you think we should go?"

"To be truthful, I do not know. The wind was in the southwest when we started."

"It may have switched by now."

"That is true."

Impatience began to overcome Dan. "We can't just sit here. No telling what those red heathens are doing to him."

Menard's answer was grave. "That also is true. What do you suggest?"

Dan got hold of himself with an effort. "We don't dare split up. That's the first thing. And the second thing is to decide where to look. There's so much dirt in the air, we can't tell which way is west."

"Maybe we best stay here until the storm goes down."

"What I hear, a storm like this might keep up for days."

"Poeyfarré has said that."

"We can't sit here while the damned Camanches are torturing Simon."

"Very well," said Menard. "You lead the way. I am with you."

They filled the vellum-like buffalo paunches with water and hung them on their saddle horns. They gave the mules a last chance to drink. Then they started into the wind.

Three days later their food gave out. The wind was still hot and grinding, all day and all night, never letting up. Their noses began to bleed without provocation. They used up their water but found a mudhole the second day.

"There have been Camanches here," said Menard.

"How do you know?"

"See the little round spots in the soft ground near the water? That's where the squaws get down on their knees to drink."

"And the warriors?"

"Always they do not trust anybody. They put their hands into the water and balance on their hands and toes. The water takes away the hand marks, and they brush away the toe marks in the dry ground. But the squaws drink from their knees. Poeyfarré says that is Camanche custom." Menard turned his back to the wind for a moment. "The pony sign is hard," he noted, "and the wind has blown away the trail or covered it up."

The next day the force of the wind abated, but the air was still filled with dirt. They found an *arroyada* that was truly an *arroyada,* for it was dry. Their water bags were empty, and the mules were braying piteously.

"There is a way, perhap', to find watair," said Menard. "Poeyfarré have told me."

"We could use Poeyfarré about now," Dan said through blackened lips.

"That Frenchman, he is wan beeg traveler. He has been everywhere. But you come. We use the knife."

They followed the *arroyada* until they came to a ten-foot-high bank on the windward side. "Dig close to the bank," said Menard.

They dug up the soft sand until they had a hole knee-deep. The sand was moist, but there was no water.

"Wait a little while," said Menard. "Water will come."

And after Menard's "little while" there was six inches of

water in the hole. They drank and filled the bags, and let the hole fill again and again. Their only food now was parched corn and a pair of mud-dauber swallows that they killed with a stick. They ate the birds raw, while the mules foraged.

They started out again the next morning, leather-lipped, cotton-mouthed. They were walking, leading the mules. The wind died down completely that afternoon, and the sun became visible as it set, a great reddish-yellow omen.

Dan stared at it. "You know what that means? We're going west!"

But Menard shook his head. "Now, yes—but not for the last several days."

"How could that be?"

"We have make a big circle, and now we're going west, all right, but we're back toward the Brazos."

"If we're that far east, we ought to be near water."

"The wind blows the water out of the ground. You can tell by watching the mules. They have not lifted their ears for two days."

They rested a while and started moving again after midnight. "The mules won't last long if we don't find water," said Dan.

"They will go a long time if you don't feed them."

Dan looked at Menard's blackened face, his cracked lips, his shrunken skin. "None of us is going much longer," he said.

Menard's eyes narrowed. "Two mules—two more days, maybe three."

They killed one of the mules that night and drank its blood, thick and purple. It gagged them, and it was salty, but it seemed to go into the dried-up tissues of their bodies. They cut off a ham and skinned it and ate it raw. Dan used the dirt to clean blood from his hands.

"It's a shame the other mule can't eat meat," he said.

Menard shook his head. "That pile of skin and bones has not much longer to live."

They killed the second mule the next day. They had crossed breaks in the earth, but there was no water in any of them, and Menard insisted that the wind had sucked it up. They ate a part of the second mule, and Menard got out his pipe and chewed on the stem. "This will be our last night unless we have some luck." His voice was hoarse.

"Do we still head west?"

"Good as any, since we don't know where we are. Texas," he said, "is a big place."

They took enough meat from the mule's carcass to carry them through another day, and staggered on west. The sun sapped the moisture out of their skin and out of their flesh, and pretty soon they knew it would begin to dry out their bones, and that would be all.

Finally, in midafternoon, Menard sat down with his back against a clump of bear grass. His voice was a croak. "I'm through, *mon ami*. Give my love to the girls in Santa Fé."

Dan, standing, looked down at him. There was nothing left of Menard but skin and bone; his face was blackened; his lips were turned inside out and were dry like old leather. "You stay here," Dan said. "I'm going to have a look. That bear grass seems familiar to me."

"Every clump of bear grass is alike. They are not like women. Women are all different, but bear grass—" He fell over on his back.

Dan pulled him off of the sharp spines. He noted the slackness in Menard's clothes, and shook his head dubiously.

He took his bearings, remembering the bear grass he had seen the day Simon had disappeared, now almost two weeks ago. Dan was still carrying his saddlebags and now he slung them over the bear grass so he would be sure to see it. Then he went southwest. It seemed he had been going southwest for many lifetimes, and this was the last journey and the longest one.

He reached the edge of an arroyo and stood looking down at it, not realizing at first what he was seeing. Then his eyes opened wide and he let out a croak. He ran back to Menard and dragged him up by the front of his shirt. "Come on, you Frenchie, there's water down there!"

"Water," said Menard, "is all alike, but women are all different. Poeyfarré said the girls in Santa Fé are best."

Dan dragged him over the prairie to the arroyo. He found a place where they could get down. He laid Menard in the sand with his hands and wrists in the water, while he himself took a mouthful, careful at first not to swallow it. He washed his arms in it. He took off his clothes and lay in it, and his body seemed to soak it up like a sponge. Menard opened his eyes. The water on his hands seemed to revive him, and presently he too was rolling in the stream. Not until an hour later did they dare to take the water into their stomachs, and finally Dan sat down and pulled on his clothes. "We're back where we started," he said. "If Simon hadn't gone for that deer, we'd be together yet."

"Is sad about Simon," said Menard. "But we have to find something to eat for ourselves."

"I'll get my rifle and we'll go up to the spring and wait. There was a chinaberry tree. Maybe another deer will come along."

"You damn Englishman." Menard smiled. "You never quit going, do you?"

"Not while I can move. You going to walk, or you want me to carry you?"

"You get the rifle," Menard said, and Dan realized from the huskiness of his voice that he was nearly gone in spite of the water. "I'll walk up the canyon and meet you." He looked at the fifteen-foot banks. "I could not climb those now."

Dan nodded. He made his way up a white-dirt draw and came out on the prairie. He saw the saddlebags and went to them. He was so intent on getting the rifle that he didn't notice anything wrong until a swarthy man stood up just beyond the bear grass and said, *"Bienvenido, Señor Shank', mi amigo francés."*

Dan stared at Lieutenant Borica. The Lieutenant had a big pistol in one hand.

"We have wait' around here several days for you, señor."

Dan looked at his rifle, half standing in the bear grass, and swore.

"Back, if you please," said Borica. "Do nothing foolish. My men are most unhappy with this abominable dust storm and the hot sun which you have caused them to endure."

"What made you think we'd come back here?"

"I knew you couldn't cross the Llano Estacado, and it seemed reasonable that you would return by the same route you used in going out. Then the storm came up, and I knew you would be lost and would probably circle, so we waited here." He smiled sardonically. "Water is important out here."

"I heard," said Dan harshly.

"Where are your *compañeros?*"

"One is out yonder somewhere. The Camanches got him."

The Lieutenant clucked sympathetically. "I am sorry. And the other?"

Dan looked at the rifle again, but Borica had moved in front of it. For a second he debated, but the answer was inescapable. Menard had to have food or he wouldn't last the next day. Dan took a deep breath. "Down there," he said.

106

Borica motioned, and two Spanish soldiers got up from where they had been lying on the ground beyond the bear grass. They ran down into the arroyo.

"What's the charge this time?" asked Dan. "We aren't violating any laws."

"You will please turn around. *Gracias.* You will see I have respect for your resourcefulness. You damned Englishmen are likely to try anything."

Dan turned around and walked slowly toward the arroyo. The other six soldiers were at the bottom of it. They had not been over half a mile from where Dan and Menard had found water. Dan went down a water-gashed draw, followed by Borica, who had his rifle.

The first two soldiers now came down the stream with Menard. He looked at Dan and smiled weakly. "It looks like they have us now, *mon ami.*"

"They've got us," said Dan. "But what for?"

"It is a pleasure to do one's duty without a thousand Indians waiting to shoot one in the back," observed Borica.

"There weren't a thousand Wichitas in that whole camp, including the dogs."

"*No obstante,* you will observe the tables are turned, and I am now able to obey the orders of His Most Catholic Majesty without interference. I arrest you for being without passports, without trading licenses, and for smuggling rifles to the Indians in defiance of the laws of the Indies."

Dan stared at him. "You must be loco! I've only got that one rifle, and I had that back at the Wichita village. I've still got it. You can't accuse me of selling rifles to the Indians."

"It is worth inquiring why you risked your lives to come into Camanche country if you did not wish to sell rifles to the Indians."

Dan hesitated. "We were looking for silver mines," he said finally.

"What would you do with silver if you found it?"

"Take it to Nacogdoches or Bexar, of course."

"That I find very difficult to believe," said Borica, "in the face of the evidence which you left behind at this camp."

"What kind of evidence?"

"You will be duly advised when you get to Bexar."

"Wait a minute. Simon Jeffreys—he's out there. The Camanches got him."

The Lieutenant smiled ironically. "By this time," he as-

sured Dan, "you have nothing to worry about on his account.
Órtiz!"

"*Sí, mi teniente.*"

"See that these men are fed. It is a shame to waste food
on such criminals, but the inspector has ordered that all
arrested men be taken to Bexar."

Dan kept still. The last few words of Borica's statement
warned him that not a very sharp line separated him from
death even now.

He looked at the west and bowed his head for a moment.
Then he said to Borica, "When do we start?"

"In the morning."

Menard's croaking voice said behind him, "We've got nothing to worry about. The food may not be very good but it
will be provided by the Viceroy. Is that it, Borica?"

"Prisoners of the King are taken care of in accordance with
the means of the country," Borica said stiffly. "As to the time,
I assure you it is out of my control. I suggest you eat. The
men killed a buffalo yesterday, and it is a long trip to Bexar."
There was an inexplicable look of satisfaction on his face.
"*El señor inspector* will be pleased to know that our trip
was not quite made for nothing, *verdad?*"

Chapter Fifteen

DAN AWOKE before daylight, with a gnawing hunger in his
stomach and a Spanish toe in his ribs. "*Levántate!*" was the
command. "Up! Get some food in your belly. It's a long
way to go today."

Dan got up, grumbling, and went to the fire, where a
Spanish soldier was stirring a savory-smelling stew in a big
kettle.

"Prairie dog," said Borica. "You like prairie dog?"

"I'd like anything right now," said Dan. "But why does that
infernal corporal of yours have to wake me up with a kick?"

Borica smiled frostily. "Pay no attention, señor. He has
little chance to exercise his authority on such a trip as this."

Dan rubbed the sore spot in his ribs. "He'd better exercise
it somewhere else or he'll find himself with his hind end
planted on the prairie."

Borica smiled again. "I would not antagonize him, señor."

108

The Spaniards did not get under way very fast. It was mid-morning before the stew was ready, and they took their time eating, squatting around the kettle and indulging in small talk.

Dan had time to learn how to roll up a thin *tortilla* and use it as a spoon to dip up the stew, eating *tortilla* and all each time.

"It is good," said Borica, "that you become familiar with our customs."

"Especially," said Menard through a mouthful of stew, "since we are likely to see the inside of a Spanish *juzgado* for the next five years."

Borica raised his eyebrows. "Is no hurry," he said. "Is a big country. Life always goes on. A man dies here and there and goes to purgatory, but life goes on. It is not a thing to fight against."

"Some die sooner than others," said Menard.

Borica shrugged. *"Es cosa de México."*

"Will there be a judge at Bexar to listen to our case?" Dan asked.

"Seguro. There is a judge in Bexar every year. Your case will be heard promptly, as soon as he arrives."

"From what I've heard," said Menard, "promptly in the Spanish language doesn't mean the same as it does in English."

"You are always in a hurry. We Spanish take our time. Life is long enough at best. Why fret about it?"

"Maybe we've got things to do," said Dan.

Borica said blandly, "Those things are no more pressing now than when you entered New Spain without a passport or a trading license."

They had trouble getting their mules together. One had broken his hobbles and strayed too far for recovery, and another had apparently been bitten by a snake, for his front leg was badly swollen.

The Lieutenant's mule was brought up, and Borica stepped into the saddle. It was astonishing, Dan noted, how the man changed when he was mounted. His whole figure assumed a regal bearing.

"I regret to say," Borica told them, "that with the loss of our two extra mules you will be forced to walk."

Dan looked out at the white plains with the heat waves shimmering above them. "You don't expect us to keep up with a mule, do you?"

"I might be forgiven if I did," said Borica. "You English

109

and French are so proud. But no, I hardly expect that. If you make six or seven leagues a day, it will be sufficient for our purpose."

"Six or seven leagues—twenty miles!"

"I trust you will not force me to be unpleasant, señor."

"I'm sure," said Dan, "you could be no more unpleasant at my forcing than you are by nature."

Menard said in a low voice, "It is going to be a long trip. We would do well to cultivate the Lieutenant's friendship."

"It isn't going to make much difference. He's got just so much cussedness to work off anyway."

They started off across the hot, dazzling plain.

"Couldn't you send a detachment to look for Simon?" asked Dan.

"You would have me jeopardize my command for one man, one Englishman? No, I don't think the inspector would approve of that."

"The Camanches—"

"I have already said that the Indians waste no food on a man they intend to kill. They have no prisons. Either they make a slave of a captive or they torture him. At any rate, I am sure your friend is a long way from here, and we do not know which way to look for him."

They made a dry camp that evening on the plains. There was no water and no wood, not even the ubiquitous mesquite or cottonwood. The soldiers gathered buffalo chips for fuel while Dan and Menard, bone-tired from a day's marching and exhausted by the heat and lack of water, lay on their backs to rest.

That night was also hot. The fire died out, and the cayeutes sang around them. In spite of his weariness, Dan found it hard to sleep. He lay on a quilt, watching the brilliant stars, wondering where Simon was that night. And twice, after midnight, he heard a killdeer cry.

Menard heard it too. "That bird never sits in a bush or a tree, always on the ground."

"Something disturbed it." Dan spoke in a low voice.

"Maybe a cayeute, maybe Camanches. Who knows?"

"*Silencio!*" growled the guard.

Dan whispered, "There's something out there."

"Maybe," said Menard. "Whatever it is, we'd be fools to go looking in the dark."

Dan rolled back.

Presently Menard whispered, "There may be an attack by the Camanches at dawn. Do you have a weapon?"

"No, they took my rifle and all."

He felt the flat, cold steel of a knife blade on his arm. "I stole two of these from the cook. Keep it out of sight, and don't use it for anything unless the Indians attack."

Dan took the knife and slid it under his belt, inside his shirt.

"See that it is at your back when they search you, for they will pat your stomach."

"All right."

He went to sleep finally, but it was an uneasy sleep, filled with bad dreams and frequent awakenings. He looked at Menard, who was sleeping soundly with his head bent down a little, at the guard who paced back and forth along the mules, at the inscrutable darkness that hid whatever was out there.

He understood a little better now why the Texas country was so inimical to man, for it was enormous and it was hostile in many different ways—from heat, from aridity, from scarcity of wood and absence of food, from wind and dust and probably from cold in the winter, from many tribes of savage Indians, from incredible distances and the ever present alkali that colored the ground as if salt water had flooded it for many years.

He stayed awake for a long time, listening for strange sounds, hearing little but the cayeutes, for up here on the dry land there were few insect noises. Occasionally, with his ear to the ground, he could hear a sound of digging, and concluded it was a badger going into a prairie-dog hole.

He slept a little more, uneasily, until he heard the cook get up and build his fire.

He thought they would be under way in a hurry that day, but it was not so. The Spaniards took their time, and again it was well into the morning before they got strung out, Dan and Menard both walking in the heavy white dust kicked up by the mules.

They had been on the move for two hours when Menard pointed at the sky ahead. "*Zopilotes.* Turkey buzzards," he said.

Borica saw them at about the same time. He pulled up his mule and stopped the column. Dan walked alongside him. "It may be a trap," said Borica. "The buzzards' being so high in the air would indicate the animal is still alive. That is

111

unusual itself, out on the plains. Generally an injured animal does not live long."

"It might be a stray buffalo bull," said Menard.

"It would be killed by the wolves in a very short time."

Dan frowned. "D'you suppose—"

Borica looked down at him. "It could be your friend. It is a favorite trick of the Camanches to find out which way a party is going and then to stake out a victim where he will be found."

Dan swallowed.

Borica sighed. "I suppose we shall have to see. You'd better come."

Dan nodded.

"Órtiz! Rubio! Dismount!"

Two Spaniards dismounted and turned their mules over to Dan and Menard.

"Santos! Morales!"

Two others fell in behind. The Lieutenant went forward at a trot, standing in his stirrups, his big rowels jingling. Dan and Menard spread out a little, staying behind him but not clouded by the white dust his mule raised.

They covered a mile. Then suddenly Borica drew up his mule. "*Allá!*" he breathed.

It was something very low on the ground. The buzzards were circling high above; half a dozen cayeutes sat up on their haunches, just out of rifle range.

"Is that what you hunt, *amigo?*" asked Borica.

Dan stared at the ground. Buried up to his neck, but still alive, was Simon Jeffreys. Hoarse croaks came from his leathery throat.

Dan slid down from the mule. With the blazing sun high overhead, he didn't know whether Simon saw them or not, for, though Simon's head was turned toward them, his eyes showed little recognition. It might have been that he was blinded by the sun, for his eyelids had been removed. Nor was that all. He had been scalped. His lips, his nose, and his ears were gone, and his tongue had been cut out. His head was oozing blood and pus, and a great cloud of blowflies arose from him as Dan ran up.

Dan dug furiously with his knife. The stench was almost unbearable. He threw dirt to one side while Menard dug on the other. They dug his arms free, while Borica watched silently. They got the dirt loose around his body, and kept

112

digging, but Borica stopped them. "I know these Caman-ches," he said. "I theenk you lift him out now."

Dan and Menard got him by the arms, and to Dan's surprise his body came up.

Simon's legs had been cut off at the knees. The lower legs were buried in the hole, and Simon had been set on top of them, his stumps twisted with rawhide so he would not bleed to death too fast. As they pulled him out, drying clay cracked off and the legs began to bleed.

Dan looked up at Borica. "We need help!" he shouted.

Borica shook his head slowly. "There is nothing in this world we can do for him. He won't last today. And if he did, what kind of man would he be?"

"We can make a litter between two mules," said Dan.

Borica looked at the sun and back at the hideous scrap of humanity. "I do not think he would want to live," he said.

"It doesn't make any difference what you think," Dan snapped. "We'll keep him alive as long as we can."

"There is no water," said Borica. "A shot in the back of the head would be quicker and easier."

"He's still alive!" shouted Dan.

Borica nodded. "Santos!"

They used a blanket stretched between two mules. Dan waved off the flies, but the hot sun was impossible to guard against. Simon had grown quiet, and his face was white. Only the croakings still came from the leathery throat and the lipless mouth.

"He's trying to say something," said Menard. "I can't hear what it is."

"I think I know," said Borica. He took out his pistol and thrust it, butt first, into Simon's hand. Dan frowned.

A change came over Simon's mutilated face. It was almost as if something pleased him. Then he put the muzzle of the pistol between his teeth and pulled the trigger.

Borica reloaded the pistol calmly. "I will give you an hour to bury him," he said.

Dan and Menard went to work. They made the grave as deep as they could. When Borica announced the time was up, they laid the mutilated body in the bottom of the hole and covered it with the whitish dirt.

"Is too bad. There are not even rocks to cover him," said Borica.

"You think the cayeutes will dig him up?"

Borica looked toward the horizon. In all quarters, sitting on their haunches out of rifle range, were prairie wolves—probably twenty in all.

"It has been a dry summer," said Borica. "They will dig deep."

"I'll stay here and beat their brains out!" Dan shouted.

"It cannot be permitted; you are a prisoner. It is not the fault of the cayeutes, anyway. Besides, they will pay, for next year there will be few rabbits and fewer cayeutes. Now, señores, if you will give me those knives—"

Chapter Sixteen

THEY CROSSED the Tock-an-ho-no that night, and the next day went around the Double Mountains and kept due south through a wide strip of mesquite, prickly pear, and post oak.

Dan and Menard were sober as they walked in the dust, and even the Spaniards did not seem as talkative as they had been. The train came out on rolling tablelands heavy with grama grass and mesquite grass, and the mules began to graze voraciously.

"I have sorrow for your friend," Borica told them the first evening they camped on the Pash-a-he-no fork of the Río Colorado. "Perhaps you know now why we do not give rifles to the accursed Camanches."

"If that's a sample," said Dan.

"And still you must remember the Camanche is only doing what he has been taught to do."

"You mean you think it's all right."

"Not all right to us. All right to him. He doesn't want us in his country, and he takes this means of trying to keep us away."

"When they turn me loose at Bexar I'm coming back," Dan said grimly, "and I'll massacre every Camanche in New Spain."

Borica dipped a *tortilla* into the eternal stew.

"Is a fine ambition," he observed, "but I theenk your anger will be cooled by the time you are released from Bexar."

They came down out of the mountains, and there, five miles across a level plain to the south, stood the small and somewhat wretched village of Bexar. Dan and Menard were still

114

walking, but, having been fed, they had toughened up, and now swung along with the mules all day without becoming exhausted.

They crossed the plain, found a path through the chaparral, and finally entered a square. Here the huts were poor Spanish or Mexican, made of stakes, without windows or window openings, plastered with mud and roofed with river grass. Brown-skinned children played leisurely among the dogs and chickens and pigs; brown-skinned men sat slumped on the packed earth, with their backs against the huts, not moving until their huge straw hats no longer protected them from the sun; and black-eyed, olive-skinned girls stood in the open doorways, smoking *cigarros* of corn shucks, wearing loose white blouses and simple red or black or yellow skirts, no stockings, and fine shoes that seemed in strange contrast to their poverty.

Menard said eagerly, "They see us, *mon ami!*"

"They can't very well help it," said Dan dryly. "They're certainly looking."

Menard was excited. "It is as Poeyfarré always told me about the Spanish women. They hunger for men of vigor."

They passed a round-domed church and crossed a bridge over a river of crystal-blue water, and went into a better part of the town, where dwellings were made of sun-burned brick.

They followed the course of the San Antonio River, and practically every street was a canal through which the water flowed and in which men, women, and children splashed, all without any sort of clothing and apparently without thought of their nakedness.

It was a warm afternoon, and they rode to the squawking of chickens and the bleating of goats, running a gauntlet of curious black eyes.

They were taken to a large building and led inside, where it was cool and dark. Borica turned them over to a grizzled Spaniard who took them to a lower floor, pushed them into a cell, and clanged shut an iron door. Dan heard the lock screech as the big key turned in it. Then the grizzled jailer's footsteps faded away on the dirt floor, and they were alone. All the sounds and the brightness of the sunshine were shut out, and it was as if they were in a different world, and those things they had just come through could not exist.

Dan looked around. "They must have been short on furniture when they built this *juzgado*."

115

Menard sat in a corner. "At least it's out of the sun, and away from the Camanches, and I suppose we'll be fed."

"I didn't ask him about getting out."

"Don't waste your time," said Menard. "We may be here for years."

"Years!"

"The Spanish don't believe in hurry."

"Do you think we'll have blankets?"

"Probably not. They expect us to buy them."

"We're not supposed to have any money."

"They know we have it anyway," Menard said imperturbably. "They expect us to buy food and knives and pay for our own washing."

"It's a strange kind of prison."

Menard lay on his back, with one arm under his head, sucking his pipe. "It's not bad, as prisons go," he said complacently. "I'll be able to get some tobacco now."

Dan paced the hard dirt floor for a while, until finally Menard, sitting wedged in a corner, took his pipe out of his mouth. "I wish you wouldn't do that. It jars the floor."

Dan stopped in the middle of the cell and stared at him. "I can't stay in here," he said irritably. "I've got a lot of things to do. There are rifles—"

"Save your energy," Menard advised, "until there is something you can do." He seemed placid and content. "You weel find Spanish prisons interesting. Not what you might expect. I've been in your damned British prisons, and they aren't fit for a beast. The Spanish prisons can be very brutal, but they can also be very comfortable if a man makes up his mind to it."

"Bars," Dan insisted, "are bars."

"Except in Spain," Menard said enigmatically.

Dan stared at him, but Menard offered no further explanation. Dan took a few more turns, studied the narrow slit that gave them fresh air and some light, and finally sat down in the opposite corner from Menard. He could not understand why the Frenchman was so imperturbable.

An hour later a soft whisper came from the iron bars that formed the door. "Señores!"

Dan got up. It must have been twilight outside, but he could see a smile spread over Menard's face. Dan went warily to the door. "Yes," he said.

A girl, vividly colored even in the half-darkness, stood outside the door. The top of her head was below Dan's shoulders, but her hair was very black, and her lips, as she looked up at him, very very red. The white, loose-fitting blouse was fresh and creamy, and her voice was a breathed whisper: *"Qué alto!* How tall you are!"

Menard spoke up. "He got that way from dodging such lovely girls as you."

"Oh, señor!"

Menard continued to suck his pipe. "A friend," he observed, "is a precious thing, and this one—" He shook his head. "How can you keep your hands at your sides, *mon ami?*"

Dan looked at him and back at the girl.

Her voice was eager. "I have sometheeng for you, señor —bread, soap, melons. What you want?"

"We can't buy anything," Dan said. He looked at her skeptically. She probably had been sent by the *comandante* to spy on them, to find out if they had money. "We're prisoners," he said with finality.

"You do not have to buy," she said in that strange, soft accent. "Is for you— a gift."

"We can't —"

Menard was on his feet. "You better let me take charge," he said. "The greatest insult you can offer a Spanish woman is to turn down a gift of food."

The girl was holding a bundle through the bars; her hands were very white. Menard took the bundle and broke into Spanish too fast for Dan to follow. The girl's smile was a glad one. *"Nos vemos,"* she said, and glided away.

Menard gave the bundle to Dan. "The first honor is yours, *muy alto.*" He added, "Her name is Panchita."

Dan sat down and began to open the square of linen on his lap.

Menard said negligently, "If you look inside the corn bread, you will no doubt find money."

Dan examined the hard, dry cones of bread. He started to break one in the middle, and it fell apart. He stared.

"You were right! A silver real!" He looked up at Menard. "How did you know about this?"

"From Poeyfarré," Menard said complacently. "I wish I had reminded her to bring some tobacco."

But tobacco came within another half hour, brought by another olive-skinned girl who said her name was Guadalupe. She had a bundle of corn-shuck *cigarros* and some live coals in a small brass bucket. She lingered at the door for some time, while Menard lighted a cigarette and smoked one with her. They talked in low tones.

"I'd give a peso for a good chew," Dan said later.

"You won't get any chewing tobacco from the Spanish. Moreover, it seems to me you are unduly critical. You certainly would never encounter such hospitality from the British—or from the French or from the Dutch."

Dan got up. "I don't know what to make of all this. What are they getting ready to do to us?"

"You are such a thickheaded Englishman." Menard sighed, obviously enjoying Dan's lack of understanding. "So if they are fattening you for the sacrifice, is that any reason why you should fail to enjoy what is offered you?" He lay flat on his back, inhaling smoke deep into his lungs and expelling it slowly so it seemed to trickle from his nostrils. "I could go to the guillotine cheerfully with a girl like that in each arm."

"I don't understand how these girls get into the prison."

"You are indeed ignorant if you do not realize the power of a smile and the swing of a pair of pretty *chiches*. Nor is that all," he said dreamily. "As soon as we save enough money to bribe the jailer, the girls will stay all night with us."

"Surely that is not possible."

Menard turned on his side. "Are you still thinking of that woman in Baltimore?"

"Perhaps."

"She's not worth it. Simon told me all about her."

"I asked her to marry me."

"You were one damn fool for asking her in the first place, and another damn fool for remembering it in the second place. What is wrong with the girls in Bexar?"

The night was warm, but Dan could find no soft spot on the floor.

"Dirt is always harder than stone," said Menard, "when it is packed down by bare feet for a few hundred years."

"Bexar hasn't been here *one* hundred years."

Menard shrugged. "So? *Es cosa de México.*"

"What does that mean?"

"Anything that cannot be explained, that is strange to anybody's way of thinking, is always explained that way: *cosa de México*—a thing of Mexico. Is very simple," Menard explained. "Since it is typically Mexican, no explanation is required. Now you will excuse me, *mon ami*. It is time all respectable prisoners are asleep."

The jailer appeared the next morning. He was a big-bellied man with a pock-marked face, long handle-bar mustaches, and a huge ring of keys that clanked at his side. He brought a pitcher of chocolate.

"It is encouraging," said Menard. "When they are mad at us, they do not serve chocolate."

Two hours later the jailer was back with a small pot of *guisado*—a thick stew with a few pieces of rank-tasting goat meat—and a pile of *tortillas*.

"When will we get out of here?" Dan asked him.

The fat-bellied man shrugged. "Is not me—the courts. Maybe the judge come next month, maybe next year. *Quién sabe?*"

"What's your name?" asked Dan.

A suspicious light came in the man's eyes, and he began to back away. *"No hablo inglés,"* he said, shaking his head. *"Cómo se llama?"*

A little of the distrust seemed to be alleviated at this use of his native language. The jailer said slowly, "Pablo Serrano."

"Well, look, Don Pablo, here's a silver peso. Tell me what the evidence is against us."

Pablo looked at the coin. "I do not know."

"You can find out, can't you?"

Pablo took the coin. "I theenk so—but may cost money, señor. More than this."

"I will pay if it's worth it."

"Muy bien." Pablo put the money in a pocket in his skin-tight trousers and went out noiselessly on the dirt floor.

"Tomorrow," Menard predicted, "you'll find out how much more it will cost."

They ate well that afternoon and evening, with several white-bloused, buxom visitors who brought more to eat than two men could ordinarily handle, but they had been a long time on the plains, and their tissues seemed to absorb food endlessly—fruit, bread, tamales, and wine.

"You never had such a fine time in Pennsylvania," said Menard. "We live like kings, and we have taken in three pesos tonight."

Dan asked thoughtfully, "Why do they give us these things?"

"Is a long story," said Menard, sipping his wine. "It is their way of rebelling against the domination of the men. In Spain the man is absolute master. He goes where and when he pleases. He does what he pleases. He has mistresses and

119

concubines. The Spanish women hate them for it, but there is nothing they can do—except take lovers."

"You learned all this from Poeyfarré?"

"The theory," Menard said dreamily, "I have learned from Poeyfarré. The facts I have ascertained for myself. One remembers better."

They had more visitors near suppertime, with a pot of *frijoles* a stack of paper-thin *tortillas*, and a heavy earthenware jug of *vino*, brought by two black-haired, graceful girls who wore lovely small shoes but no stockings, and who lingered outside of the door and talked to them in broken English and some Spanish until the slit in the wall showed that it was dark outside.

"I like that Juana," said Menard, "but I miss Lupe, too. It may be she has a jealous husband."

Dan said, frowning, "It's a strange kind of jail where you can have all the visitors you want and they can bring you anything."

"It's a game," said Menard, "with unspoken but well-understood rules. Borica doesn't care what we do as long as we are here when his superior takes a notion to dispose of our cases. When that time comes, we must be on hand, or Borica will suffer. So why should they keep us in chains? It's too much trouble. We're a thousand miles from the capital, and nobody will know the difference. Only when the judge rides in, or Oconor comes to town, will they put on a show to demonstrate their zeal for the King. Otherwise, why bother? Life is long and life is tragic, and why make it any harder?"

"But prisoners—"

"Are marks on a report. If they were severe with us, it would cause inconvenience to Don Pablo and possibly to Borica. They'd have to feed us more, and that would mean money out of Borica's pocket, for he draws so many pesos a month for feeding us, and if he doesn't have to feed us, he can put the money in his pocket." Menard lit a *cigarro* from the coals. "It seems a very complicated thing, but in reality it is very simple."

"Maybe—if you get used to it. But I don't like being locked up. I get plenty to eat and drink, but I've still got rifles to find."

"There are also women," said Menard. "We'll have those soon enough, and in plenty."

120

"But a jail cell—twelve feet by twelve. I'd like to stretch my legs."

"You will soon be able to," Menard predicted.

"I thought you said we'd be locked up for years."

Menard's answer was offhand. "I did not say 'locked up,' *mon ami*. I said we should be in prison."

Dan stared at him. "What's the difference?"

Menard answered, "In a Spanish prison the difference may be great."

"But—"

"Don Pablo comes to collect his further stipend."

Dan subsided. He heard then the soft shuffle of the jailer's straw sandals, and Don Pablo came down the dirt stairway with a small square lantern that had glass windows and a burning candle inside. He came close to the door, until his fat belly rested against the bars. "I can find out about the evidence, señor, but is very risky," he said. "The Governor has his headquarters in Bexar, as you may know, and he is also *comandante* of the soldiers here. Therefore the Lieutenant is of necessity on the alert."

Menard, still lying on the floor, glanced at Dan and forestalled the skeptical comment he was about to make by asking, "How dangerous, Don Pablo?"

"I shall have to bribe an orderly in the Lieutenant's office."

Menard sat up and began filling his pipe with tobacco brought by one of the girls. Dan glanced at him, recognized his elaborate unconcern as a warning, and said quietly, "How about a gold quadruple-piaster piece?"

Pablo said, "You understand it is not for me, señor. Did you say gold?" The *carcelero's* eyes glittered in the yellow candlelight.

Dan gave him a small gold piece.

"In the morning, señor, I shall have news for you."

He shuffled off along the hallway, and they heard him go up the dirt steps. They were in darkness except for the twinkle of the stars through the narrow slit of a window above their heads. "They brought us candles," Menard noted, "but we don't need them just yet, unless you have some letter-writing to do."

Dan thought of Sarah, but he couldn't think of anything to tell her. He remembered his mother and sisters, but he didn't want to worry them. "It will keep," he said.

121

From the iron bars came a high-pitched voice, clear and musical: "Señores."

"*Quién?*" Menard asked without getting up.

"Guadalupe."

"Are you the one who brought the tobacco?" asked Menard.

The answer was quick, almost eager: "*Sí.*"

"*Bienvenida,*" said Menard, getting up. He went to the bars. "Isn't it late for you to be out, señorita?"

"My *mamá* thinks I am home asleep," she whispered.

Menard held his pipe in one hand. "What is the news that brings you here at this hour?"

Her skin was a dusky blur in the darkness as she moved, and excitement was suppressed in her voice. "I have a key from Don Pablo, if you weesh to come outside, señor." She added softly, "The moon is very pretty tonight."

Menard threw his pipe into the corner. "Let's see if the key works, señorita." Dan heard the key in the huge old lock, the tumblers screeching, then the rusty grating of the iron door. Menard said, "Lupe, I am forever in your debt." Then the two figures moved together, and Dan heard the sound of a kiss.

Menard turned back. "I take it, *mon ami,* you are not interested in going walking with Lupe."

Dan didn't answer.

"*Bien,*" said Menard, and there were both resignation and anticipation in his voice. "I must do my duty." By this time the resignation was absent. "We'll stroll the streets of the village and then I'll be back."

"What if Pablo comes down and finds out?" asked Dan.

The girl's voice came, a little muffled. "Pablo won't be back tonight, I am sure."

Dan listened to the soft footfalls of Menard, the tiny sounds of the girl's slippers. He pulled the door back into position, and for some reason the sound of its rusty hinges grated on his nerves. He went back and stared at the stars through the slit of a window. . . .

He was awakened by the door. Menard came in. "I am at peace with the world," he announced. "This is the most lovely prison in all America."

Dan looked at the slit in the wall. It was turning daylight. "I didn't know the streets in Bexar were so long," he said.

Menard was stretching out on the floor. "They are as long

122

as one wishes to make them, *mon ami,*" he said dreamily, and went to sleep.

Dan did not feel the same peace, but he went back to sleep to the sound of birds' twittering in the growing dawn, and awoke later to the splashing of water and the chattering of Spanish women as they bathed in the canal outside.

Pablo brought them chocolate, and Menard gave him a coin. At noon he was back with a *guisado* so hot with chili peppers that it burned the lining of Dan's throat. Pablo said guardedly, "I have at great cost found what is the evidence against you, señores."

"Let's hear it."

"It has taken all the gold you gave me, and I—"

Dan tossed him another peso.

Pablo brightened. "It is that there are two rifles in a long box of wood which was found at your camp, señor."

Dan took a step toward him. "Two rifles? What make? What year?"

"I do not know, but they are new. They still have the lard on them."

Dan shook the bars of the door. "But what make? What   "

"I have sorrow, señor. My old eyes could not see the words, and besides, I cannot read," he said sadly. "Moreover, I have not seen these rifles with my own eyes."

"Where are they?" asked Dan.

"In the Lieutenant's office."

"Where is that?"

"Beyond the church—across the town."

Dan asked, knowing the inevitable answer, "How can we get a look at those rifles?"

"That is not easy," said Pablo.

"What's the difference?" Menard asked. "They're rifles, aren't they? Somebody planted them on us."

"If they are rifles of a certain make," said Dan, "there will be a lot more like them somewhere—perhaps in a warehouse in New Orleans. If I could find—"

"That's not important," Menard insisted. "Borica found them somewhere and had to bring them back. It would look bad for him to bring the evidence with no prisoners, so he found us in Camanche country and considered us as good as any."

"Either that," Dan said, "or he was paid to bring us back, and the rifles were put so they would point to us."

Menard sat up straight. There was admiration in his voice.

"You are getting ver' smart to this country. You theenk that man from Natchitoches—"

"Poeyfarré wouldn't do it, would he?"

"Positively not. Poeyfarré never did that to a man who has fight with him."

"Then it was Meservy. He planted the rifles on us and he told Borica to follow us."

"Is maybe right," Menard said thoughtfully. "I have think it was strange that Borica should go into Camanche country, for the Spaniards do not like Camanches."

"I've got to find out who made those rifles, and in what year."

"Is not much difference."

"It makes a difference to me," Dan insisted. "I can trace those rifles down and take them back to Pennsylvania."

"And are there enough to be worth the trouble?"

"Somewhere," Dan said positively, "there are hundreds. You saw how many he brought to the Wichitas—a handful. Oconor's activities are undoubtedly making it hard for him to trade freely in rifles."

Menard considered. "It may be a while before you get out, and in the meantime you will need something to keep you occupied."

"What do you suggest?"

"My friend Lupe says Beatriz, the girl who left two pesos, is asking about the *hombre alto*."

"Why hasn't she been back?"

"She is of an old family and cannot so easily come to you unless you ask her."

"She came once."

"That was a courtesy call—a little daring for a girl of her position—and you must allow a woman her pride. If she did not stir any emotion in your manly breast—"

"What's her last name?"

"Is that important?"

"Well—"

"She is of the original families that settled here from the Canary Islands. That should be enough for you to know. She is no *campesina*."

"It may be—" Dan began doubtfully.

Menard bounded up. "Excellent! I will tell Lupe you are pining away for a sight of her inspiring presence!"

"Now, don't—"

"For two pesos," Menard asked, "is not a lady entitled to a few comforting words?"

Dan finally smiled. "All right, but—"

"Lupe will be happy. She was worried about you, *mon ami.*"

Dan, remembering the music in Beatriz' voice, asked, "When will Lupe be back?"

"Tonight, and perhaps every night." Menard sighed. "I like women. It is wonderful how they relieve the monotony of life. But they can be demanding, too."

There were two visitors that afternoon, but not Beatriz, and Dan found himself getting impatient. Lupe arrived immediately after dark, and unlocked the door. Menard, leaving, said to Dan, "I shall deliver your message."

Dan nodded, and listened to their footsteps up the stairway.

They had no more than got out of sight when Pablo came down. "There is a chance tonight, señor."

"To see the rifles?"

"*Sí.* The Governor has gone to look into the contrabanding, and the Lieutenant left this afternoon for a scouting trip among the Apaches. If you should wish—"

Dan gave him another peso. "I wish."

The door swung open. Pablo did not seem to notice that it was unlocked. Dan followed him outside, along one of the canals, like silver in the moonlight, and across the bridge, and within the thick walls of the old church. Pablo lighted his lantern from a candle burning in a recess of the long, low hall. As they crossed the center aisle Pablo genuflected and crossed himself quickly. Then he tiptoed through another door. "Your promise, señor, that you will never reveal how you have learned this thing."

"I promise," Dan whispered.

They went out into another hallway and into a larger room. Pablo looked nervous in the yellow light from the candle. "The box, in the corner."

The lid was loose. Dan lifted it. Two long rifles, heavily greased, lay there.

"Please hurry," said Pablo.

Dan took one of the rifles out of the box and held it near the lantern. With the heel of his hand he rubbed the lard from one side of the breech and looked for a name. He saw none. He turned the rifle over and rubbed the lard from that side, and held the rifle closer to the light. In fine, flowing

125

script engraved in the steel were the words: "Wm. Watts 1772."

Dan stared for a moment.

"Please, señor."

He laid the rifle back in the box and replaced the lid. He followed Pablo outside. Pablo had blown out the candle. He looked up at Dan and asked, "Is it what you weesh?"

Dan rubbed his hands in the dirt, scrubbed them clean together, and wiped them on his buckskin breeches. He looked down at Pablo, puffing along in the moonlight, at his swarthy, pock-marked face and his protruding belly. "Yes," he said grimly, "it is exactly what I want. Now I have to find a way to get out of here and locate the rest of the rifles."

"And the one who has done this thing to you?"

Dan stared at him. Apparently it was common knowledge. "Him too," Dan said harshly. "There will be a day of reckoning."

Chapter Seventeen

THE NEXT NIGHT Beatriz came with Lupe. She was a little shy at first, but walking along the canals that shimmered in the moonlight, listening to the steady song of the crickets and sometimes the howling of the cayeutes out beyond the edges of the village, smelling the ripe blooms of jasmine and hibiscus, she began to talk and ask him about himself. "You are married, no?"

"No."

"You have a family in England?"

"In the colonies—a mother and sisters."

"And you have come out here to do what, señor?"

He hesitated, wondering if she had been sent to spy on him, to get an admission. "Well, I—" He stopped and looked down at her. He couldn't say he had come to trade, but as he looked at her face, thrown into shadows by the moon at her right and leaving her eyes like wide pools, he knew she was asking out of interest, and then he forgot the whole thing and said huskily, "You are so beautiful."

He was holding both of her arms with his big hands, and she did not try to back away. There were kindness and sympathy in her eyes, and it had been so long . . .

126

He kissed her, a little abruptly and awkwardly. He drew back, but the pressure of her lips seemed still to be on his mouth. He did not take his arms from around her, but kissed her again. Her arms held him, and presently she put her head against his chest and said softly, "There must be so much you want to tell, and you are *muy hombre.* Tell me now about you."

He was cautious and said nothing about why he had come, but he told her about Arkansa Post and the Osages, about Poeyfarré, about Chamillard and Dartigo, about going west and getting lost on the Salt Plains in the storm, and then at last about the terrible thing the Camanches had done to Simon.

She clung to him tightly, and her voice was filled with compassion when she murmured, *"Pobrecito!"*

"He was a good friend," Dan said grimly. "I wish we could have kept him alive."

She shook her head. "Man is born to die." She crossed herself. "There is a time and a way for all of us."

"It wasn't right, him being cut up like that."

She put her soft finger upon his mouth. "You must not make yourself fight what is to be, Dahn. It is not for us to know what is best."

He kissed her again before they reached the jail. He passed the snoring Pablo, sleeping on a pallet on the floor, and went downstairs. He opened the iron door and went inside—and fell over the outstretched legs of Menard.

The Frenchman rolled to his feet. *"Mon Dieu,* you idiot Englishman! I thought the Camanches were back."

"Sorry."

Menard felt in the corner for their stock of corn shucks and tobacco, and began to roll a *cigarro.* "So," he said with satisfaction. "When the damned English do fall, they fall hard."

Dan stretched out on the floor. "If you had kept your feet out of the doorway—"

"Then I would be deprived of the pleasure of seeing your reaction to the beautiful Beatriz."

Dan said, "She's nice to talk to, but—"

Menard groaned. "Don't tell me you *talked* all night."

"We weren't out all night."

Menard, on his knees, blew on the coals in the brass bucket and lighted a twig. "Then," he said, looking hard at Dan, "why is the sky lightening up in the east?"

Dan stared at the slit window. Incredibly enough, Menard was right. Their window faced the east, and he could see the stars beginning to fade out. "We had a lot to talk about," he said finally.

Menard lay back, inhaling the cigarette smoke. "Anyhow, you are a man. I was beginning to wonder."

"But there are more important things. When do we get out of this place?"

Menard sighed. "Such a *señorita simpática*, and you want out."

"I've got a job to do," Dan said stubbornly.

"I will give you more advice, my friend. Suppose you were to escape. Which way would you go?"

"I don't know."

"You would not dare travel toward Chihuahua or Nuevo México."

"How about north, the way we came?"

"Through those accursed Camanches?" Menard shuddered. "Not to mention the Osages. I think it would be a difficult trip for two of us."

"Where, then?"

"Natchitoches is nearly a hundred leagues, and they would be looking for you."

"What about the *contrabandista* traders along the Trinity River?"

Menard spoke carefully. "That I think is the only hope. We could follow the Camino Real to the Trinity, and then down to Arkokisa. But there are still problems."

"There are always problems."

"In such a vast country as this, a man must plan well for an escape. You must have horses, food, weapons, a guide—"

"We don't need a guide. We can follow the trail."

Menard shrugged. "All right, no guide. But what of horses and weapons?"

"The girls—Beatriz and Lupe."

Menard sighed. "In time, yes. I'm sure neither of them could put her hands on enough money immediately. And why should they? You walk the canals all night with Beatriz, and you expect her to help you escape the next day?"

Dan was silent, thinking of that walk.

"There is always the possibility that the judge will come and set us free. If he does not, then will be the time to escape."

Dan said, "I'll wait a while, but—"

Menard propped himself up in the corner, singing softly, *"Cae la tarde lentamente sobre el mar . . ."*

"You need a guitar," Dan muttered.

"Don't worry, *mon ami.* Tomorrow will bring a guitar. I have suggested it."

The guitar came the next night with Lupe—an instrument with an almost straight, boxlike body, a thick neck, and seven strings.

But in the days to come, Menard did not play favorites. He walked with Margarita, Panchita, Alicia, Soledad, and a dozen others. And from time to time Beatriz came to see Dan. Life in the *juzgado* was hardly monotonous. They had food and wine and new moccasins and clothing and small amounts of money—which Dan carefully saved, burying it in a hole in the floor and covering it with the brass bucket. Always he clung to that fierce determination to get away.

But the months went along swiftly, with the gentle Beatriz to keep him company. Winter came, but in Bexar it was hardly noticeable. On the few cold days, they had plenty of wool blankets. Then the spring came, and it was cool in their cell during the daytime. At night he walked the dusty trails around the village with Beatriz, breathed the fragrance of the mesquite blossoms and the heady *huele de noche,* and bathed in the canals.

That fall a rumor stirred the village. Beatriz told Dan about it first: The judge would come to Bexar in the early summer.

"Then," said Beatriz, "either you will be sent to Spain as a prisoner or you will be released and allowed to go. In either event"—she hesitated—"in either event we shall see each other no more."

"Early summer," Dan repeated, and took a deep breath. "Early summer. . . ."

With the financial assistance of Beatriz and Lupe and the others, and with the money he had saved under the brass bucket, Dan set up business as a cobbler, determined to accumulate as much money as possible toward release or escape, for he still had a job to do. He made a good profit, which he quietly converted into gold, one piece at a time, and hid away in their cell. The Lieutenant allowed him, on his word of honor not to escape, to rent and operate a shop on the street, and there he never lacked for a feminine audience. Sometimes Menard helped, but more often he courted the audience.

Winter came briefly. Then the flowers and shrubs and trees became clothed in a profusion of green foliage and many-colored flowers. "Early summer," Dan told Menard, "will soon be here."

Menard was not so happy. "What about those rifles over in the church?"

"I have talked with a lawyer," said Dan, "and he doubts that the court will convict us, for the rifles were not in our possession when found, and at least two other parties—those of Poeyfarré and Meservy—were in the vicinity at the same time."

Menard did not answer.

"You needn't look so sad," said Dan, feeling good. "There are other towns and other girls."

Menard eyed him. "Such as Baltimore?"

Dan didn't answer.

Then one day in the shop, while Dan was finishing a pair of cowhide boots, Pablo waddled in, scowling importantly. "You weel come with me," he told Dan.

They went, leaving three girls staring big-eyed after them. Pablo offered no explanation, but this time, when he put them in their cell, he locked the door carefully.

They looked at each other, puzzled. Then a dried-up, wrinkled, gray-haired old Mexican came in with a hammer and some straps of iron. Two men with him brought an anvil and a small forge and bellows. They set up the forge and built a hot charcoal fire. The old Spaniard fitted a band of iron around Menard's left leg and riveted it with the hammer. He put one also on Dan's left leg, and Dan, dumfounded at this turn of events, asked him what had happened.

The old Spaniard did not even look up. *"No sé."* His words were punctuated by the ringing of the anvil. "It is orders from the Lieutenant."

When he finished, each man had fifteen feet of heavy chain attached to one leg.

Pablo came back about dark, and Dan questioned him. "What are the chains for? What have we done?"

"I do not know." Pablo shook his swarthy head. "Perhaps it is that you have done nothing, but you are *inglés.*"

"Is that a crime?" asked Dan.

Pablo's black eyes were inscrutable. "The English colonies

130

in America have rebelled and are fighting against the King. There is going to be a war."

"Rebelled! You mean the colonies?"

"*Sí, señor.*"

"All of them?"

"As far as I know."

Dan stared at Menard. "The war has started!"

Menard nodded wisely.

Dan turned to Pablo, who had set the *olla* on the floor and pushed it through the wide bars. "We had nothing to do with that. Anyway, it's the King that Spain doesn't like —not the colonies."

Pablo backed away from the door. "Señor," he said, "you have been a good prisoner, and I have sorrow, but the Council of the Indies does not know which side is best to take. The British we hate, for they have destroyed our Great Armada. But also the colonies we fear. If this rebellion lasts a long time, it may spread to New Spain. There could be bad results for the Spanish colonies. The *comandante* has been ordered to take no chances. You must both be kept in heavy irons. It is the order from the Viceroy."

"How long does this last?"

"I do not know. You will be taken to Chihuahua and then to México, to await a decision by His Most Catholic Majesty."

Dan shook the bars of the heavy door. "We've waited long enough already!"

Pablo backed off and shrugged. "The English are always in such a hurry."

"And the Spanish," Menard said sarcastically, "have got forever."

Pablo shrugged again. "*Es cosa de México, señor.*"

Chapter Eighteen

IT WAS NOTICEABLE that no girls came to see them that evening, and there was nothing to do but talk over their troubles.

"The way it looks to me," Dan said finally, "we're really in for it now. No matter if the judge does come, he won't listen to our case. The decision will have to come from Seville, and it may be five years."

"And in the meantime," said Menard, "they may send us to a prison in Spain."

"I thought you said all Spanish prisons were alike."

Menard shook his head. "I was talking about the New World. I have heard bad stories about the Spanish prisons. They say the Inquisition—" His lips tightened. "I don't like this, Dan."

Dan said slowly, "Maybe the judge—"

"The judge won't touch it now that the Viceroy has issued an order."

"Then," said Dan slowly, "the only answer is to escape from Bexar."

Menard said soberly, "Perhaps I should have agreed to that when you first wanted to do it."

"That's not the question," Dan pointed out. He had never before seen Menard so dejected. "Let's talk about getting away now."

Menard looked at the *olla* and up at the slit window. "We're in chains now," he said. "There's not a chance. There would have been a chance before."

"The chains can be got rid of," Dan said with assurance that he did not feel.

Menard sounded utterly hopeless. "I don't know how."

"The first thing," Dan said, "is to find out how long we have."

The next morning he held up a silver piece of eight where Pablo could see it. "Don Pablo," he said, "when do we go to *Chihuahua?*"

"*Gracias.*" Pedro took the coin. "I will let you know," he said.

Menard watched him go up the stairway. "What good will it do to find that out?"

"We'll know how long we have to get ready," Dan said tersely. "Can you still play that guitar?"

"I suppose so, but my heart won't be in it."

"Never mind. Play it and sing. Sing loud, so the ladies will know we're down here and lonesome."

Menard stared at him, then listlessly picked up the guitar.

"Make it sad," Dan said. "Make it as sad as you look."

Menard put the instrument in his lap, began to pick at the strings, and presently sang mournfully.

He stopped after a while and said seriously, "If you want to get one of the girls to help us escape, you better deal with Beatriz."

132

"What's the matter with Lupe?"

"Lupe's a very fine girl," said Menard. "Beautiful, warm, affectionate, willing. Her only trouble is that she's too willing. She'd do the job for us, but there's no guarantee that she wouldn't fall in love with the Lieutenant and give us away."

"You don't think Beatriz would do that?"

"I know she wouldn't," Menard said positively. "Beatriz is a one-man woman."

That evening they had visitors again. Lupe was first, with the key, and beside her was Beatriz. They gasped when they saw the chains, and Beatriz cried silently. Dan would not have known it if her warm tears had not fallen on his arm.

They wrapped the chains around their waists, with the loose ends under their belts. The four went upstairs. Pablo was nowhere in sight. The two couples separated at the canal. Dan and Beatriz walked westward, holding hands. Presently she said, "You are very solemn tonight, Dahn."

They sat on a stone, shielded by a clump of jasmine.

He found it hard to answer. How would she take it when she found out that he wanted her to help him leave her—when he could promise nothing?

The fragrance of the night blossoms lay lightly on them. The soft, warm breeze from the south was like a healing hand.

"You are angry weeth me, Dahn?" she asked.

"Oh, no! No, it isn't that."

"It is, then, about the chains?"

"Partly."

"I have fixed that," she said. "The old *herrero* will be back day after tomorrow to inspect them, and he will hammer the rivet heads until they are very thin. Then you can file them off, and you need wear them only when the *oficiales* come to the jail." She bent over and looked up at him. "This makes you feel more better, *sí?*"

He smiled briefly. "It helps, Beatriz, but there is also the matter of going to Chihuahua."

She gasped. "I did not hear that news."

"It is what Pablo said."

"You do not know when?"

"Not yet."

She grasped his arm with both hands. "It must not be, Dahn. They would have you in prison for the rest of your life."

That wasn't the worst, he was thinking. Somewhere in

133

New Spain was almost a year's output of Watts rifles—two years' now, perhaps—while back in New England they were fighting a war without enough rifles to go around. Certainly the King's soldiers would be well equipped. He was filled with the urgent need to find those rifles and ship them back to Theophilus Radnor.

He chose his next words with care. "How can I avoid going to Chihuahua?"

"You must escape! Go to the trading camps on the Trinity. From there you can get to New Orleans."

He was gratified that she had suggested it, but he did not want to accede too quickly. "That would take a deal of preparation," he observed.

"It is nothing," she said fervently. "I will help you. But I do not know—" she stopped.

"I can get money," he told her cautiously.

She shook her head. "It will take so much. You must have two mules to ride."

"We can walk," he said, testing her, "and get along with one mule for a pack animal."

"No, you cannot. The soldiers would hunt you down. You must have good mules to ride, and another to carry supplies. You must have rifles, powder, lead. You can depend on game for food all the way to the Trinity. This time of year the deer will be fat, but you must be careful of the bears. And the Camanches from the west—"

He was completely astounded. "How did you get to know so much about traveling?"

She put both hands on one of his. "I was born in Texas. My mother died here. My grandfather lives at El Paso. All my life I have seen expeditions come and go. I have heard the war whoops of the Camanches. This is my country, Dahn, and I know it to the least blade of grass."

He was halted for a moment by the intensity of her feeling. Then he asked, "How about the Camino Real? Can we follow it to the Trinity?"

"You can, but you must not travel on it. The road leads northeast; stay south of it, for Oconor's squads might meet you on the road. And, Dahn—"

"Yes?"

She was facing him now, her face on one side white in the moonlight, on the other shadowed. She looked up at him. "Dahn, will you ever come back to Bexar?"

He smiled easily—too easily. He had expected a question

134

like that. "It would be hard to keep me away, Beatriz." It was an evasion, for of course the Spanish government would never forgive him for escaping. But he didn't want to hurt her, nor did he want to lose her help.

"I will help you," she said. "It will take several days, perhaps, for I will have to buy mules from a man who will not talk, and I will have to pay a high price to keep him from talking."

"How much money will you need?"

She thought for a moment. "Perhaps a hundred and fifty pesos each for three mules."

"Two will be enough," he said.

She shook her head. "It will take a third to carry your supplies."

"We won't have any supplies."

She turned to him with strange intensity. "You must! I know this country. You must have three mules. If you have not the money, I will get it myself."

"I can manage," he said. The cost was not worrying him much. He had nearly two thousand pesos buried under the brass bucket, but he did not want to tell her that.

"I think I can get two rifles without paying. You do not have to worry about that. You have knives?"

"Yes."

"You will not need water bags. It is nowhere more than a day's ride to a stream. But much dried beef and parched corn. And powder and lead and a bullet mold." Her eyes were flashing with excitement. "When will you be ready?"

"When you get the mules."

"And the money?"

He took a deep breath. "I'll give that to you tonight."

She stood—gracefully, as she did everything. Her head was thrown back and her eyes shone in the moonlight. "Oh, Dahn, I am so happy you are going to get away!" She put both arms around him and hugged him. Her arms were surprisingly strong.

Back at the jail, she waited in the dark shadows outside while he went in past Pablo, who reeked of wine and snored like a mule learning to bray. With his knife he dug up the gold pieces until he counted five hundred pesos, then replaced the dirt and put the bucket of coals back over it. The sack of gold was heavy. He put it in her hands and said, "Let me know when it is arranged."

135

She was strangely quiet when she said, "I will let you know, Dahn. Good night."

She was a woman of changing moods. Lupe seemed always the same—always happy, always willing. But perhaps Lupe had her bad moments too. He thought of other women he had known, trying to remember their moods. Yes, even Mrs. Cotlow had been unpredictable. He wondered if she had got another husband yet.

"*Mon Dieu,* you burro! Must you continue to stumble over a man's legs when a man is trying to sleep?"

"Menard!" he said in a low voice.

"But no, of course not. This is Lupe—or Margarita, or even Pablo or Pablo's fat wife. What in hell is the matter with you, my friend? Are you moon-struck?"

"Maybe I am," Dan said worriedly. "I just gave Beatriz money for mules."

"Well, don't worry about it. You have nothing to lose. You won't need that money in Chihuahua, anyway."

Pablo was down in the morning. "Four days from today," he said, "the Governor will send a cart train to Chihuahua with an escort of soldiers. You will go with them."

"*Gracias.*" Dan gave him the usual peso.

There was no word from Beatriz that day. The blacksmith came in the next day and readjusted the collars on their ankles. The rivets were hammered down until the heads were thin, and Dan gave him a gold piece. Menard got Lupe to buy a file, and after a couple of hours' work they were able to slip out of the chains at will.

Dan was worried that night. It was nearly forty-eight hours since he had given the money to Beatriz, and there had been no word. "What do you suppose happened?" he asked Menard.

"How do I know? She's not my woman. If it was Lupe, I'd know she had given it to the Lieutenant."

Dan asked abruptly, "Does Lupe know of our plans?"

Menard snorted. "Do you think I'm such a fool about women as you are? I wouldn't trust her across the canal."

"But Beatriz—"

"Maybe she can be faithful to you long enough to get us out of here. If she turned you in, the *soldados* would be down here in no time." Menard lay back, rolling a cigarette. "Breathe easy. You're like a filly losing her first race to a stallion."

Menard spent the next day and night making farewell

appearances along the canal, while Dan paced the floor of the cell and sometimes walked up and down the street. He asked Lupe if she had seen Beatriz, but Lupe only smiled oddly and asked if he wanted to walk with her instead. "No," he said. "I want to see Beatriz. If you see her, tell her I'm waiting."

"I will do it." She added, "You would not have to wait for me, Dahn."

He frowned. Damn it, he wanted those mules and rifles, and this little Mexican beauty insisted on making sly remarks.

It was after midnight of the third day, and Dan was debating the wisdom of their striking out on foot, when he heard soft steps on the dirt stairs, and a familiar whisper: "Dahn!"

He leaped to the door. "Beatriz?"

"Yes, Dahn. I am back."

She was opening the lock and rushing into his arms. "I am sorry to be so long. I had to make a trip to the San Miguel River to get mules without brands so they could not be traced. I have had to drive them back at night, and it has taken so very long!"

She was shaking. He put his arm around her, but she continued to shiver as if she were cold. "I'm only tired," she said, rubbing her eyes. "It was so long a trip, and there was so little time."

Menard was digging up the money and slipping off the chain.

"Where are the mules?" asked Dan.

"Across the river, beyond the church. I did not dare bring them through town."

"All right." Dan threw the chain into a corner. "Can you go with us to show us where the mules are?"

"Yes."

They filed out. Pablo was drunk again, for Dan and Menard had kept him well supplied with wine money.

"He'll get hell from the Governor," said Menard.

"He is used to it," said Beatriz. "Is nothing." She gave a breathless chuckle. "He is not half as scared of the Governor as he is of his fat wife."

Dan grunted.

"Dahn," she said, "would you want your wife to be fat?"

"Not me," said Dan. "No fat wives. Now which way do we go?"

"To the left. I know the dogs on that side."

They walked quietly up the street. Most people were in bed, and nearly all the huts were dark. Only the dogs were prowling, and these Beatriz miraculously kept quiet. They came to the big bridge and crossed the river quietly in the darkness.

"How about the rifles and stuff?" asked Dan.

"They are with the mules—everything."

"Where did you get rifles?"

She turned right. "An old servant of my grandfather's works in the church. He has taken the two rifles they were to use as evidence."

Dan grinned. "The Watts rifles! They shoot dead center."

They passed the church. Its round dome shone brightly in the rising moon, but there was still darkness under the trees. "I have hurried so fast," Beatriz whispered, "for the caravan of the judge is to arrive tonight, and there will be more soldiers."

They went north into the mesquite thickets. She found the mules, and Dan examined them hastily but expertly. A rifle was slung on each saddle, and the third animal was loaded with food, extra moccasins, and powder. "You've done a good job, Beatriz." Dan hugged her briefly. "How will you get back home now?"

"Past the church," she said.

"Isn't that risky?"

She smiled. "I have done it twice tonight."

"You could go around."

"There are soldiers on post on both sides. I cannot go so far into the mesquite for fear of the Camanches. But I will be all right, Dahn." She spoke his name slowly, and her tongue tip lingered over the word.

Dan got into the saddle. *"Mil gracias, Beatriz."*

Menard whispered hoarsely, "The caravan!"

They came from the south across the bridge, iron-shod hoofs thudding on the boards, the heavy coach of the judge rumbling. Dan stared. There were eighteen or twenty mounted soldiers, and there was great activity about the church. Servants with flaming torches ran back and forth.

Dan dug his heels into the mule's sides, but then he hauled back on the reins. "Beatriz, what will you do now?"

She was shaking again. She looked up at him, her eyes bright with fear. "I am all right, Dahn." Her teeth were chattering. "Do not worry about me. You must go quickly, before they discover the rifles are missing from the box."

138

Dan wheeled the mule until he faced the church. "Hell of a lot of shouting going on down there now," he observed.

Beatriz said, "I am so scared. You go, please, quick!"

"Wait a minute!" said Menard. "They *have* found the rifles are gone! Hear that? *'Fusiles!'* "

She whispered, "Please hurry, Dahn."

"If they know the rifles are gone," said Menard, "they'll have patrols out all over the country. She won't be able to get back home at all tonight."

"And if they find you out here," said Dan thoughtfully, "the whole damn town will remember we're friends, I suppose."

"You may be friends," said Menard, "but I can guarantee that's not what they call it in Bexar."

"Please, Dahn!" She kicked the mule in the flank, and it plunged through a small mesquite tree.

Dan brought it around and rode back to her. "If it's like that," he said, "they'll blame you for the escape anyway."

"I do not know, Dahn. I only know that you must hurry." Her voice was trembling with urgency. "You see? They have already sent two cavalrymen to the jail to see if you are gone!"

The horses thundered over the bridge, their riders yelling, and the dogs of the town on the other side of the river—the jail side—began to bark in a sudden burst of sound that seemed to come from everywhere at once. Dan watched for an instant. Then he wheeled the mule toward Beatriz. "Get on behind me!" he ordered, giving her his hand.

She came up light and sat down easy. . . .

It was a big mule and carried them well. They alternately walked and trotted, and by dawn had covered a good many miles. Beatriz directed them to pull across the road. Menard looked for footprints. "Nobody passed here lately," he said.

"They are not brave to come into this part at night," Beatriz said, "for the Camanches. But it is Oconor's men you have to watch for now."

"There's a stream up ahead," said Dan. "We better pull up for a while and graze the mules. We'll have to rearrange the packs, too, so Beatriz can ride the third mule."

"Will he ride?" asked Menard.

"Yes," said Beatriz, sliding off. "I have tried them all."

At midmorning they saddled up the mules and rode on. "Is one funny damn thing," Menard observed, and there

139

was puzzlement in his voice, "how everything worked out so you would have to come with us, Beatriz."

Dan looked at Beatriz. She looked at him and answered happily, *"Es cosa de México."*

Chapter Nineteen

THEY RODE through chaparral until midafternoon. Beatriz found trails through the tangle, insisting that they must stay away from the road. A little after noon they stopped to let the mules graze.

"How long will it take us to get to the river?" asked Dan.

"Three more days, I think."

"If the mules don't balk," said Menard.

"They won't balk with that corn inside of them," Dan pointed out.

Beatriz came up from the spring with a can of water, and Dan, counting carefully the twenty round bullets, and giving ten to Menard, took time to notice that she was as graceful climbing a grassy slope as she had been walking along the canal. She would make a good pioneer wife, he thought. She would never lose her attractiveness nor would she ever have to have help in doing her part of the job. Dan glanced at Menard. Maybe someday the Frenchman would want to settle down.

"What are we having for dinner?" asked Menard as she set the can of water on the fire. "Baked unborn colt with *aguardiente,* or breast of chicken *à la* viceroy?"

"You shall have small cakes made of *pinole,* and *higote colorado* which I myself have prepared."

"And no doubt," said Menard, obviously goading her, "it will take the hair off a hog without being warmed up."

She retained her good humor. "It is excellent food. You will be glad for it before we reach the Trinity."

Dan glanced quickly at Menard and saw an odd expression on his face as the Frenchman talked to Beatriz. Dan puzzled over it. It was not Menard's usual cynical expression or the amused gleam customarily in his eyes when he had talked to Lupe. It hit Dan suddenly that Menard was in love with Beatriz. It bothered him for a moment, but he shrugged it off. Somebody would have to marry Beatriz when they got to civilization, and it might as well be Menard. No doubt he would make a good husband.

That afternoon they left the chaparral behind. The mesquite trees became scattered until they looked like peach trees; then they grew smaller, and by evening they had disappeared, and the country was an undulating prairie.

"We must watch carefully to avoid meeting anybody," Beatriz reminded them.

"It isn't too dry yet," said Dan, riding behind her. "We won't kick up much dust if we stay on the grass."

"If soldiers come, there will be at least a squad," said Menard. "We could see their dust a long way."

They slept in blankets that night in the shelter of an oak motte, and Dan awakened to find the sun in his eyes.

He sat up and looked around. It was good country, with the pale green of the prairie, the darker green of the oaks, the blue sky with scattered white clouds, the early sun sending almost golden rays across the dew-freshened grass. Dan put on his moccasins and got up. No doubt the other two were still asleep.

But they were not, for he smelled coffee. Beatriz, then, must have got up early. She was a jewel. When he came back from the spring, he found a small fire on the southeast side of the motte, where it was screened from the road. Beatriz sat with her legs under her, discreetly covered by the red-and-yellow skirt, and Menard lay on the ground across the fire from her, smoking a *cigarro*. They were talking intently.

Dan frowned. For a moment he was angry; then he got control of himself, for there was no reason for him to be concerned. Menard was his friend and had stood by him. Undoubtedly he would be as good for Beatriz as any Mexican in Bexar. He walked up behind Beatriz and asked, "Coffee ready?"

She looked up at him. "Almost. You slept well?"

"Like a log." He looked at Menard and asked shortly, "How about the mules?"

Menard raised his eyebrows, looked at Dan, and drew on the cigarette. "All gathered, fed, tied, and ready to be saddled." He kept his eyes on the fire.

Dan squatted and poured some coffee. "You've been up quite a while, then."

Beatriz laughed; it was a birdlike chirrup. "It is necessary that you should sleep, Dahn. We have much way to go."

141

He gulped down the rest of his coffee. He didn't like their both getting up before him, and quietly so as not to awaken him. Damn it, he knew how Menard was about women. Not that Beatriz wasn't old enough to take care of herself, but after all, she was different, and he was in a way responsible for her. He stalked from the fire and went to saddle the mules. . . .

They had their brush with the military the next day. It was Beatriz who spotted the dust column, and they stopped to study it.

"It would not be Indians," said Menard, "for they would not travel bunched up."

"It's moving too fast for a caravan of families," Dan said. "They are soldiers."

They rode their mules due southeast at a walk to avoid raising dust, until they found a low place where the mules would be out of sight of the road. Dan warned Menard not to let the mules bray, and Menard snapped, "How the hell do you keep a mule from braying?"

"Keep his tail down," said Dan. "A mule can't bray without raising his tail."

He walked back toward the trace of the so-called Royal Road, found a clump of thistles, and threw himself to the ground behind it. In half an hour he could make out the crossed belts of the soldiers, and he lay quite still until they had passed. Then he edged back until he was covered by a rise. He got up and returned to the mules.

"Beatriz," he said, "you have mighty good hunches. If we had stayed on that road we'd have been on the way back to Bexar by now."

Menard's eyes were narrow. "Was that Borica?"

Dan nodded.

Menard looked at the Watts slung under the saddle leather. "This time," he said, "we'd have had our rifles in our hands."

"Two against nine," Dan reminded him. "And us with a woman to protect."

Menard turned away abruptly. "We'd better move."

The Trinity was fifty yards wide, with high, steep banks, and therefore probably deep. That judgment was sustained by the presence of a raftlike ferry, which they caught sight of as they reconnoitered upstream. The river had fine timber, and in the valley it was easy to keep under cover.

They drew together in the protection of the thick trunk of a huge old black-walnut tree.

142

"How far to the trading camps now?" Dan asked.

Menard answered, "Is hard to say. They move, you know. Perhaps fifty leagues, perhaps twenty."

"The only thing to do," Dan observed, "is to stay in the saddle until we hit sign." He looked at the sun. "We can ride for three hours yet. Let's move."

They strung out downstream, Dan ahead, Beatriz in the middle, Menard behind. They stayed in the bottom to keep out of sight.

They reached camp the next afternoon. A hunters' camp, by the looks of things, for there were no fields of foot-high corn, no lean-tos against the cabins for the shelter of one or two animals that would be precious to a family, but rather stacks of hides on a rack built above the ground, round pens for horses, and a herd of cattle spread out down the valley. From the corner of one cabin hung half a dozen scalps.

They rode out into the bare ground between the river and the biggest cabin. Dan stayed on his mule and shouted, "Hello! Anybody home?"

The broad copper-colored face of an Indian squaw looked out of the open door and stared at them, then disappeared.

"There's a white man living there," Menard noted, "or she'd be outside working."

A minute later the man appeared, a lean man of medium height, deeply and heavily wrinkled, but not with age. His hair was still black. It was uncombed, and he hadn't shaved for several days. His feet were bare as he stood in the doorway, obviously having just been awakened. He glanced at them and went back into the cabin, and a moment later appeared in cowhide boots, carrying a long rifle. He came outside, squinting his eyes against the sun. "Whadda you want?" he growled.

"Lookin' for Clermont," Dan said promptly.

The man walked all around them. His black shirt was wrinkled, his buckskin trousers greasy. He glanced at their rifles and at the trappings on the mules, and examined the animals for brands. "You sure got Spanish stock," he said finally, "especially this little *chiquita* here." He leered at Beatriz, and Dan tightened up. "But it ain't soldier stuff. Where you from?"

"Bexar."

"How'd you dodge Borica?" the man asked instantly.

"We were on the lookout for him. We didn't travel the road."

"Smart, eh? Where'd you pick up the little Mexican wench?"

"In Bexar," Dan said stiffly.

The man was narrow-eyed for a moment. He looked Dan over contemplatively, glancing at the brass hatchet that had hung on his hip from the time they had left Bexar—one of Beatriz' thoughtfulnesses. "Where'd you git that?"

"In Pennsylvania."

"How long you been gone?"

"About two years."

"Do you know what's goin' on back there?"

"Can't say as I do."

"The colonies rebelled, and it's turning into a full-fledged war."

"Who's winning?"

"It doesn't look good for the colonies, I hear. How can they beat the King's soldiers? They've got no supplies, no money, no rifles." The man leaned on his gun. "How'd you get to Bexar?"

Dan said impatiently, "If you don't want us here, we'll move on."

The man looked at Beatriz. "Maybe I want you here—but I want to know who you are. If you got business here, all right. If you're spies for the Spanish"—he grinned, his mouth making a wide straight crack across his face—"the woods are full of my men."

"We've been in prison. The girl got us out."

"You don't look pale."

"You don't know much about Spanish prisons," said Dan.

"All right. Tell me how you got to Bexar."

"Through Arkansa Post."

The man considered. "Two years ago, eh? Anybody up along the river then?"

"Harry Blundin, Poeyfarré, Chamillard, Dartigo, Menard here—"

"Menard!" The man squinted. "You *are* Menard, at that. Well, 'light! What are you waitin' on?"

They got down stiffly. "I'm Clermont," said the man. "There's an empty cabin over there for you and your squaw."

"She's no squaw," said Dan.

Clermont contemplated her. "All right, she's no squaw yet. But you can use that brush cabin. How long you stayin'?"

"Not long," said Dan.

Clermont raised his voice. "Star!" he shouted.

The broad-faced Indian woman came out of the grass-thatched cabin. She was younger than Dan had thought. "She's Caddo," Clermont explained. "I don't talk Caddo, and my interpreter isn't here, but she savvies what I want." He turned to the Indian woman and motioned toward the mules. "Get them saddles off and leave them in the other cabin. Turn the mules out to graze." All this with many flourishes of the arms.

The Caddo woman watched carefully, and nodded. She caught up the reins and took the mules to the other cabin.

"I'll go with her," said Beatriz.

Clermont's eyes followed her. "Mighty nice squaw you got there—mighty nice."

"I said she's no squaw."

Clermont, scratching himself, looked up. "Sure you did. Want a chew?"

"We've had nothing but corn-shuck cigarettes for a long time," said Dan, sinking his teeth into the carrot.

"Now, what are you here for—to get out of the country?"

"That," said Dan, "and something else."

Clermont was rigid for an instant. "What else?"

"You saw our rifles?"

"Watts, by the look of them."

"How do they get into the country?"

"They're not my rifles," said Clermont.

"They came up the Trinity," said Dan. "You'd know about them."

"Even so, why should I cut my own throat?"

"For five hundred pesos in gold," Dan said, "you can afford to cut your own throat."

Clermont stared at him. "Five hundred? You want to know right bad."

"I want to know where they come from."

Clermont scrutinized Menard and shook his head. "Why would you be interested in those rifles unless you're workin' for the damn Spaniards?"

Dan took a chance. "Because they're my rifles," he said.

Clermont looked at him and slowly put the carrot away inside his shirt. "Your rifles?"

"A man sometimes called Meservy runs them into Texas," Dan said coldly. "I don't give a damn about Texas, but I want my rifles. I know that Oconor has made it difficult to bring rifles in here for a couple of years now, so Meservy, or whatever he calls himself, must have plenty in reserve. For

145

five hundred pesos you can afford to tell me where they're kept. You're not making any money out of them, anyway."

He watched Clermont for a moment, but the man shook his head. "It's not my game. I got my own sources. Anyway, I can't tell you where they come from. They come up the river and go up to the Red, but that's all I know. I do my own trading. These here Watts rifles are no part of my stuff."

"Then you can't tell?"

Clermont showed that wide, ghoulish grin. "Not by a damn sight—but I know somebody who can. I'm lookin' for him this evening."

Dan looked up. "Meservy?" he asked sharply.

The grin became wider. "Not Meservy. D'Etrées. He can tell you anything you want to know—if you can persuade him."

Chapter Twenty

BEATRIZ was smiling when they came up to the cabin. "All is clean," she said. "The floor is dampened. The chair is dusted."

She had a fire going outside, and strips of meat hanging over it. Water was simmering in a brass pot. "I have bought real potatoes for our supper," she said proudly.

Dan stared at her. "What with?"

"I have bring money of my own. Is all right, no?"

Dan nodded. "I'll pay you back when we get to New Orleans."

She pursed her lips. "Is nice in New Orleans. I have an uncle there."

Menard frowned.

"An uncle?" repeated Dan.

"Yes," she said, smiling in pleasant recollection. "Don Eustacio. He was my grandmother's brother."

"Well, now, wait a minute. That cuts out New Orleans."

She looked at their faces. "I do not understand."

"It means we can't go to New Orleans," Dan explained.

Menard added, "The Spanish rule New Orleans the same as they rule Bexar. They'll be looking for you there."

But she did not act alarmed. "Is not the same. New Orleans

146

is under the Captain General at Havana, not under the Viceroy of Mexico. It is like two different governments. Besides, my uncle Eustacio would not allow them to take me. I shall be quite safe there, I am sure. Then a nephew of my grandfather in El Paso is commandant at Rapide."

"If you are right," said Dan, "there remains only the small matter of getting you into the right hands."

"That will be easy with two such strong men. I am not worried, Dahn."

"All right, don't you worry." Dan leaned over and sniffed the stew. "You're a good cook, Beatriz," he said, looking up.

"Oh, *gracias,* Dahn."

"I'm going up to see Clermont," he said to Menard. "You keep an eye on Beatriz."

"A woman like this out here," Menard muttered, "is like a soap bubble in a hailstorm."

"I won't be gone long," Dan assured him. "I want to borrow a stone to sharpen up my tomahawk."

Beatriz stared at him with sudden fear in her big eyes. "You are not going to fight, Dahn?"

"Just getting ready in case it comes," he assured her.

The sun was low now, and mosquitoes were beginning to hum in the backwaters. Clermont met him outside. "You'll might' near have to build a fire in the house," he said, "to keep the mosquiters out."

"Maybe," said Dan. "You got a hand stone?"

Clermont nodded, his eyes mere slits. "You want to borrow or buy?"

"Either."

"Then I'll loan it. I'm waiting for a shipment of trade stuff. It might come in with D'Etrées." He watched Dan hone the edge of the tomahawk for a while. "You said you'd pay five hundred pesos to find out where those rifles came from."

Dan tested the edge with his thumb, then spat on the stone and began the circular motion. "That's what I said—but I might get it from D'Etrées cheaper."

"Nobody gets anything cheap from D'Etrées. You know that, Shankle. I heard you saw him at the Wichita village. He had a bad place on his forehead when he came back from that trip," he said suddenly, "and he was in an ugly mood. One of my men asked him about it and he carved the man's stomach right out of his body, then walked down to the river and rinsed off his knife and finished eating."

147

Dan did not look up. "He's ugly, eh?"

Clermont spat. "He's a killer," he said. "Like a diamond-back."

Dan tried the blade, stroked it a few more times, tried it again. "Will Meservy come with him?" he asked.

"Meservy?"

"He's D'Etrées's boss."

"Oh him! He was here once, many years ago, but that was not his name."

"He doesn't make this trip, then?"

"Not when I'm here."

"He goes through Natchitoches?"

"It's not for me to say. Why are you asking about Meservy?"

"Because he's the one I'll have to see eventually."

"I wouldn't worry about him until you get through with D'Etrées."

"You're afraid of D'Etrées, I take it."

"Ye'd be a fool," Clermont said angrily, "to think me afraid of anybody. But I don't put my head in the lion's mouth until I have to."

Dan looked up at him. The tomahawk was in his lap.

"You're right," he said. "I know you're afraid of nobody, else you wouldn't be here on the Trinity for so long." Dan gave the tomahawk a final inspection and dropped it through the rawhide loop. He handed the stone back to Clermont. "Thanks."

The deep lines in the man's face were deeper, and his eyes were glints. "If I had the information, where would you get five hundred pesos to pay for it?"

"You haven't got it," Dan said cheerfully, "or you'd have started negotiations long ago." He got up. "Whenever I promise you money, my friend, be sure that I can get it for you."

Two bearded men came out of the woods across the river and put their horses in the water without taking off the bridles. The horses were soon swimming, and presently came out on the near side, dripping, and started up toward Clermont's cabin.

Clermont walked to meet them. The man's feet were again bare. "What have you learned?"

The nearest man wore a fur cap. "Mataliche is expected at the mouth of the Trinity with plenty of goods."

Clermont nodded. "And D'Etrées?"

"Down the river about a league."

"Fellow here lookin' for him," said Clermont.

The fur-capped man turned to inspect Dan. "They say D'Etrées is easy to find and hard to lose."

"I've heard that," Dan said pleasantly.

Beatriz' clear voice rang across the grass like a bell.

"Dahn! Supper is ready!"

Both men turned in their saddles to stare at her. The fur-capped man said, "So we're gonna have something besides Indian squaws around here."

The second man pulled his long mustaches and took a harsh breath. "It's about time."

Clermont looked sidewise at Dan. "Gent here says she's all his."

"That's not exactly what I said," Dan told them, "but it puts across the general idea."

The two men continued to stare. They walked their horses past the cabin, watching Beatriz.

"They don't see many white women," said Clermont, watching Dan. "They might forget their manners."

Dan said, "The man who does will wake up with this hatchet in his brain. That goes for you too, Clermont." They stared at each other a moment. Dan said, "Thanks for the stone," spun on his heel, and walked away. One thing he did not do: underestimate Clermont. If D'Etrées was like a rattlesnake, Clermont was like a water moccasin, and fully as dangerous. That was apparent in the gleam in his eyes, the slackness of his mouth. He was a dangerous man and a clever man. As for D'Etrées, perhaps he was only dangerous.

Menard was walking up from another cabin with an earthenware jug. "A little rum," he said.

Dan took one drink and then another, but he refused a third one. "This is not a night to get drunk," he said.

Menard said, "It might be my last chance to drink with Beatriz—but it shall be as you say."

"It has to be that way," said Dan. "We're in a mare's nest."

"What does that mean, Dahn?" asked Beatriz.

"It means we've got to keep our eyes open. This is a smugglers' camp. They're all killers and they all expect to be killed someday. It isn't too important when."

They sat around the fire for a while after supper. It got dark swiftly. Beatriz went inside.

"We shoulda got her out of here," said Menard.

"Can you think what would happen to us traveling at night along a river that none of us knows?" Dan began to roll a *cigarro*. "We'd never reach the bay."

"Why not? These brigands?"

"Were you any better, up on the Arkansa?"

Beatriz came back.

"Perhaps not," Menard said slowly, "but somehow it was different. We weren't so deadly."

"It doesn't look the same to you any more. You've lost the spirit of the wild man."

"Was Menard once like those?" asked Beatriz, rolling her own *cigarro*.

"No," said Dan, amused. "He was never that old."

She was sitting with her legs under her, and now she leaned over and lighted the cigarette with a twig.

Dan watched Menard looking at her. "I have a feeling he's about ready to settle down. He's through his wild days."

Smoke drifted from her nostrils. "He only needs to find a wife, then."

"That's all I need," said Menard.

"And you, Dahn, will you ever settle down?"

He opened his mouth to speak, then closed it. It was on the tip of his tongue to tell her about Sarah, but suddenly he realized that had been two years ago, and he'd better be sure Sarah was still of a mind for marriage. At any rate, there was no point in telling Beatriz now. He'd tell her when he got out of this mess.

Menard said slowly, "Mules are coming. That'll be D'Etrées."

Dan stood up. He seemed to be looking down on Beatriz from a great height. "Keep the rifle," he said. "If anybody approaches you, shoot."

She jumped up, frightened. "You are going to meet him, Dahn? You may be killed!"

"Maybe, but I don't think so." He didn't tell her just how important this fight was. If he should be killed, the *contrabandistas* would overwhelm Menard, and Beatriz would be left to men like Clermont.

Menard too was thinking that. He was on his feet, feeling for the handle of his knife. "Maybe you don't have to fight him. Maybe you stay here—no trouble."

"There'll be trouble," Dan said quietly. "He probably knows I'm here already—and Clermont says he hasn't for-

150

gotten about that knot on his forehead. If I don't meet him, he'll be hunting me."

He felt his knife in its sheath, the tomahawk in its loop. He took the tomahawk out and balanced it in his hand, then dropped it back. "You carry your rifle and come with me," Dan said.

"It's danger," said Menard.

He knew Menard was thinking of Beatriz, and he was too; but he had to have somebody back him when he met D'Etrées. Two of them were far too few as it was, but they might brazen it out, and Beatriz would have the rifle. Moreover, they would not be gone long.

"There's not a chance for one man," he said to Menard.

The Frenchman's eyes dropped. *"Oui.* You are right, of course."

He led Beatriz into the cabin. "Sit there in the dark," he told her, "and do not come out unless I tell you to."

"Está bien. No tenga pena." She was very quiet.

"I'll be back," he told her lightly.

Suddenly she dropped the rifle against the wall and stood on her toes to put her arms around his neck and kiss him. He thought in wonderment that her lips were warm. Then she pulled back into the dark.

Dan straightened and set off down the valley, but he had an uneasy feeling. He looked back at Clermont's cabin and saw the man standing in the doorway with the firelight on his deep-lined, bristly face. He stared at the man until Clermont looked at him, and he thought Beatriz would be safe from Clermont until the fight was over.

It was a quarter of a mile to the place where D'Etrées and his men were building a big fire, and long before Dan and Menard got close, the fire was blazing high. Dan saw D'Etrées standing before it, drinking coffee, while some of his men unloaded the mules. Then a murmur ran around the group, and it began to open toward Dan. He walked steadily toward the fire, and the murmur died, and abruptly there was no sound but the crackling of the burning branches. The *arrieros* stopped unloading their mules. Then the mosquitoes hummed higher and higher, and the frogs struck up a steady chorus. Somewhere down the river a bull alligator bellowed, and Dan walked into the full light of the fire and faced D'Etrées.

The man stood across the fire and turned his cold eyes on Dan. He was very tall, and the firelight, throwing shadows upward across his face, made him look more sinister. His hair had not been combed, but pushed back from his forehead with greasy hands, so that it projected like the collar of bristles on a boar's neck. His eyes showed sardonic pleasure at this meeting. His mouth was a thin quarter circle turned down; his sloping shoulders added power to his frame and menace to his posture.

Dan stopped, his hands in the open, and said, "I hear you've come from New Orleans."

"You might hear anything around here," D'Etrées said, and made the opening thrust: "What do you want?"

There was, as Dan had anticipated, no compromise in his voice. Dan looked across the fire at him and saw the red mark on his forehead, and he realized abruptly, as he had not before, that there would be no halfway measures. A man like D'Etrées, carrying that mark, would never be satisfied until he had avenged it. Dan said, "I'm looking for Meservy."

"For what?"

"I want to talk to him about rifles."

"If you want to buy, you can talk to me."

Dan hesitated. Then he said, "I don't want to buy."

"Then talk to me anyway."

Fourteen or fifteen men had drawn around them in a circle—men with ragged deerskin clothing, bearded faces, nondescript hats and caps, wild eyes; men who did not know the meaning of loyalty, but who would be quick to finish off the man who went down. Now they were watching and waiting.

Dan did not look behind him. He knew Menard was there with the rifle. He kept his eyes on D'Etrées.

"Where is Meservy?" he asked.

The man said, "Minding his own business."

Dan sprang across the fire, drawing the tomahawk from its loop. D'Etrées slid to the left, as Dan had expected. D'Etrées's right hand came up with a knife, his left with a pistol. Dan swung the tomahawk fast, and the pistol blazed at his middle. The fire singed his whiskers, but he closed his eyes before the heat reached his face. He felt the ball jerk at his right hip. Then the tomahawk had completed its arc, and D'Etrées's left arm was hanging loose, cut almost in two above the elbow.

The man's face never changed. He attacked furiously with

the knife, thrusting, hacking, cutting. The blood was pouring out of his arm.

The *contrabandista* stood where he had been struck, fighting it out, but Dan parried with short swings of the tomahawk. He felt blood running down his right leg, but D'Etrées's slashes were showing less speed and less power, and finally D'Etrées, making a wild swing, slipped in his own blood and fell across the fire. He tried to rise. He got up on his good elbow, but, his face working horribly, fell back.

Dan dragged him out of the fire. "Where's Meservy?" he shouted.

But D'Etrées's eyes were beginning to glaze even while Dan put his hands around the stump of an arm to stop the bleeding. Dan swore. He had not wanted to kill the man, only to make him talk, but now he saw that there had been no chance to make D'Etrées talk from the beginning. The man had been too strong.

The body went limp, and Dan straightened up and searched the faces around him. A voice at Dan's shoulder said, "Him! He was with D'Etrées at the Wichita village."

Dan saw a brown-skinned half-breed, and took one step toward him. He watched the man's eyes change, and knew he had not wasted his effort. He grasped the man by the front of his leather shirt and shook him. "Where does Meservy keep the rifles?"

The man had intended to be stubborn, Dan thought, but he looked down at D'Etrées's body and faltered. "In New Orleans," he said fearfully.

Dan shook him. "Whose warehouse?"

"Juan Pisero's," the man said.

Dan took a deep breath. "One more question. Where's Meservy?"

The man licked his dry lips and looked around for help, but these were not the kind of men to give help to somebody else. The man looked back and said, "On the Arkansa."

Dan studied his eyes. He thought the man was telling the truth. He pushed him backward to throw him off balance. Then he went around the fire and through the lane opened for him.

Chapter Twenty-one

THEY WENT BACK up the meadow. The cabin was dark. Dan went to the open doorway and called in a low tone, "Beatriz!"

There was no answer.

Dan stepped inside. He saw nothing but darkness. Fear shot through him and left his knees weak. He called more loudly, "Beatriz!"

He sensed movement at one side, and reached for his tomahawk. "Whoever you are," he growled, "come out before I come after you." He took one step inside.

"Don't come any farther," said Clermont's harsh voice. "I'm holdin' a pistol on you. You too!" Obviously now he was addressing Menard. "I see both of you against the fire. Drop that rifle, you Frenchman, before I shoot your guts out."

Dan heard the rifle grounded on the dirt. His own hand was on the tomahawk, but he did not draw it out of the loop. "Where's the girl?" he demanded.

"Don't know. Move over to the other side, away from the door."

"Where's the girl?" Dan shouted.

"Remember, I've got the pistol. Move away from the door."

Dan moved slowly, farther into the cabin, trying to see in the darkness. There were no windows in the cabin, and the interior was black except for the faint light that came from the distant fire. If he could have seen the man, he would have leaped, but this way he had no chance. He took one step to his left on the balls of his feet. Menard moved behind him.

"I can see you both," said Clermont. "I'm comin' out."

"Clermont," Dan growled, "if you've touched that girl I'll kill you."

There was a rustling, and Clermont was outlined in the door. He was carrying a pair of saddlebags, and quite plainly, from the weight of them, they contained the gold that Dan had brought. He breathed a sigh of relief. But where was Beatriz? He froze up again.

Clermont backed through the door, holding the pistol on them. Dan and Menard together could easily beat him, for he

154

had but one load in the pistol, but Beatriz needed the protection of both of them to get through the outlaw country. One man and one woman . . . He shook his head.

Clermont was outside the door. He was moving slowly, knowing, no doubt, that fast movement might precipitate action. Dan watched him tensely, ready to leap if he got a chance.

Then Beatriz' clear, high voice came from outside. "Hands up or I shoot!"

Clermont must have calculated his chances. He must have identified the voice and decided to risk it, for suddenly he spun. He might have made it if he had not been burdened by the weight of the gold. As it was, the rifle thundered before he was all the way around. Dan sprang toward him. Clermont stumbled and went down. Lying there, he tried to raise the pistol, but Dan jumped on his wrist with both feet, and the pistol ball went into the ground. Dan's tomahawk was in his hand. "Get some fire," he told Menard.

He turned Clermont over. The heavy ball had come out of his back. He might live. Dan looked at the lined face and the shifty eyes. He laid the razor edge of the bloody tomahawk against Clermont's Adam's apple. "You said you had an interpreter. What's his name?"

"Antonio Flores."

"Where is he now?"

He watched Clermont's eyes change as the man tried to decide what to do. Dan pressed a little harder on the tomahawk. "In El Atacapas," Clermont said.

"How do you get there?"

"Go down the river to Arkokisa. Follow the trail east across the Mexican River to the Opelousa country."

Menard muttered, "You think he's telling the truth, or shall I shoot him?"

Dan looked down. The tomahawk had cut through the tough skin on Clermont's throat, and a few drops of blood were running down his neck. "It's a temptation to cut his throat and finish him off," Dan said. "I don't think he'll live long anyway."

"I told you the truth," Clermont said hoarsely.

Dan got up. "It jibes with what Simon told me. Let him go."

Clermont got to his feet and started for his cabin, but he collapsed within twenty feet.

"Come and get him!" Dan roared.

Two squaws hurried out of the cabin. They picked Clermont up and carried him to the cabin.

Dan looked down at Beatriz. His arm was around her shoulders, and relief at knowing she was safe made him suddenly weak.

"Oh, Dahn!" she trilled. "I was so glad to hear you call my name. It sounded as if you had the great fright for me."

He let his arm drop slowly. "Think nothing of it," he said.

But her eyes were laughing, and she put her own arm around him. Then suddenly she drew it away. "Blood!" she cried. "You have been hurt!"

Dan didn't feel very good. "I got a bullet from D'Etrées," he said, "but it went on through," and he fell over. . . .

When he came to, his buckskin shirt was pulled up out of his belt, and Beatriz and Menard were tying a prickly-pear poultice over the bullet holes on both front and back, holding it in place with rawhide strings. Dan grunted and sat up.

Beatriz stood back, her face filled with concern. They had built up the fire, and he could see them both clearly. "Find anything?" he asked.

"No. The bullet went through above your belt, and it was a clean hole in your shirt. No leather went in with it. You're all right."

"Thanks."

He got to his feet with one arm on Menard's shoulder and Beatriz on the other side. He made it to the cabin and lay down on the blanket, and soon he slept.

They rode out the next morning, Dan resting most of his weight on his left leg, for his right side was sore in an area as big as his head.

"We could wait over a few days," Menard suggested, and Beatriz nodded, her dark eyes filled with trouble.

"We wait, and word gets to Meservy. Then I won't be able to find him. We've got to leave now."

"What's to keep somebody else from getting there first anyway?"

"Us," Dan said grimly.

"You can't do it. You lost too much blood."

"I'll gain it back."

And so he pushed them on down the Trinity to Arkokisa, and then they took the Opelousa trail east across the swamps and the canebrakes. They found Flores, Clermont's interpreter, in El Atacapas. With his work done by Negro slaves

156

and his few financial needs supplied by Clermont and a few scattered traders who came his way, Flores had grown corpulent. He sat in the humid heat of his Indian hut and smoked a pipe with them. Yes, he would sell tobacco. The price would be a little high, for he had to bring it down from Natchitoches, and the King took a heavy duty. He watched with deep eyes bright in his fat face as Beatriz rolled her own *cigarro*. "You do not come here to buy tobacco, yes?"

"Of course not," said Dan. "We want three fresh mules."

Flores said calculatingly, "Mules are hard to get in El Atacapas."

"They're hard to get anywhere," Menard retorted.

Dan was about to dismount. "How much?" he asked.

"A hundred pesos and the mules you have."

"Fifty," Dan said, and sat back in the saddle. "Not a cent more."

"Your animals are tired and have lost flesh," Flores pointed out. "They wouldn't be much good in a race."

"Fifty pesos."

"I have kept these animals for some weeks, and have even fed them corn. I will take seventy-five pesos."

Dan got down. "You never fed a grain of corn to a mule in your life—but I will give you sixty pesos. And we will try the animals before accepting them."

"Make it seventy."

"I will go sixty-five, and that is my limit. Moreover, they will have to be mules as good as these."

Flores shrugged. "It is hard to make a profit with such as you. Unpack your animals."

Dan dismounted and loosened the cinch strap. Flores turned and yelled something at the grass huts beyond his own. Half a dozen Indian women popped out. His high, feminine voice called: *"Zhá'ä!"*

"That's the Lipan word for 'mules,'" Menard observed.

Dan nodded. "Probably they're Apache women, bought maybe from Meservy, who got them from the Wichitas for rifles, who in turn got them from the Camanches."

"And the Camanches?"

"Captured them by killing and raiding down around Bexar."

Beatriz seemed to shudder as she moved closer to Dan. He said, "You've got no worry."

"It is always a worry around Bexar," she told him.

"Many Mexican women are carried away by the savages, and sold into slavery." She said vehemently, "I would kill myself."

"Well, don't worry," Dan said soothingly. "As long as we're here, nothing will happen to you."

They brought up the mules from the canebrake, and Dan looked them over with Menard. He picked out four, and turned to Beatriz. "What do you say?"

"That one," said Beatriz, pointing, "is no good. He would balk."

Dan looked at Flores, who shrugged. "How can I do anything against such a combination?" he asked. "A sharp-eyed Frenchman, a hard-headed Englishman, and a beautiful sq—señorita."

Dan said, "We'll have to see if they're all broke for riding."

Beatriz said, "You saddle them. I will ride them."

Flores' eyes opened wider as he saw Beatriz drop into the saddle. The first mule began to buck, but she belabored him with a short stick, and stuck to his back like a cocklebur in buffalo wool until he came in tired and subdued. "She is a *mesteñera*," said Flores. "Maybe I would give you ten mules for her."

"A hundred wouldn't touch her," said Dan, watching her sack out the second mule. The color was high in her cheeks from the excitement, and she was truly a beautiful girl.

She finished the job and said, "One is a little jolting on his foreleg—perhaps a stiff knee—but he's strong and willing. I think we'll get along with them."

Dan gave Flores the sixty-five pesos.

"You are staying here tonight, of course," Flores said in his whining voice. "It is late to set out on the prairies."

"We've had enough of thieves' dens," Dan said sharply. "We're going east to New Orleans, and the man who follows us does so at the risk of his life. We've come too far to be stopped now."

"You came through Arkokisa?"

"Yes."

"From Bahía or down the Trinity?"

"Down the Trinity."

Flores hesitated. "You saw Clermont?"

"We saw Clermont. He's lying in his cabin now, trying to recover from a bullet wound."

For a moment Flores showed no sign of having heard. Then he swallowed. "You saw D'Etrées also?"

"I saw D'Etrées," Dan said coldly. "He's back there feeding the buzzards. I cut off his arm with the tomahawk."

"You talk big," Flores said finally, but it was a feeble thrust.

"Maybe," said Dan, "you know where Meservy is."

He fastened his eyes on the fat man, and Flores stood up under it for a moment. Then he shifted uneasily. "I have heard he is on the Arkansa, but that is only talk."

"You hear a lot of talk," said Dan, "and some of it is true."

"I know only what I hear," said Flores.

Dan produced a quadruple-piaster gold piece. "Have you heard in what warehouse Meservy keeps his rifles?"

Flores' mouth opened. He looked at the gold piece. "Juan Pisero's, I have heard, but I do not know."

Dan tossed him the gold, satisfied now that two men had told him the same. "See that we are not followed."

Flores stepped back, eying Beatriz with a last longing look. "If you have business with Meservy's rifles," he said finally, "you'd better finish it before Meservy gets back from the Arkansa. He's a more dangerous man than D'Etrées."

Dan laughed in his face. "There are few like D'Etrées. As for Meservy, I'll take care of him when I find him. See that I don't have to take care of you first."

He knew what was eating at Flores. The interpreter wanted Beatriz, and was disappointed at not getting her, and now he was trying to save his face. Nevertheless, he was right: Meservy had not grown to his present position in the contraband trade by dalliance or softness. He would be a more dangerous killer than D'Etrées, because he wasn't handicapped by hatred. He would kill coldly and efficiently.

They got out on the broad prairies of the Opelousa before dark, and found a spring in a clump of yellow persimmon trees. They made camp and hobbled the mules. They had a cold meal of wild turkey, cooked the day before. Beatriz washed the coffee can in the spring, and Dan said, "We'll have to keep watch against that Flores. I don't think he'll follow us, but you can't be sure."

"It would not do to take a chance," said Menard.

"There's a rise on both sides—east and west. I'll take the west. You take the east. We can watch in all directions, and keep an eye on the mules. Beatriz will stay down here in the trees."

"We can take care of tonight all right," Menard said heavily, "but there's something else I'm worried about. You're heading northeast instead of east, aren't you?"

"Yes. I said that to throw off Flores."

"You're planning to hit the Red River between Natchitoches and Rapide, *oui?*"

"Yes."

"From Rapide the natural course would be across country to the Washita, and up that river to the Arkansa."

"That's what I figured."

"Why not go directly to New Orleans for the rifles?"

"We have to have the warehouse receipt from Meservy before we can get the rifles from the warehouse."

"Have you figured out what to do with Beatriz?"

Dan stared at him. "How do you mean?"

"You wouldn't want to take her on to the Arkansa, for if you and I got killed, she would be taken over by the *contrabandistas.*"

"No," Dan said slowly. "Of course not."

"Likewise you cannot take her to her uncle in New Orleans, for there is not time. The word would get to Meservy that you are looking for him—and with only two of us, our only chance is to take him by surprise. *Oui?*"

"It sounds reasonable," Dan admitted, "but it doesn't sound good."

"We do not have passports," Menard reminded him. "We cannot ask the protection of the military. I might pass for Spanish, but you never would."

"No."

"Then what are we going to do when we hit the Red?"

Dan got up slowly, favoring the healing wound in his side. They had put on a new poultice that evening, and it seemed to have a deal of drawing power. "Damned if I know," he said. "Maybe I can figure that out while we're watching the mules."

Chapter Twenty-two

BUT HE SAW no answer as he sat under the stars that night. If he took Beatriz on to New Orleans, he would surely lose the chance to confront Meservy. If he sent Menard to New Orleans with Beatriz, they would be splitting their forces— and they had mighty little to split. It was audacious enough for two men to go after Meservy in the stamping ground of the *contrabandistas*. It would be suicide for one—unless he could be incredibly lucky.

It wasn't only his own hide he was looking out for. He had come to this country two years before to find rifles. Now the people who had needed those rifles needed them ten times as much, and it would be criminal to pass up the chance to get his hands on them.

And yet—what of Beatriz? It was strange how a woman complicated things. If only they could have left her in Bexar . . . He put that thought away. It had happened this way, and he owed her a debt. But for her, he'd still be in prison. Perhaps, he thought, she had served her destined purpose in getting him released. Perhaps it was enough to get her to the Red, and worry about her no further while continuing the project of finding the rifles. And yet it wasn't quite that easy. Perhaps he was more grateful to her than he had any obligation to be. Well, he'd take care of that. Gratitude was one thing. A burden was something else. He'd do his duty by her some way, but he'd have to leave her when they reached the river. That was clear enough, for there was no sense in him, a man who had asked another girl to marry him, worrying about her. He'd see that she was restored to civilization, and that would end it. He nodded to himself, sitting under the stars, and bit a chew off of the twist. Yes, that would end it. He needn't feel any further obligation. He'd give her some money, and she could get to her uncle.

He saw the fire die down by the spring, and Beatriz curled up in her blanket by it. There was no use denying that he felt a very strong protective instinct toward her— probably similar to that felt by a father toward a daughter —but the decision had been made, the die had been cast.

From now on he would have to work it out so that the securing of the rifles would be foremost. . . .

On their way northeast the next morning, he asked her about her uncle.

"He is called Eustacio de Orieta. He was a merchant in Mexico and a very wealthy man."

"Why did he go to New Orleans?"

"My cousin was raised by him, and when my cousin was appointed to the government, Don Eustacio retired from business and moved there to be near him. Don Eustacio is very fond of his grandchildren," she said.

"Well—" Dan braced himself and tried to sound business-like. "We're going to have to leave you at the Red River, and your cousin can get you to New Orleans."

She looked stricken. "Dahn! You're going to send me away by myself?"

"I—we—" He hadn't quite bargained for this. It had not occurred to him that she would have her own preference. "There's no choice," he said. "We're going on up to Arkansa Post. It's a long, hard trip, and there'll be fighting at the end of it."

"Then you will need me to take care of you!"

"No." He was firm. "It won't do." He compromised. "Perhaps we can put you with a caravan for New Orleans."

"Dahn," she said quietly, "do you want to be rid of me?"

"I have no choice," he said. "It's out of the question to take you to the Arkansa."

"And you must go?" she asked.

"I must. It's a duty."

"Very well. I will give you no trouble, Dahn. You may leave me at Rapide."

He tried to catch her eye, but she was looking straight ahead and refused to meet his glance. Menard rode along soberly on the other side. Dan wondered why he had offered no conversation in the matter. It left him quite uncomfortable, and that feeling was not alleviated by her detached and impersonal attitude for the rest of the trip across the prairies.

Rapide was a smaller village than Bexar, and they had no trouble finding the commandant's house. Beatriz' cousin was a powerfully built, virile-looking, swarthy-faced man of hardly over thirty years, with handsome black mustaches. He was effusive in greeting Beatriz, and she introduced him to Dan: "Lieutenant Ambrosio de Orieta y Sandoval."

162

"These men"—she indicated Dan and Menard—"have been shipwrecked on the coast and escaped from the Indians. They rescued me from the Apaches, who took me to Arkokisa, and I have asked them to bring me here."

"My most profound and humble thanks to both of you," said Lieutenant de Orieta, and asked a barbed question: "Why did you not return to Bexar, where my cousin's father lives?"

"Oh, Ambrosio," she said lightly, "you don't know how it is in the Texas country now. Rípperda has removed settlers and soldiers from the Louisiana frontier to stop the contrabanding, and the horrid Indians are on the warpath. It is worth one's life to travel through that country now."

"It is true," Orieta said thoughtfully. "Rípperda moved the capital from Los Adaes and abandoned the settlement. Of the Indians we hear little. Our communications with that region are limited."

"The country is upset," Menard said.

"No doubt Beatriz' father has offered a handsome reward for her return," Ambrosio said. "If you gentlemen will be my guests for a few weeks, I will see that you are paid just as soon as I get word from Bexar."

"Father has been in Vera Cruz on business for some months," said Beatriz.

Dan shook his head. "We didn't do it for a reward," he said. "All we want is a passport to New Orleans. Then we get a ship and go back to France."

But Ambrosio shook his head. "I am sorry, señores. I cannot provide you with passports. Only De Mézières in this part of the country may issue a passport. But I will be glad to send you to him with an escort of soldiers, and I will give you a letter explaining the situation."

"Ambrosio," said Beatriz, putting her hand on his arm, "these men have saved my life, and they want to get to New Orleans in a hurry."

"But it is only two or three days to Natchitoches."

She said impressively, "They have information that rifles are being smuggled up the Trinity."

Orieta scrutinized them thoughtfully. "It is true there is much smuggling, but we have not enough forces to stop it."

"Do you know anything about a man called Meservy?" Dan asked.

"Meserbi?" Orieta sighed. "He is one bad man. De Mézières forced him to stop going through Natchitoches,

163

and now he is on the Arkansa. Only a few nights ago he was reported to leave the Camino Real at the Mexican River and go in Arkansa territory with three hundred and sixty horses and mules and twenty-two Apache women."

Dan concealed his satisfaction at this verification of his information. "You know this?"

"We can do nothing, señor. The Mexican River is in Texas, and the Arkansa territory is not our responsibility."

"Can you not give them a pass to New Orleans?" asked Beatriz.

"Perhaps I can give them a pass to the commandant at Baton Rouge."

"I was sure you could," said Beatriz, sighing as if that were the end of that. "And I think they are in a hurry."

"Very well. In the morning, then."

"But—" Dan began.

"Señor, I could not permit you to leave so soon, after having done this so great a service to my family. In the morning your pass will be ready. Tonight you are my guests." This with a bow and a great sweep of his big arm.

Dan nodded. *"Bien, señor teniente.* It shall be as you say."

They feasted that night on duck, turkey, roast pork, and many wines, with a final cup of coffee and brandy and an excellent fat Cuban cigar. Beatriz avoided their eyes while Orieta asked meaningless questions about their experience.

They left the next morning. Dan was disappointed that Beatriz was not at hand to watch them leave. They turned their mules downriver until they were out of sight of the village; then they cut across the prairie land northeast and headed for the swamp country of the Washita.

"The Lieutenant didn't believe a word any of us said," Dan told Menard.

Menard shrugged. "What could he do? We claimed his hospitality as saviors of his cousin—which she proved by her own story. He had no choice. He had to accept it. But *mon Dieu!* What a woman Beatriz is to tell a story! I do not think I would ever trust her on her sacred oath!"

"She did it for us," Dan reminded him.

"She did it very prettily, too. I could almost believe her myself."

"I almost gave it away when I spoke to him in Spanish," Dan remembered. "He stared at me when I did that."

"I wonder," said Menard, "if the big ox will try to make love to her."

Dan chuckled. "With a wife so young and so fat, he won't get a chance. Anyway, they're cousins."

"Very distant cousins," Menard grumbled.

They reached the Washita, a winding river of swamps and lakes, of alligators, pelicans, and small red deer, of cypress swamps and massive oaks hung with Spanish moss, of flowering dogwood and big-leafed catalpa. They went around the swamps and kept to the north, watching out for wandering Quapaws or Osages as they neared the end of the Washita.

They crossed over a ridge and went down into the valley of the Arkansa.

Menard looked at him as they sat their mules. "The hunt is about over, *mon ami*. How do you feel?"

Dan touched the tomahawk swinging at his hip. "I feel like seeing it through to the end," he said.

"It may not end the way you want it to."

"I'll take that risk," Dan said soberly.

They followed the river down along the high bank on the south side, and camped on the ridge that night. The next day about noon they came to the big oak tree under which the Osage children had been stalking the wild turkey. A man came out of the blockhouse across the river, looked at them, and spoke to a squaw pounding corn on the top of a stump. She went inside a smaller cabin. Dan called, but there was no answer. "Let's swim it," he said. He took the bridle off the mule and put him down the steep bank into the water. They came out on the sand bar. The mules shook themselves, but Dan took them on through the lagoon and rode out on the shore.

The squaw came out of the cabin and said something in a low voice. A square, energetic figure came out of the blockhouse.

"Pocyfarré!" cried Menard.

"Menard, you half-wit Frenchman!"

They embraced each other, and Poeyfarré held him at arm's length. "I expected to find your scalp hanging from a Camanche shield," he said. "I thought you were dead."

"Not Menard. I been taking it easy in one of them Spanish prisons you like so much."

"Good!" said Poeyfarré. "But how did you get out?"

"I'll tell you sometime. You know this *inglés?*"

Poeyfarré scrutinized Dan. "Sure, the big tall one. I know him. You both look fine. They fed you good in that Spanish prison, eh?"

"*Bueno*," said Dan.

"You both sound like Spaniards. You been in Mexico since you went to find the damn Camanches?"

"Until lately," said Menard.

Poeyfarré grinned. "I have always said the best way to learn the language is from the women. Men don't always understand each other. Men and women always do."

"We tried," said Dan.

"And now you want what? You have no goods, no money?"

"Not much," said Dan.

"I owe you for some mules." Poeyfarré grinned. "I'd just as soon the Camanches got you—then the mules would be mine. Anyway, I charge you one mule for bringing them back. Five are yours if you want them."

Dan held Poeyfarré's eyes. "There's something I want a lot more."

Poeyfarré met his eyes for a moment. Then he turned to Menard. "What happened to Simon?"

Menard's jaws clamped for a moment. "The Camanches got him. Where's Blundin?"

"Blundin?" Poeyfarré looked regretful. "I had to kill him a year ago. We had an argument over a squaw. He wanted to keep her; I wanted to sell her—and I'm the one who captured her at the risk of my scalp." He dismissed Blundin with a gesture of his arm. "Anyway, he was getting too old for this work."

"You're running the camp, then?" asked Dan.

Poeyfarré looked at him warily. "*Oui.*"

"We're looking for a man," Dan said.

Poeyfarré shrugged. He swept his thick arm through a half circle. "Help yourself—if you can."

"Not just any man. John Meservy."

Poeyfarré's eyes became suddenly veiled. "He is the one who came from Natchitoches when we were at the Wichita village."

"That's right."

"I know nothing," Poeyfarré said flatly.

"I do," said Dan. "I know he's been on the Arkansa, and I know he's due here about now with a big herd of animals and a large bunch of slaves."

"I know noth—"

"I'm not trying to cut in on your business," said Dan. "This is a personal matter."

Poeyfarré studied him, obviously trying to weigh all the factors. "A herd of animals and some slaves. They are not mine."

"You owe me five mules," Dan said. "Tell me where to find Meservy and you can keep the mules."

Poeyfarré considered. "I do business with Meservy. I don't know you."

"I know he has over three hundred animals," said Dan. "What happens to them if Meservy is killed?"

A small glint of greed came into Poeyfarré's eyes and began to grow. "Those are many animals."

"If I am killed," said Dan, "then there is this mule I'm riding."

Poeyfarré looked the animal over. "It is not much."

"You can lose nothing," Dan insisted.

Poeyfarré asked Menard, "You have been with this man since you went into Camanche country?"

"Oui."

"You think he's telling the truth?"

"If he's not," said Menard, "he's fooled me bad."

Poeyfarré looked at Dan and said slowly, "He came down the north side of the river last night."

"He'd have to have grazing land," Dan said thoughtfully. "He'd be camped over on the prairie beyond the swamp."

"I warn you," said Poeyfarré, "if you're trying to get my business, I'll cut your liver out and feed it to the birds."

Dan put one hand on Poeyfarré's hard shoulder. "After what the Camanches did to Simon, I don't scare so easy," he said harshly.

Poeyfarré's eyes were narrow. "I'm not afraid of Indians. If you have business with Meservy, settle it, but don't try to buy his stock or his squaws. He has agreed to sell to me if he does not take them down to Manchac."

"All right. Menard, you know the way?"

Menard led the way past the blockhouse and took a trail into the swamp. Poeyfarré shook his head as they rode off.

In the swamp, insects arose humming as they progressed, and brown water bugs darted across the still surface. A snake slid silently into the brown water ahead of them. The sun was hot, and there was no wind, and the dank smell of wet reeds rose smotheringly around them, while big blue flies buzzed over the remains of a dead pelican, probably stalked and killed by a wildcat.

Menard kept mostly on dry ground, with the mules' hoofs crunching the crisp stalks of marsh grass and swamp iris. "We're almost out," said Menard.

"I see horses on the ridge."

"Are you going to use the rifle?"

Dan's hand went to his hip. "I've got the tomahawk."

"It's not my business," Menard said, "but it would be easier to shoot him."

"I didn't come to kill him," Dan said. "If he wants to fight, it will be a fair fight."

"Maybe you better tell *him* that."

Dan pulled his belt tighter. "If it doesn't go right, tell Beatriz—"

"Tell her what?"

Dan said thoughtfully, "If I can't tell her myself, I guess there's nothing to tell her." He swung his arms to loosen them, then unbuckled the wide belt with its many gadgets and small containers, took off his buckskin shirt, and threw it over the mule's withers. He disengaged the tobacco pouch, the bullet pouch and powder container, the awl and sinew bag and salt bag, and slipped them all into his saddlebag, then fastened the belt back in place and saw that the knife was in its sheath and the tomahawk hung right. He felt the sun hot on his bare back, and it felt good.

They rode through a clump of cottonwoods. They saw the horses and mules spread out over the prairie for a mile up and down and as far north as the ridge. Half a dozen buffalo-hide tepees clustered on the prairie at his left, a little way from the swamp. Dan took the lead and rode toward them. The squaws were busy with hides or with the preparation of food. They heard him and Menard approach, and heads began to bob up here and there. In a moment all were watching. Dan rode steadily forward.

A man came out of one of the tepees. He took one look at them approaching and snapped, *"Lä'n!"*

An Indian woman came out of the tepee and ran around behind it. Half a minute later she returned, leading a black horse, which Meservy mounted. He rode to intercept them.

Dan did not change the mule's pace. As Meservy drew near, Dan looked at the squaws behind him—all short, heavy-set, all with straight black hair—and no children anywhere. "Apparently you're in the slave business," Dan said. "What did

168

you do with the kids—kill them or leave them to starve?"

Meservy's cynical eyes were cold as Dan measured him. The man must have spent most of the last two years in this country, for the sun and the wind had tanned his face into a leathery scowl. "You want something?" he asked.

"Yes." Dan dropped his hand to his saddle horn. "You see the rifle under my stirrup? That's one of the rifles you planted on me in Camanche country. I've come to pay you back for that. Also, I want the warehouse receipt so I can draw the rest of those rifles from Juan Pisero."

Meservy made a swift movement with his hand, but Menard's rifle cracked, and Meservy swore as his smashed pistol dropped to the ground.

Dan said quietly, "You're a good shot, Menard."

Meservy leaped from the saddle, a knife in his hand. Dan lunged toward him, and they fell between the animals. Dan's mule shied and moved away. They rolled on the ground. Meservy, grunting like a hog, stabbed at him with the knife, but Dan kept his hand on Meservy's right wrist while he snaked the tomahawk from its rawhide loop. They strained against each other and got nowhere. They pushed apart and began to circle. Dan, balancing the tomahawk, saw an opening and darted in. Meservy side-stepped and spun on his heel, stabbing hard at Dan's body.

Dan felt a thump as the hilt of the knife struck his back. For a moment he felt no pain, but he knew the knife was in him. He twisted away from Meservy, pulling the knife out of Meservy's hand.

Meservy was circling, trying to get his hand on the knife. Dan tried to raise his arm to swing the tomahawk, but a muscle hit the knife blade and made his shoulder jerk. He could not force his arm against it, and he knew he shouldn't, for it might cut the muscle. He lowered his arm and tried to get his mind off the white fire that was in his back now. Meservy was still circling, warily now. He had another knife in his hand.

Dan tried to raise his arm again but failed. Meservy saw this and slashed at him. Dan dodged back toward Menard, who was still mounted. He backed a step and shouted, "Take the knife!" in a voice unlike his own.

Menard reached down and gripped the knife in his back. It scraped across Dan's raw nerves. He opened his mouth to scream, but stopped the sound and clamped his jaws together. Meservy was coming at him.

169

Dan moved out of the way, leaving the knife in Menard's hand. He wondered how much blood he was losing. His back was numb.

Meservy rushed at him. Dan held his ground and swung the tomahawk, and Meservy halted just short of the brassy arc it made in the sun. Menard sat his mule, looking worried. Meservy feinted. Dan motioned with the tomahawk but did not swing it, for that was what Meservy wanted: to get him to swing and rush in while he was off balance.

For a moment they maneuvered silently. Poeyfarré was standing at the edge of the swamp, watching. The squaws, now gathered in a group, watched from a distance with no emotion showing on their faces.

Dan heard his blood dropping to the ground. Meservy looked at Dan with a new light in his eyes, a calculating glint, and Dan knew what that meant: Meservy could wait him out, as he had waited out D'Etrées. He was not bleeding as much, but it would tell. He knew that.

He crowded Meservy, swinging crisscross hacks at the man's face but careful to keep the strokes short so he could retain control of the tomahawk. Meservy backed, side-stepped, striking with the knife. Dan felt his strength beginning to go. Perspiration began to run down his chest, and he opened his mouth to get more air. He lowered the tomahawk as if he were too tired to hold it up—and Meservy leaped in.

Dan had time for one swing, lightning fast. He made it, and the sharp edge of the ax caught Meservy in the act of stabbing, and cut a slice from the top of his head.

Meservy staggered. The blood poured from his open scalp and covered his face. He fell forward, and Dan jumped back out of the way. Meservy sprawled at full length. A band of pigeons flew over from the swamp. Bees were humming across the prairie. Dan reached out a foot and kicked the knife out of Meservy's hand. The knife fell into the grass, and Meservy did not move. Dan put a knee in the small of his back and felt for a heartbeat. There was none.

He got up. He rolled the body over and felt inside the man's buckskin shirt. He found half a dozen folded documents on heavy rag paper. He scrutinized them quickly, found the warehouse receipt, and put it under his own belt. "Twelve hundred Watts rifles will make a difference back in the colonies," he observed with satisfaction.

Big blue flies were settling on Meservy's head. A large shadow crossed the ground, and Dan looked up to see two buzzards. He was beginning to feel faint. He walked over and wiped the blood off the ax on Menard's saddle blanket. "How do I look in back?" he asked.

"Bleeding some. Are you spitting any blood?"

"No."

"Then he missed your lungs and you're probably all right. Be sore for a while, though."

Dan started to put the tomahawk in the loop, but the twisting motion nauseated him. He swayed, and looked at Menard from under lowered eyelids. "Take it," he said.

Menard was on the ground. "Can you get back to Poeyfarré's?"

"I think so." He put one hand on the saddle horn and walked. The vertigo lessened. Menard helped him into the saddle and they went through the swamp. Poeyfarré said, "I am damn glad you finished that fellow. He had decided to be boss on the Arkansa, and I would have had to kill him if you didn't."

"Maybe for that," Dan said, "you've got a drink of rum."

"For such an occasion we have the best."

"Let's get at it," said Dan, "before this thing starts to ache."

Dan had a tin cup full of rum, and it eased him considerably. "One of Blundin's squaws," said Poeyfarré, "will put a poultice on it for you. I keep her here because she knows the remedies. She'll go out in the swamps and gather some herbs, and make a concoction that would kill a mule— but it will be good for your back."

"Anything," Dan said, "so I can get going tomorrow."

Poeyfarré shrugged. "You're in a hurry."

Dan nodded and poured another cup of rum.

"There was a man from Virginia here last week looking for rifles," Poeyfarré recalled. "He says there is much fighting in the English colonies and they need arms."

"If he comes back," Dan said, "tell him to look somewhere else. Meservy is a damned Tory and wouldn't sell to him anyway."

They traded the mules to Poeyfarré for a canoe and a supply of corn and boiled meat. They started at sunset, and went past Fort Carlos III at night under cover of the high bank, dipping their paddles quietly. It did not take long to reach New Orleans, and the exercise, Dan said, kept him from getting stiff.

They left the canoe above the American section and walked the rest of the way. The American section was composed of a few houses and as many saloons. They stopped for a drink and Dan inquired about Pisero's warehouse.

"You'll find it in the French section," the cadaverous bartender said. "But you may have to have papers to get in."

"Maybe," said Dan.

They went to the Gate of Tchoupitoulas and said they were laborers for Juan Pisero. They were allowed within the rampart, and walked down the narrow, black dirt streets, where garbage was thrown into the open, to the benefit of the many dogs. They found Juan Pisero sitting quietly in his office next to a coffeehouse. He was a small, thin man, dressed as most men in the French section dressed in those days, in heart pantaloons and silk coat.

Dan said, "You have some rifles here in the name of Meservy."

Pisero said cautiously, "I have goods in his name. It is not my business what the goods may be."

"It says here, 'Six hundred boxes of iron goods.' "

Pisero did not reach for the paper, but looked at Dan.

"My business is providing storage space, not performing the duties of a customs officer."

"Let's not combat each other. I have received this paper from Meservy, and I want the goods it represents."

"You shall have it upon payment of the charges."

"How much?"

Pisero did some calculation with a turkey-quill pen. Then he looked up. "A hundred and forty pesos."

"That's high storage for iron goods," Dan commented.

Pisero shrugged. "It was agreed between us."

Dan counted out the gold. "Can you recommend a place to get mules?"

"You are expecting to go overland through Natchez?"

"Yes."

"I would not advise it. The British have control of the left bank of the Misicipi."

Dan studied him.

Pisero said, "I suggest you go directly to Governor Unzaga and tell him you have bought these rifles and want to ship them to Philadelphia. He looks on the colonists with considerable favor. I think he would see that you got permission to load these goods on a ship."

Dan hesitated. Pisero had only to report him to get him in plenty of trouble. On the other hand, Pisero was no

172

doubt guilty of contraband activities of his own. He said, "I'll think about that."

Pisero signed the receipt, and Dan put it back in his shirt. They went outside. "If he's talking straight," Dan said, "the next thing we have to do is find a ship."

"Preferably a fast one that can outrun the British men-of-war."

"Yes. Let's walk down along the levee."

"He took you for an agent of the colonies," said Menard.

Dan nodded. "It shows, I think, that there is considerable activity in New Orleans for supplies."

They spied a brigantine lying at anchor, and Dan hailed her. The master came to the rail. "What d'ye want, mate?"

"Is this ship for hire?"

"That she is, if you can get your cargo cleared."

"She looks fast."

"Fast enough to outrun the damned British. It won't be long, though. They're beginning to draw like flies at a pickle barrel."

"When can you sail?"

"There's usually a breeze at dawn. All we need is enough to get out in the current."

"You're hired," said Dan, and he added, "I hear Unzaga is favorable toward the colonies."

"So far."

Dan gave Menard some gold. "Get blacks and load those rifles on the ship. You should be ready to go by midnight."

"Where'll you be?"

"I'll be getting clearance from the Governor, and attending to some other business."

Menard looked at him searchingly. A sad light grew in Menard's eyes. "All right," he said.

Dan found hospitality at the Cabildo. He got permission to reship "six hundred boxes of iron goods" to Philadelphia. Then he inquired for Don Eustacio de Orieta.

A few minutes later he was using the brass knocker at the front door of a one-story stucco house two blocks from the Place d'Armes. A black girl came to the door. Dan said, "I'd like to see Don Eustacio."

She disappeared into the dimness of the interior. A few moments later a small, white-haired old man padded to the door.

"You are Don Eustacio de Orieta?" asked Dan.

The old man looked at his ragged buckskin clothing. *"Sí, señor."*

"No tengo mucho tiempo," said Dan. "I would like to speak to the Señorita Beatriz."

"You have business with her?" Don Eustacio asked dubiously.

Dan was fumbling with his fur cap. "I wanted to say something to her before I leave."

"I—"

"Dahn!"

She came flying, all black hair and black eyes and olive skin. He held out his arms and she came into them. He smoothed her hair with his rough palm, and when she raised her face her eyes were shining through tears.

Don Eustacio was fluttering around. "This is the *inglés* who rescued you from the *bárbaros?*"

"Es verdad, tío mío."

His arms, which had been empty for so long, now felt satisfied for the first time in his life. "Beatriz," he said, "I'm going back to a hard life, for there is a war going on, and there are Indians, and there is the Bloody Hamilton on the northwest, and the entire frontier will be ringing with gunfire and tomahawks—but I would ask you to go with me."

She drew back and looked at him with the color suddenly draining out of her face. "You are asking me to marry with you?"

"That's it. I'm going to need somebody who can help, and somebody I want to fight for. You're the one."

"Oh, Dahn!"

"Pues," said Don Eustacio, smiling paternally, "we must have a little brandy for this happy occasion."

They were eating dinner later when Menard found them. He was introduced to Don Eustacio and his wife, and looked sharply at Dan and at Beatriz. Finally he said, "We're all loaded and ready to sail whenever there's a wind."

"You were fortunate to find me."

"It wasn't hard to guess."

"We'll have another passenger going back," said Dan.

"There's plenty of room," said Menard. "Six hundred boxes of iron goods don't fill up a ship."

"I have ordered a priest," said Don Eustacio. "He will be here any moment."

"A priest!" Menard's eyes were wide. He turned to Dan. "You are going to—"

Dan nodded solemnly.

Menard shook his head. "I'll be damned. I never believed you would have the sense, you thickheaded Englishman."

"A toast!" cried Don Eustacio.

While the glasses were being filled, Dan gave Menard the port clearance. "I forgot to get the name of the ship. I didn't notice."

Menard filled it in slowly, painfully: the *Sarah Evers.* Owner, Theophilus Radnor. Destination, Baltimore.

Dan stared a moment at the name: *Sarah Evers.* Then he roared. He picked up Beatriz with his big hands at her waist and held her high. Then he set her on her feet and kissed her.

Don Eustacio looked bewildered.

Menard frowned. "I have never seen the name of a ship make such a celebration," he observed.

But Beatriz was not puzzled. She smiled quietly at Dan, as if she had known all the time what had held them apart, and as if, now that she had him, she had never had any real doubt of the outcome.

THE END

175

Noel M(iller) Loomis was born in Oklahoma Territory and retained all his life a strong Southwestern heritage. One of his grandfathers made the California Gold Rush in 1849 and another was in the Cherokee Strip land rush in 1893. He grew up in Oklahoma, New Mexico, Texas, and Wyoming, areas in the American West that would figure prominently in his Western stories. His parents operated an itinerant printing and newspaper business and, as a boy, he learned to set lead type by hand. Although he began contributing Western fiction to the magazine market in the late 1930s, it was with publication of his first novel, *Rim of the Caprock* (1952), that he truly came to prominence. This novel is set in Texas, the location of two other notable literary endeavors, *Tejas Country* (1953) and *The Twilighters* (1955). These novels evoke the harsh, even savage violence of an untamed land in a graphic manner that eschewed sharply the romanticism of fiction so characteristic of an earlier period in the literary history of the Western story. In these novels, as well as *West to the Sun* (1955), *Short Cut to Red River* (1958), and *Cheyenne War Cry* (1959), Loomis very precisely sets forth a precise time and place in frontier history and proceeds to capture the ambiance of the period in descriptions, in attitudes responding to the events of the day, and laconic dialogue that etches vivid characters set against these historical backgrounds. In the second edition of *Twentieth Century Western Writers* (1991), the observation is made that Loomis's work was "far ahead of its time. No other Western writer of the 1950s depicts so honestly the nature of the land and its people, and renders them so alive. Avoiding comment, he concentrates on the atmosphere of time and place. One experiences with him the smell of Indian camps and frontier trading posts, the breathtaking vision of the Caprock, the sudden terror of a surprise attack. Loomis, in his swift character sketches, his striking descriptions, his lithe effective style, brings that world to life before our eyes. In the field he chose, he has yet to be surpassed."